BEAUTY
AND THE
STREETS

Kim K

Buy

for Melodrama

BEAUTY
AND THE
STREETS

Kim K.

This is a work of fiction. All of the characters, organizations, and events portrayed in this novel are either products of the author's imagination or are used fictitiously.

www.melodramapublishing.com

Library of Congress Control Number: 2014943117
ISBN-13: 978-1620780411
ISBN-10: 1620780410
First Edition: December 2014
10 9 8 7 6 5 4 3 2 1

Interior Design: Candace K. Cottrell
Cover Design: Candace K. Cottrell
Model Photo: Marion Designs

BOOKS BY

Kim K.

ONE

Khye stared out her bedroom window clad in her panties and bra and dreamed of a place better than her own. The weatherman had said temperatures would reach one hundred degrees, with the humidity just as high. It felt like she had fallen into the pits of hell. Khye sighed. She was frustrated and sweating like a runaway slave. The only relief she had in the scorching bedroom was sitting by an open window. It was only a few weeks before summer officially started, and already the city was having its first major heat wave. It wouldn't have been so bad if the air conditioning worked, or if she'd had a fan that didn't blow out hot air. Just moving from one side of her room to the other, Khye felt like she wanted to pass out.

She had locked the bedroom door. She wanted to escape from her family. She wanted to be alone. Her sisters, Ava and Maisie, were knocking on the door repeatedly, complaining about wanting to come in.

"Khye, open the damn door! Why are you hogging the room?" Ava shouted angrily.

"Stop being a bitch, Khye!" Maisie shouted too.

"Go away!" Khye retorted.

"No, you go away!" Ava spat. "We live here too!"

Khye threw a pillow at the door and frowned. It was too hot to deal with her little sisters. Ava was fifteen, and Maisie was thirteen; both girls had their father's complexion and coarse hair texture, and they were pains in the ass. Khye tuned out her sisters' griping and continued to gaze out the bedroom window, wishing she was in a different world—a luxurious world that was totally opposite from her own. Her stomach growled because there was no food in the fridge, and although she was a beautiful young woman, she felt insecure because summer was right around the corner and she had nothing nice to wear—not even a pair of decent sandals to show off her lovely feet.

Khye was nineteen years old, and she'd been living in the States for ten years. Her parents moved her and her two little sisters to America when she was nine years old for a better life. London was too expensive a city to live in, so they moved to Harlem thinking life would be better for them. Khye remembered a lot about London, and sometimes she did miss home. But she felt she was cursed; she had the beauty but not the lifestyle of a Queen. Her family was dirt poor, and she wished she was born into royalty. Khye would sit alone and daydream for hours, thinking, what if—what if she had been born into the British royal family, and lived in Buckingham Palace? She daydreamed about going on lavish shopping sprees at Harrods in the UK, going in and out of popular stores on Oxford Street, and making her way to the exclusive stores on Saville Row and Bond Street. She daydreamed about traveling to all the wonders in the world and staying in five-star hotels. And her major fantasy: getting married to a prince and having her wedding at Westminster Abbey or St. Paul's Cathedral with the entire world watching.

Yes, that was the life for her, what she wanted. But they were only dreams and what-ifs, and her reality felt like a perpetual nightmare.

"Khye, I'm telling Mummy on you," Maisie threatened.

"Go ahead, you bloody snitch, she don't care what you do anyway," Khye retorted.

She heard Maisie kick the door so hard, it felt like her foot went through it. Khye didn't budge. She sat by the window and looked outside at Harlem burning hot like eggs in a skillet. She wiped the sweat from her brow.

"Fine, be that way, Khye! Be a bloody fuckin' bitch," she heard Ava yell.

Finally, they were away from the door, giving up on their attempt to occupy the bedroom with Khye. When Khye wanted to be alone, she stayed alone. She wanted to be entertained by her thoughts and her fantasies. Ava and Maisie would go running to their parents, but her parents weren't Clair and Cliff Huxtable—in fact, their parents were more like Peter and Lois Griffin, or Al and Peggy Bundy—the realistic version of *Family Guy* and *Married… with Children* combined.

Things weren't much different when they lived in England; they were always poor and lived in a bad neighborhood. Lincoln Projects in East Harlem weren't much different than council flats in London. There was violence, people using the elevator as a bathroom, and drug dealers plaguing the area to sell dope. There were poor families trying to make an extra dollar by any means necessary.

Khye didn't have all bad news about moving to America. When they first moved to the States, their pounds, once exchanged, went further in dollars. And a long time ago, they'd lived in a really nice neighborhood in Harlem and rented a four-bedroom co-op apartment on a tree-lined block. Then it all changed drastically—living in the co-op was short-lived.

Khye's father, Adewale, who was thirty-seven, had been born in Nigeria and moved to London where he met her mother, Sarah. Adewale loved his Nigerian heritage and Khye's mother, who was a white woman with piercing blue-gray eyes, high cheekbones, and thick blonde hair. She loved black men and fell in love with Adewale. He was tall and well-built like a Yoruba warrior, but he didn't have the credentials of a king. He was a poor man but had big plans to make millions someday.

When he met Sarah twenty years ago, he immediately fell in love with her. She was beautiful, and most important, she was white. Though he was a beautiful black man with chiseled features and magnificent black skin that wrapped around him like a moonless night, he hated his dark skin and coarse hair. However, Sarah loved the contrast of their skin color and features. Adewale treated her like a princess and when they married, like his queen. He had promised her the world; he had big plans to make millions in some profession. However, Sarah had gotten pregnant really young, and she chose to drop out of school. Adewale completed his mandatory UK education at sixteen, after that, he took an optional year of schooling called sixth-form college so that he could go to a university in order to secure a better future for his new family. All Sarah talked about was leaving the UK for the States, so when Adewale got a company to sponsor his visa, they packed what little they had and flew over seven thousand miles to their new lives.

In America, at first, things were great. Adewale was a computer tech with a fledgling software company until his arrogance got the best of him and he continued to clash with the company's CFO. After he was fired, he worked odd jobs and some good jobs. When his work visa was revoked, Adewale was able to convince a relative, a U.S. citizen to sponsor his family's green cards. Adewale was determined to provide for his family. He caught another break and started working in construction, but once again, he was let go from his job. Their savings dwindled and the family ended up moving into the projects. With mouths to feed and children to shelter and clothe, to support his family, Adewale resorted to credit-card scams. And for a short while, life was good, and then it wasn't again. He had gotten caught, tried, and convicted. He did his time, got out, went back to doing something illicit again, got caught again and did more time. Now the U.S. was threatening to have him deported.

The American dream soon started to dissipate and fade for Adewale, and it didn't take long for him to start drowning his sorrows away in liquor. He became a functioning alcoholic and landed a janitorial job at a local public school.

Now, the defined features and flawless black skin Adewale had once had was gone—substituted with a protruding gut, bad skin, and a puffy face from the alcohol consumption. He refused to accept that he was a drunk and believed no one knew it, constantly hiding his liquor and sneakily taking a swig when he believed no one was looking.

Khye was ready to come out of her panties and bra and lie around butt-naked. It was only noon and it felt like the sun was giving the earth a personal bear hug and refused to let go. She looked in the mirror, and although she was beautiful, she was insecure about so many things. She had light skin, high cheekbones, a thin straight nose, and long, dark, silky hair that she wore naturally curly. She looked like a model. Growing up, a lot of African-American girls in the neighborhood were jealous of her light skin and hair. They always tried to jump on her, beating her up until she learned how to fight back.

Khye gazed at her image in the mirror, then she slowly peeled away her bra and panties and stood naked. She had no tattoos, no scars, and she was curvy everywhere. She got her curves, undoubtedly, from her Nigerian side of the family. Her mother always told her that her looks would get her far in life and that her beauty would get her the man of her dreams—any man. At nineteen, she was desperately looking.

As Khye stared at herself, she heard the rugrats come back. This time, they were attempting to pick the lock from outside and burst into the room. It had to be Maisie; she was the youngest and the most mischievous. Khye threw back on her panties and bra and raced to the door.

"Maisie, you little sneak, I know what you're tryin' to do," Khye hollered.

"It ain't just your room, Khye, it's ours, too. And I want to come in!" Maisie hollered. She kicked the door again.

"Well, for the bloody moment, it's mine. I need my personal space," Khye shouted back.

"So move out!" Maisie yelped.

"No, you move out," Khye quipped.

"I'm only thirteen."

"And?" Khye became sarcastic.

Her English accent was still thick. Ten years she had spent in America, and it hadn't phased out. It attracted the boys and made people pause with infatuation when she talked. They always asked her to repeat certain phrases. Her first month in America, enrolled in grade school, Khye had raised her hand in class and asked, "Can I use the toilet, Miss?" The students laughed. They had never heard anyone call the bathroom or restroom, *the toilet.* But it got worse, *trainers* were called *sneakers* and *chips* were called *french fries.* It took some time for Khye to adjust, but she did, though every now and then, certain English phrases would spill out accidentally.

Khye heard her sister kick and bang on the door harder. Maisie was the impatient one. Khye knew her little sister wasn't going to stop until she got what she wanted. They were all spoiled, but Khye was spoiled the most.

"I swear to god, I'm gonna kick this damn door down, Khye…let us in!" Maisie demanded.

"All right already!" Khye shouted.

She marched toward the door, unlocked it, and swung it open like she wanted to rip it from its hinges. Maisie and Ava stood there frowning with their arms folded across their chests. They pushed Khye to the side and stormed into the room like they were on a mission.

"That's rude!" Khye hissed.

"Fuck you!" Ava retorted.

"Arsehole!" Maisie said, meaning *asshole.*

Khye rolled her eyes and left the room, snapping back, "I got some place to be anyway."

"Go then," Maisie replied with her smart mouth.

Ava and Maisie got their looks from their father, and fortunately for Khye, she inherited her mother's beauty. She was the firstborn. She had the beauty. She was proud to look like her white mother with her light eyes and light skin. Ava and Maisie were dark-skinned with coarse hair. Both sisters resented Khye because their parents always favored her. It seemed like Adewale and Sarah despised Ava and Maisie, but they adored, catered to, and spoiled Khye as much as humanly possible. Ava believed that because of Khye's light skin she had a better chance of achieving success and snatching up a rich man. Their parents looked at Khye as their savior from poverty. They were always telling Khye how beautiful she was, and would give up their last nickel to make her happy.

"Where's Mum?" Khye asked.

"Where you think she is?" Ava snapped back.

"Upstairs?"

"Yes. Why, cuz you need to borrow money?" Maisie asked with an attitude.

"None of your business."

Khye walked away from her sisters and into the living room. Her family was dysfunctional with a capital D. Her father was a broke-down drunk, and her mother was a slut. When she walked into the living room, like expected, Adewale was passed out on the living room couch. He was lying face down in his work attire, looking dead to the world, snoring, and in a deep stupor. He would remain like that for hours.

Khye needed money. She didn't have a dime to her name. She walked over to her father and slowly reached into his pocket. She effortlessly removed his wallet, opened it up, and wasn't surprised that he didn't have a single dollar on him. Khye sighed with frustration

"Damn, I hate this family!" she hollered.

TWO

"Damn, I like that, ma. I definitely do," Gino said with a huge smile across his face while grabbing his growing erection.

His eyes were fixed on Sarah walking into the living room butt-naked and wearing a pair of red pumps. He loved what he saw and his dick became so hard, it looked like a steel pipe pointing vertically between his legs. His dick was big and black, and his hunger for Sarah was even bigger.

"You like what you see?" Sarah asked with a teasing smile.

"You know I do, ma," Gino said.

Sarah seductively strutted his way in her six-inch pumps. Her sexual appetite was bigger than his. She was ready to devour his dick and deep throat him until it couldn't go down her throat any farther. Gino was too sexy, just her type—a roughneck, swathed with menacing tattoos and battle scars on dark skin like a chocolate bar. His body was ripped with muscles with his protruding, thick chest, a six-pack, and defined arms. He was twenty-one years old and a notorious Blood gang member. The color red and his gangster lifestyle was manifested all throughout his apartment—a Glock 19 on the small table, a pound of weed and a roach in the ashtray, a massive flatscreen, X-Box, and naked pictures of ladies plastered on his wall. It was the perfect bachelor pad—disorganized, filled with drugs and loud music.

Sarah could hardly wait to taste his dick. Gino had been rubbing himself with one hand and staring hungrily at his white woman. He was physically and emotionally excited. His cock was very impressive. She could see his veins throbbing through the skin. He wanted her. She wanted him.

"Ya beautiful, ma," he uttered.

She smiled. It felt good to be wanted. "I'm going to suck and lick your hard cock in my mouth until you are begging me to fuck you, yuh hear?" she said.

"Damn, I like that."

Her English accent was a strong turn-on. It made Gino super hard just to hear Sarah talk, and her snow white skin and curvy body was so enticing, it could lead any man into temptation. It was what she did best, seduce men. It didn't matter that she was a married woman. Her husband was a drunk. She became the town whore. Her white flesh and blue eyes made African-American men weak. Sarah never worked a day in her life, and even in poverty, Adewale kissed her ass and catered to her. Sarah was lazy. She could have gotten a job years ago to help support the family, but she didn't. Adewale gave his wife his entire paycheck each week. She would give him a couple of dollars so that he could buy his liquor and be content, and then she would run off and have some fun with his money. When her husband was drunk, he stayed out of her way and it gave her free room to carry out numerous affairs and get her freak on with different men in the city. There was Gino—the Blood gang member on the fourth floor above their apartment, James—the retired cop who lived in the Bronx, and Marcus—a married man with kids who lived in Queens. Sarah loved black dick, the bigger, the better, and she loved dark skin, the darker the better. All her men were black.

Although Sarah loved to fuck black men, she no longer felt any connection to her husband or her two daughters, Ava and Maisie. Khye was her favorite. Khye was beautiful just like her, and Khye had the strong sex appeal and attractiveness to snatch up any baller she wanted. Maisie, her youngest daughter—it was obvious she was going to be a little pudgy as she got older, and Ava didn't have the sassiness and eye-catching figure of her older sister. Sarah was always praising Khye and telling her how beautiful she was. Khye was a younger version of herself. They both had no ambition, wanted to find a man to take care of them, and heavily relied on their looks and freakiness to keep a man.

Young Khye was always spoiled and told that her beauty would get her far. And both mother and daughter figured out quickly that their accents garnered attention.

Sarah was addicted to gambling at card games and frequenting the casinos—Atlantic City was her favorite place to be. She would constantly lose her husband's entire paycheck each week so her family had to suffer, the refrigerator was always empty, and her kids didn't have enough clothes for the summer or the winter—they looked like refugees most times. However, when things got really bad, Sarah didn't have a problem getting a few dollars from any nigga, especially Gino or her cop friend—and if they didn't have it, she wasn't a stranger to giving a blow job or a hand job to the young hustlers in the building. She would borderline prostitute herself for a quick come up, and soon, everyone in the neighborhood started to clown Sarah and her family. It was embarrassing to Khye at first, but then she'd gotten used to it and no longer cared. Most times her mother was giving hand jobs for something Khye needed. Also, Khye had her own scandalous reputation in Harlem; she was beautiful but insecure, and easily fell prey to anyone praising and complimenting her beauty, especially a drug dealer. She was fucking niggas just to get a fresh pair of sneakers and a quick come up—demonstrating the old saying "She get it from her mama."

Sarah situated herself on her knees between Gino's legs and began to softly and gently lick the mushroom head, licking it like a soft-serve cone and expertly using the tip of her tongue in his slit.

"Ooooh shit . . . I like that, ma," Gino said.

She began swirling her tongue around the head, getting it wet and slippery with her spit; stroking him to full hardness with her hand. She looked up at Gino with a sexy look in her eyes, wrapped her full lips around his big dick, and took his entire length into her mouth in one stroke.

"Oh shit . . . ugh . . . ugh," he groaned.

She took a deep breath and went farther down, deep-throating Gino with a technique that would make a porn star jealous. Her head rapidly bobbed up and down in his lap, completely consuming him. She continued to wet his dick with her saliva and tickled the tip with her tongue, making Gino squirm in her grasp. He was so excited that he hardly recognized the strangely new high pitched moaning that he was making. He didn't care. It turned him on that she could do that to him.

"Damn ma, suck that fuckin' dick. Ooooh, do that shit, that's what the fuck I'm talkin' 'bout," he said.

He was breathless, feeling himself about to come quickly. Sarah began her technique of licking, sucking, and stroking his dick in a way that made him want to lose his mind. The pleasure was unspeakable—insane. Her lips, her tongue, her mouth, and hands all worked together to suck with the right pressure, to lick the right spots, to give him the sloppy, wet sensuous pleasure that made Gino coo loudly.

"You gonna make me come!" he hollered.

At that moment, there was hard knocking at the door, and it quickly interrupted the freakish and lustful mood in the room.

"What the fuck?!" Gino exclaimed.

Sarah stopped her pleasures as Gino jumped up to his full height, startled by the banging at his apartment door. He quickly pulled up his pants and grabbed the Glock 19 lying on the table. It sounded like police were outside.

"You expect company?" Sarah asked.

"Nah," he replied, nervously.

With the Glock gripped in his hand, Gino walked toward the door, shirtless and frowning about putting his nut on hold when it was really getting good. He cautiously moved closer, looked through the peephole, and sighed with relief knowing it wasn't the police or a rival threat.

"Yo, it's ya fuckin' daughter, Khye," he said.

"Khye?" Sarah was confused.

Gino opened the door to a frowning Khye.

"My mum here?" Khye asked.

"Yeah, what's up Khye? You know you got perfect timing," Gino said.

"Like I care," she replied.

Gino opened the door wider and stepped to the side to let her in. Sarah was covering her nudeness with one of Gino's T-shirts. Khye looked her mother's way with unconcerned eyes about her mother's whorish ways and simply said, "Mum, I need twenty dollars."

"Twenty dollars?"

"Yes."

"For what?"

"Sammy and I wanna go to the park and chill," she said.

"Park?" Sarah replied.

"There's this basketball game going on in Rucker's Park, and everybody's gonna be there. I need to go, Mum, it's gonna be smashing," said Khye.

Khye found Gino standing a little too closely behind her with his shirt off and his body shimmering with sexiness. His tattoos were appealing. He had *Blood Nation* tattooed across his thick chest and his gang affiliation was provocative. Khye found him attractive, but she wasn't about to take sloppy seconds behind her mother. Sarah already claimed him. Khye was ready to chase after other eligible hustlers who her mother didn't fuck.

"Why you hangin' out wit' the faggot?" Gino said, referring to Sammy.

"He's my friend. My best friend," Khye replied.

"He's a fuckin' faggot," Gino repeated.

Ignoring his last comment, Khye spoke to her mother. "Anyway, I'm hungry and there's nothing to eat in the fridge, like usual."

Knowing that her mother was with Gino, she figured he had to break her off with something. Gino was a drug dealer and he was known to always carry hundreds on him. He wasn't big-time, but he was doing okay for himself.

"Yo, I got you, ma…you ain't even gotta worry," Gino said, while looking at her candidly. It was no secret that Gino wanted to fuck her too. He wanted the best of both worlds—mother and daughter, be able to brag amongst his peers.

Khye placed her hand on her hip and stuck out her hand with her palm up, waiting for Gino to drop some cash into it.

He chuckled. "You a trip, ma."

"I know, so pay me," Khye quipped.

"So what's up wit' you and me?" he asked, unashamedly flirting with Khye while her mother was scantily clad in his apartment. He didn't have any morals when it came to pussy.

"Gino!" Sarah called out. "Don't, I'm standing right here."

"C'mon, ma, I was just playin'. I ain't tryin' to go there wit' ya young'un," he said.

"Uh-huh, whatever." Sarah rolled her eyes and sucked her teeth.

Khye was still waiting with her hand out, becoming impatient to get her hands on some cash. She didn't want to go out to Rucker's park a broke bitch. Her stomach was growling and she wanted to have some fun.

"Just give her something so she can leave and we can do us," Sarah urged.

Gino smiled. "Yeah, I feel you, ma."

He walked into his bedroom while Khye and Sarah stood in the living room looking at each other. Khye knew if her mother didn't get to Gino first, then she would have been the one occupying his apartment, sucking on his big dick and riding it until he exploded inside of her. Gino was a catch—thuggish eye candy that made both their pussies wet. But finders keepers, losers weepers.

"Is your father still sleeping?" Sarah asked.

"He's not going anywhere anytime soon, Mum. You know how he is."

"I know."

Sarah appreciated knowing that her daughter would never tell her father about any of her affairs. Their marriage had been crumbling for a long time. They weren't having sex at all, but she stayed because of his paycheck and it was expected, and twenty five years together was a long time—longevity was the only thing they had together.

Gino came walking out of the bedroom and placed a twenty-dollar bill into Khye's hand.

"That's it?" Khye complained.

"You only asked for twenty, right?" Gino said.

Khye sucked her teeth and crushed the bill into her fist. "Cheap!"

"You goin' to Rucker's now, right? Then be thankful, ma," said Gino.

Khye wanted to blurt out, *"Fuck you!"* but she kept her mouth shut, ungrateful for the twenty dollars she received. She expected Gino to break her off at least with fifty dollars.

She pivoted on her shoes and made her way toward the exit. She didn't even utter a goodbye to her mother or a thank-you to Gino. Khye marched out of Gino's apartment and heard the door shut behind her.

While her mother was getting the business in an air conditioned apartment, Khye was hot, sweaty, and frustrated. She caught an attitude. What could she do with twenty dollars in her pocket? It sucked to have her options limited. Everything cost. Khye was desperate for a change, and she hoped that by going to the basketball tournament in Rucker's Park, she could latch onto a fine, paid man who didn't mind looking out. Simply put, she was out to find a nigga to take care of her.

THREE

Marching out of the building lobby in her bargain center dress and Payless shoes, Khye got on her prepaid cell phone and called Sammy, her best friend. Sammy lived in the building next to hers on 135th Street, and he was as gay and flamboyant as Miss Jay from *America's Next Top Model*. The two had been best friends for years. Growing up, a lot of African-American girls in the neighborhood were jealous of her light skin and long hair, so Khye never had any girlfriends. Sammy, who sometimes liked to be called Sandy when he was feeling fabulous, was the only one who befriended Khye during troubled times. They had a lot in common. They both felt like outcasts in Harlem; he was just as poor as she was; and they were different, being called freaks—Khye because of her English accent and Sammy because of being homosexual.

The second she was in the sun, she started to sweat, feeling the sun's heat barreling down on her like heavy rain. Khye huffed; it didn't make any sense that it was so hot outside. She just hoped it cooled off before the first basketball game started at the park. Khye was excited; a basketball tournament at Rucker's park always brought out the superstars—the celebrities, the shot callers, and the street ballers, along with the players and niggas with money. The games always attracted the hoochie-mamas and the thirsty bitches that would be showing off skin and booty and yearning to snatch them up a fine, rich man. Khye knew she wasn't going to be the only one on the hunt, and she felt so far behind the competition because of her off-brand wardrobe and weak shoes. She felt like a diamond stuck inside a piece of coal.

Khye pressed the cell phone to her ear and let it ring, waiting for Sammy to pick up. She walked toward his building. Sammy was her crutch. When she felt down, he was always there to bring her up, make her laugh, and comfort her. She didn't care that he liked dick. He was very open about his sex life—always flaunting his sexuality. If you felt uncomfortable around him, he would flaunt it even more. He didn't care who judged him. He would always shout, "I'm gay and I'm black, but fuck with me. Laugh at me now and I'll have you crying later, bitches."

Sammy was a colorful guy. He was outgoing and showy, but could be sincere like a nun when it came to his family and his friends. He had visions of flashing lights and fame; he wanted to become a fashion designer. He wanted to become bigger than Tommy Hilfiger and Ralph Lauren put together. Sammy was known for always buying cheap clothes and then adding his own fabric and sequins to make them, only in his mind, couture.

Khye stood outside her friend's building and waited for him to pick up. He lived with his mother. Sammy's father had left a few years ago and disowned his son when he found out he was gay. It was a crushing feeling to Sammy. His own biological father wanted nothing to do with him and would constantly curse and criticize Sammy, saying cruel things like, "My faggot fuckin' son, you're an abomination to Christ! You hear me? I don't have faggots for sons! You AIDS-infested bitch. Faggots will always go to hell! Why don't you be more like your brother? Be a fuckin' man, you fuckin' faggot!"

It crushed Sammy. His father tried to beat the gay out of him on numerous occasions, but there was no changing Sammy. No matter what his father tried or said, Sammy was comfortable with who and what he was.

"You see, he don't know me, Khye, and he will never understand me. You supposed to love your son unconditionally, no matter what they are. That muthafucka never loved me. I hate him. But he the one that's gonna burn in hell, Khye. He the one that don't understand the world is changing, and that muthafucka is the real faggot," Sammy would complain to Khye as he cried on her shoulder and poured out his feelings.

For Khye and Sammy, as long as they had each other, they felt they could overcome anything.

"What, bitch?" Sammy answered lively and jokingly.

"I'm downstairs. Hurry up."

"Bitch, don't rush me. I'll be down there in a minute. You know it takes a diva some time to get ready for an event like this. You know I gotta look fabulous for these fine niggas out here," he said.

Khye laughed. "Don't have me waiting long out here in this blazing sun while you get all dolled up."

"Jelly?" Sammy mocked.

"Please, never that."

"Anyway, you know how some of these bitches is put together easily like Lego, and falling apart… not this bitch, so I gotta show off and stunt today, Khye. I need me a boo to take care of me," Sammy said.

"You and me both."

"Give me ten minutes and I'll be down there," he said.

"Okay."

"And, bitch, when you see me…don't hate," Sammy said.

Khye laughed. "I never do."

"That's why I love you," he proclaimed.

"And I love you, too," she replied.

Khye hung up and waited for Sammy in the lobby of his building. It was too hot to be lingering outside. She lit a cigarette, took a few pulls, and wished she had access to a pool. She wanted to wash away the sweat and cool off from the heat. What she would give to ride around in an air-conditioned luxury car—a Benz or a Lexus—close her eyes, and feel the blast of coolness against her skin. She could dream, but she didn't want to dream anymore. When would her dream become a reality?

Sammy stepped out of the elevator and Khye was blown away.

"Wow," she uttered.

"You like it, bitch?" he asked.

"I love it," she said.

Sammy twirled in front of her, going vogue. He wore straight-legged shorts so tight, you could see his bulge and a fitted shirt designed with pink rhinestones and a stylish sequence of hearts and flowers underneath a bright green vest. His nails and toes were polished, and his eyeliner and glossy lips looked flawless. Everything was put together by him in his own, unique flavor. When a crowd of people were around, he loved twerking like a big-booty bitch, popping his ass cheeks up and down. Sammy was a character.

Sammy wanted to own the room and expected every eye to be on him. He loved the attention.

"You not gonna be hot in all that?" Khye asked. "I mean, it is brilliant."

"Bitch, I'm brighter than the sun right now. Chicks gonna need shade from me when I step through," Sammy said.

Khye laughed. "You're so silly."

"Like Martin on *Def Comedy Jam*, now you know that's my nigga."

Sammy gazed at Khye's clothing; she looked like the Salvation Army had spit her out. The only thing going for her was her massive mane of hair and the lip gloss on her lips. Khye read her friend's look and said, "I know, but I had nothing else to put on."

"Girl, we gonna work with you this summer."

"I need work, huh?"

"Yes you do. Bitch, I'm gonna be your fairy godmother and work magic on you," he said, and tugging on her dress with rapid hand gestures.

She smiled.

Sammy continued with, "I'm ready to get these glossy lips on some nigga's dick tonight."

"You are a hot mess, Sammy."

"The hotter the better . . . feel me bitch?"

"Yeah, I feel you."

"You got any cash on you?" Sammy asked.

"Twenty dollars."

"That's it?" he said.

"I tried."

"A bitch is hungry like a starving slave."

"I am, too," she said.

"Girl, I hope this doesn't become a long, fucked-up day," said Sammy.

"I hope so, too."

They exited the lobby and decided to walk to Rucker's Park near the former Polo Grounds. It was a twenty-block walk, and in the unbearable heat, it was almost suicidal. But with only twenty dollars between them, they needed the money for something to eat and water to keep from dehydrating. They were determined to make it to the basketball tournament and have a fun time.

It was early evening, and Rucker's Park was getting underway for another night of exciting street basketball. The area was bustling with traffic and people. The high end cars and bumper to bumper traffic were lined up and down Frederick Douglass Blvd. Every flashy car had music blaring rap or R&B, causing people to stop and quickly dance to their favorite song playing. The dope boys and hustlers were already out in full force, looking like rap stars in their gaudy jewelry and urban clothing. It looked more like a video shoot than a basketball game was happening.

Across the street, rising out of the ground were the once-famed Polo Grounds; four thirty-story housing projects known as the Polo Ground

Towers loomed ominously over Holcombe Rucker Park.

Fans on the street were willing to wait for hours to squeeze inside the small park and watch basketball in its rawest form. A Rucker's Game—an Eastside Basketball Club event— brought out everyone from renowned NBA players, such as Ron Artest, Vince Carter, Wilt Chamberlain, and many more. The celebrities and rap stars showed their presences at big games—some rappers and music moguls even coached teams—and major bets were made on the games. It was better than the NBA in most eyes. Rucker's Park on tournament night—it was the place to be in Harlem, and Khye and Sammy made sure they were going to be front and center.

Khye's eyes lit up like gold seeing all the activity happening around her. Everywhere she turned, there were people, cars—nice cars; Benzes, Lexuses, Range Rovers, Porsches, and BMWs—even a Ferrari and a couple of Bentleys were parked on the street. She envied the fly bitches stepping out of the high-end cars, latched to their men and looking like divas. She wasn't going to let the glitzy scene intimidate her, though she was dressed like an orphan. Khye walked with her head held as high as if she were wearing Prada and Chanel. She wanted the attention, too. Niggas were posted up on their cars like they were about to do a photo shoot with their vehicles.

She and Sammy didn't care what people thought as they passed, going toward Rucker's Park. Sammy's flamboyant attire manifested his gayness full-scale. He switched harder than most bitches in the street and saw a few male cuties he wanted to get with. His lip gloss was popping, and his clothing definitely caught attention. The men scowled and frowned at him walking by, but no one had the balls to say anything to him, until they got near the entrance gate.

"Fuckin' faggot!" someone exclaimed.

Sammy heard the muthafucka loud and clear. Khye did too. He said it intentionally for it to be heard. Sammy stopped walking and said, "Oh,

I know this nigga ain't just come out his mouth at me. Bitch, do he know who the fuck I am?"

He pivoted on his sandals and was ready to confront the man. The man with the harsh comment scowled at Sammy, ignoring his friends' warning. "Yo, nigga chill, don't start wit' him."

"Fuck that faggot!" he exclaimed.

Unbeknownst to him, Sammy was connected and not to be fucked with. Sammy had a brother named Able, and Able was totally the opposite of his little brother. Able was a thug—a hardcore gangster. He was Blood, notorious in the streets and he had a best friend named, Jason, who everyone called "The Gun." The Gun was a hired killer for the local thugs, the gangs in Harlem. His name rang bells and he was greatly feared. Able was bad news. Able and The Gun, together, were a problem.

Everybody knew Sammy and Able were brothers, and the hood looked the other way when Sammy came through with his gayness. No one disrespected him. If they didn't like his lifestyle, they kept it to themselves. They didn't want any dealings with Able or The Gun. Able was always screaming on his brother for being a faggot, but deep down inside, he deeply loved his little brother and somewhat respected him for being who he was, despite what their father might have thought of him. So Sammy was protected in the neighborhood because of his brother, and it gave him freedom to go wherever he wanted and not be humiliated or disrespected.

Sammy marched toward the man, ready to go ham for being called a faggot. Khye was right behind him. She didn't want the drama, but Sammy was her best friend, and if he had beef, then she had beef.

"Nigga, who you calling a faggot with your ugly self?" Sammy barked, with his hands moving through the air at him.

"Yo Sammy, he ain't mean no disrespect," the friend chimed, stepping in between the two and trying to defuse the drama.

"Yes he did. He got that mouth; he can speak for himself, Benny… that's your friend? You know who the fuck I am?" Sammy questioned.

The thug continued to scowl. "Yo, nigga, you need to fall back, Christmas-tree looking gay-ass faggot," the man said, not willing to back down.

"What? Oh no he didn't," Sammy exclaimed. "Nigga, I will fuck you up."

Before the confrontation ensued, the heavy police presence made Sammy and his adversary fall back. There were cops everywhere, and once a confrontation looked like it was about to happen, NYPD would come running over. No one wanted to get arrested today. It was too hot, and Khye wanted to have a good time.

"C'mon, Sammy. He's not even worth it," Khye said.

"I know right? Like ill. There are too many fine-ass niggas out here right now for me to be focused on some ugly buster," Sammy said.

Khye and Sammy proceeded to make their way toward the park. Khye's stomach was growling, and she wanted someone to take her out to eat, and with a basketball court full of sweaty men, and hustlers on the streets, she felt her odds were good.

The two decided to linger outside the park for a moment. Khye yearned for some attention. Even though she wasn't dressed stylishly, she was extremely beautiful, but so was almost every chick there—the competition was fierce. There were so many beautiful girls everywhere, all wearing extremely tight outfits with huge booties like there was a booty sale at the plastic surgeon's office. No way all those chicks were born that way, Khye thought. The women were wearing much better clothing, dressed in booty shorts, tight jeans and spandex, high heels and long weaves, carrying designer bags, and one girl was showing off in her six-inch gladiator Louboutins.

"Girl, you ready to go in, cuz I need me a seat," Sammy said.

"Wait a minute," Khye replied.

"Why, who you got your eye on, girl?" he asked.

She smiled. Khye caught eyes with a few ballers lingering outside the park, but it was hard to keep them simply focused on her and get their undivided attention. With so much ass and skin around, she seemed average. Khye pretended to be in a deep conversation with Sammy while glancing at one guy seated in a 2014 Range Rover nearby. She ran her hand through her long hair and laughed out of the blue.

"Bitch, you crazy?" Sammy asked. "Who you trying to impress?"

"Somebody," she said.

Khye and the driver made eye contact a few times and she threw him a welcoming smile. He was cute, with light skin and hazel eyes. Her welcoming smile didn't cause him to bite. He diverted his attention somewhere else, and Khye's heart sunk into the pit of her stomach. She thought she had him. She didn't want to look desperate. She was taught men should always approach you, not the other way around.

After trying to snatch up some ballers' attention outside with no results, the two finally decided to enter the park. The problem was, there was a ten-dollar admission. It sucked. Khye paid her and Sammy's way in. She wanted to be at the game and try her luck inside. Now that she was completely broke, her stomach growled louder and it was embarrassing. She was so hungry that she felt faint, but she stayed strong.

There were a few dozen spectators already lounging around the steel and plastic bleachers. The park filled fast. The slight breeze coming off the Harlem River felt good. Khye and Sammy were able to get seating in the back of the bleachers. The game was about to start. The two rival teams took the courts in their colorful jerseys, and each player towered with finesse and height.

"Damn, all them goodies on the court, foul me! Ooooh, foul me any day," Sammy hollered.

He stirred up some laughter around him. Khye laughed too. "You're so silly."

"Girl, I think I need to become a referee, so I can get up close and personal. They hiring?" he continued to joke. Today he was definitely Sandy.

It was getting late, the daylight hour transitioning into hours of darkness and the heat wave steadily declining to something normal. The streetlights were on, and the music was going. The referees took the court, the ball in their hands, each team standing on opposite ends of the court. They were ready to play and give the crowd something to cheer about. The park was swelled with spectators from every end, looking like a fat man in tight jeans about to burst open. The referee bent his legs slightly as the long-time EBC announcer, Ethan Lango, picked up the microphone, ready to make it happen.

"Welcome to Rucker Park, the start of the greatest outdoor tournament in the world." His husky voice shredded through the summer air, jolting the listless crowd.

The ball was tossed up—a knuckleball—and climbed toward its apex before a pair of large hands met it on the way down. The game had started. It was tipped backwards in a slow, soft arc.

Khye tried to focus on the game, but she was more focused on the fine men scattered around the park. Some were on their cell phones, some were talking and laughing with each other, some were with their girlfriends, and many were making big bets and observing the standout players on the basketball court doing voracious dunks and sinking three-pointers from the top of the key.

Ethan Lango made the crowd laugh with his silky voice and witty remarks. The game was exciting—players were dunking wildly and the crowds of spectators were roaring.

Sammy and Khye weren't even pretending to watch the game; they were both annoyed. They didn't come to watch basketball, they came to change their lives. Sammy knew there were a lot of down-low niggas in Harlem, who weren't openly gay as he was, but chose to remain trapped in the closet and pretend that they were something that they weren't. But Sammy knew with the right stare and the right words, there was always one that wanted him in secret, where they could be themselves somewhere private, away from judgment, and please each other—two dicks playing swordsmen, along with pillow biting and asshole thumping.

Two hours later, they were leaving the park and were ready to go back home. The day was a failure to them both. Khye caught niggas looking her way, but she wasn't enough to fully capture their attention. With her stomach growling like a lion roaring in the wilderness, and no food in the fridge at home, she wanted to cry.

With the game over, hordes of people started to pour out the exit from the sidewalks into the streets. Music blared from every direction, and people were mingling, networking, and hooking up. As Khye made her way toward 155th Street, she felt someone gently grab her hand and say, "Hey gorgeous."

At first, she wanted to keep on walking. She was frustrated and annoyed. She was more interested in the hustlers out front with their expensive cars. But when she turned to face the guy grabbing her hand out of nowhere, she fell silent and was in awe at his features. He was too fine—tall and handsome.

"I know you ain't just gonna walk away from me, beautiful," he said.

Sammy stood behind her, admiring. He wished he could have a piece of him, too, but it was obvious he wanted Khye's attention. So he stood quietly with his arms folded across his chest and let Khye have her moment.

"And you are?" Khye said in her thick English accent.

"Oh shit, damn… I love ya accent. Where you from?" he asked.

"Originally, I'm from London. But I've been living here for years now."

"Well, welcome to America. I'm Floyd. What's ya name?" he asked.

"Khye," she said.

Her eyes were transfixed by his handsome features. He had soft, black hair that he kept low and cinnamon-colored skin, a thick mustache, and a heavy scar on his left cheek that gave him that edge. Khye immediately knew he was a bad boy. He was clad in cargo shorts, a V-neck T-shirt, and white shelltoes that looked fresh out of the box. His physique was lean and defined with tattoos that started at his wrists and crawled toward his slender biceps. He was six feet tall with a lithe upper body that resembled that of a tennis player.

Car or no car, Khye felt Floyd was definitely worth her time.

"Floyd, huh…like Mayweather," she said.

"Yup, but only better," he said with his bright, white smile showing.

She was tempted to ask if he had money like Floyd Mayweather, but she didn't want to come across as a gold-digger. She wanted him to believe she was an innocent foreign girl from a different country who was still getting used to living in the States, though she'd been living in Harlem for ten years. Floyd thought he hit the lottery when he heard Khye talk. She was known for exaggerating her English accent to lure the men in. She would enunciate her words to garner much attention for herself. They always loved something different, and when Khye talked, she was something different.

"So what brings you to Rucker's Park?" she asked.

"I love the game."

"I do too," she lied.

"So what's good wit' you, you single, dating, or what?" Floyd asked frankly.

"I'm single at the moment."

"Oh, word?" Floyd replied with a heavy grin. "So what you doin' right now? You busy?"

"Not really."

"You hungry?" he asked. "You want to get something to eat? It's my treat, baby girl."

Those were the magic words she'd been longing to hear all day. She was starving. It felt like her stomach was in cardiac arrest. It was hard for Khye to contain her smile. She was about to give up and go home hungry and exhausted, but Floyd became her refuge. She was ready to jump on his horse and ride with him to wherever.

"Yes, I am," said Khye, coolly.

"A'ight, let's go then," Floyd said.

She started to walk off with him, forgetting about Sammy standing behind her, who was waiting patiently for her conversation to end with her newfound friend. She didn't even have the courtesy to introduce Sammy to Floyd.

"Khye," Sammy called out, looking at his friend with a slight attitude. "Where you going?"

Khye turned around and uttered, "Oh, he's gonna take me out for something to eat."

"Really, Khye? You know a bitch is hungry, too," Sammy griped.

Floyd nonchalantly stared at Sammy and he wanted no parts with the faggot, even though he was Khye's friend, he was ready to let him starve. Khye was his only interest.

"Sammy, I'm going to call you, okay? Cheerio," Khye said, using an archaic British expression.

Sammy scowled. "Cheer-i-o?!"

"Yes!"

"Really?"

Sammy was pissed. He watched as Khye walked away with Floyd, arm-in-arm, the two already becoming too friendly with each other, looking cozy as they walked up the block.

" 'Cheerio.' I like that. What that mean?" Floyd asked.

"Oh, it means 'goodbye.'"

Floyd laughed. "Damn, I like you."

"I'm glad you do, and I like you too," Khye said, grinning from ear to ear.

When Floyd walked toward his CL600, it was hard for Khye to hold back her smile and excitement. It was a beautiful car. It was dark blue with chrome rims and slightly tinted windows. It screamed "baller" in Khye's eyes.

"Nice car," she said.

"Thanks," he replied.

Floyd hit the button to deactivate the alarm and opened the passenger door for Khye so she could slide into the seat. It was a good feeling to be treated like a lady. He didn't even know her, and she didn't know him, but it felt like he was the one already.

Floyd got behind the wheel and started the car. The engine purred like a kitten. The cream color leather seats and the illuminated dashboard had Khye feeling like she was in a spaceship. Floyd pulled away from the curb, and Khye couldn't help but smile, thinking to herself, *Mission accomplished.*

FOUR

my Ruth's, the renowned soul food restaurant on 116th Street, had some of the best dishes in Harlem. The place was semi-crowded when Khye walked in with Floyd. The smell of collard greens, chicken wings and waffles, and barbecued spare ribs overran Khye's nostrils and made her mouth water. She couldn't wait to eat. The two grabbed a corner table and the waiter immediately came over to get their drink order. Khye was only nineteen, so she ordered fruit punch. Khye wanted to try everything on the menu; Floyd already made it clear that money wasn't an issue with him. She ordered chicken wings and waffles, and a cornbread.

Sitting opposite of Khye, Floyd gazed at Khye's beauty. She seemed so innocent and pure. Khye was quickly smitten by his kindness and his swag. He had "roughneck" written all over him, but there was this gentleness that surfaced.

"I gotta be honest," Floyd started.

"Honest about what?" Khye asked.

"One of the reasons why I approached you is because of your style," he said.

"My style?" she was confused by his statement. She didn't have a style, so she thought. She felt plain and subpar.

"Yeah, you weren't like all the other ladies out there wearing expensive clothing and shoes, having heavy makeup on. You were just cute and simple, being yourself. I like that," he declared.

She chuckled. "You do?"

"Hells yeah, and then your accent was like whoa, what the fuck. That's a definite turn-on," he said.

"I'm glad you like it."

"I love it."

She smiled. Her plainness paid off. She didn't think in a million years it would. Today, everything was in her favor. Floyd seemed like a nice guy who knew what he wanted in a woman. She sat across from him with her innocence oozing out, constantly blushing from his compliments. He oozed sex appeal, and his confidence was so strong that Khye felt her pussy dripping.

They continued to talk until their orders arrived. Khye wanted to devour the chicken and waffles that were placed in front of her. She was so hungry that she could eat a horse and still have room for dessert. Floyd had the barbecued spare ribs.

The chicken Khye ordered was delicious and the waffles were sweet and tasty.

"Where are you from?" Khye asked. She never saw him around in Harlem.

Floyd took a drink of juice and then responded, "Brooklyn. Bed-Stuy, do or die. You ever been out that way?"

"Not really," she said, with her accent catching the attention of others in the surrounding area.

"You definitely need to come out to Brooklyn. I got you out there. That's my home," he said.

"And you come to Harlem regular?" she asked him.

"Yeah, I love it out here, too. I go to the studio not too far from here."

"Studio?" Khye said with her raised eyebrow.

"Yeah, I do music," he said. "But I'm not a rapper or a singer. I'm an engineer."

"Oh, you are? Nice."

"Yup, love it, trying to become the next Dr. Dre out here."

Hearing Floyd say he was in the music business turned Khye on even more. His style, his jewelry, his sneakers . . . yes, he was perfect. She continued to throw her virtuousness at him like a baseball pitch. Khye had a way of playing the same role when she met a man. She pretended to be sheltered from America's harsh ways—the personification of innocence, almost virginal. Floyd foolishly believed she was untouched, pure. Instantly, he wanted to take care of her. There was something about her that was unquestionable. He wanted Khye to experience the good life through him.

As they dined, Floyd's cell phone went off against his hip. He stared at the caller I.D and decided to ignore the phone call. It wasn't the first time his cell phone had rung. His phone had been blowing up all night. He was a really busy man, but she wasn't bothered by it. She was just happy to occupy his space and get a free meal. She figured he had a girlfriend. He was too fine and rich to not have someone special in his life.

"Girlfriend?" she said.

Floyd chuckled. "Nah, just business."

"I see."

"I'm serious. I'm a single man, Khye, waiting for that right someone to come into my life and steal my heart away. It might be you," he said.

She grinned. His game was tight. His words were convincing. He regularly made eye contact with Khye when speaking. He didn't stutter, and he seemed comfortable with himself. Khye didn't care if he had a girlfriend; it would be only a minor obstacle in her way to making Floyd hers. So far, everything was going well.

"So tell me more about you, Khye." Floyd leaned closer to her across the table, transfixed by her light eyes and dimpled cheeks.

"There's nothing much special about me," she returned simply. "I'm an up and coming fashion designer, and trying to get into school soon," she lied.

"Oh word? That's what up."

She decided to take Sammy's ambition. She didn't want to come across as stupid and lazy. She understood a man loved a woman with goals for herself. So she made her friend's goal hers.

"You got sketches or sumthin' I can look at?" he asked.

"I had, but I lost everything when our apartment caught on fire," she lied again.

"Oh shit, sorry to hear about that. How that happen?"

"Faulty wiring in the building," she said.

"Damn, but I'm glad you came out okay," he said.

"Barely," she replied.

Khye was on a roll. She had Floyd's undivided attention and planned on keeping it for a long while. They spent an hour dining in Amy Ruth's. Whatever Khye wanted, she ordered that night, from dessert to something extra to take home. At the end of the meal, Floyd pulled out a wad of hundreds to pay for the meal, and Khye was impressed. He was definitely legit. Jackpot!

They exited the restaurant into the balmy night. Floyd pulled out a cigarette and lit it up. Khye looked his way and said, "Can I get a fag as well?"

"What?" he responded, thrown off by the word. "You want what?"

She giggled. "Cigarette," she corrected.

"That's what y'all call it in London? A fag?"

She nodded. "Yes."

"Wow, that's crazy. I'm gonna love being with you," he said, smiling.

Floyd and Khye started to walk toward his car. When he hit the alarm to his CL600, there was one problem; she was embarrassed to tell him where she lived.

"I'm fine, I'll take the train home," she said.

"Nah, I got you, love. I'll take you home," he insisted.

But Khye was determined to walk home because she didn't have any money on her.

"I'd rather take the train," she said.

Rather than debate with her any longer, he said, "You sure?"

She nodded.

He reached into his pocket, pulled out his wad of hundreds and peeled off three hundred dollars. He put the cash in Khye's hand and said, "If you don't want me to know where you live, that's cool, but take a taxi home. It's on me."

Khye had no problem taking his cash but she feigned an objection. "This is absolutely too bloody much money. I mean, this is a week's paycheck."

Floyd chuckled. "This is pocket change; that's what this is."

"But I don't want to take all your money. What will you have left?"

This was a first for Floyd and he had to admit he liked it. What chick turned down a handout? "Don't worry about all that. I got me. And, if you let me, I got you too."

Khye continued to resist before ultimately accepting his offer. It was a needed blessing. "Thank you."

Before Floyd climbed into his Benz, he said, "So when I'm gonna see you again?"

"You have my number, call me."

"I definitely will."

Khye grinned. She didn't want to leave him, but she had to. It was late and she wasn't stupid, figuring he had a girlfriend at home. That wasn't going to stop her from getting her come up. Floyd got behind the wheel and started the ignition. He pulled away from the curb and headed toward the Brooklyn Bridge. Khye watched him leave with butterflies in her stomach. A warm feeling stirred up inside of her. She had a good feeling about Floyd. The first thing she wanted to do was call Sammy and tell him everything about tonight. He would be pissed, but knowing Sammy, he would get over it. She couldn't pass up on a golden opportunity. It's what they always talked about; finding that rich and fine guy to sweep them off their feet and take care of them. Floyd had the potential to be her bailout. Yes, she couldn't wait to see him again.

She walked toward the nearest train station to jump the turnstile feeling on cloud nine. With three hundred dollars in her pocket, it was a new outfit, some sneakers, shoes maybe, and other needed accessories for the summer. If things kept going the way they were going with Floyd, Khye felt it could become the best summer of her young life.

***

Khye walked into her family's apartment with her belly full and money in her pockets. Her father was motionless in his underwear on the shabby couch, with an empty vodka bottle tipped over on the carpet. She shook her head in disgust and went to her bedroom. Inside, both her sisters were sleeping. She had to share a bed with her sisters—two beds, three girls, do the math. It was uncomfortable and tiresome. Ava talked in her sleep, and Maisie couldn't keep still, always hogging up the covers and moving around constantly like she had ADD in her sleep.

Khye sighed. She needed her own room.

She shut the door and went into her parents' room. Her mother wasn't home. She was still upstairs in Gino's apartment, probably still getting dicked down.

She closed the door to her parents' room and pulled out the money Floyd gave her. She grinned like Scrooge McDuck. There was no way she was going to share any of it with her family, although her two sisters were also starving in the house.

Even though she dissed him for Floyd, she wanted to call Sammy. She couldn't wait to spill everything in his ear about Floyd. Bluntly speaking, she wanted to brag. Picking up her prepaid cell phone with only a few minutes left on it, she dialed Sammy's number. It rang a few times before he answered with an attitude, "Oh, so now I'm relevant, bitch?"

"Yes you are, Sammy, and always will be. I'm sorry," Khye said, sweetly.

"Bitch, um . . . fuck your sorry. How you gonna diss me like that?"

"Did you bloody well *see* him, Sammy?" she said.

"Yeah, he was kind of cute," Sammy replied dryly.

"Kind of? He was fine!"

"Whatever, bitch. Did you fuck him?"

"No, not yet. But come over, I wanna talk to you," Khye suggested.

"Diva, it's almost midnight, you know I need my beauty sleep, and besides, you ain't my favorite person right now."

"Sammy, I got a lot to tell you. So, stay the night over here. My mum's upstairs and my father is passed out drunk again. And I'm sorry; I'll make it up to you, promise."

Sammy sucked his teeth, feeling reluctant. "I don't know. I still feel salty."

"Please," Khye begged him.

"Ho, I love it when you beg, and he better have a friend for me," said Sammy.

Khye laughed.

Fifteen minutes later, Sammy was at her door and Khye let him in and they both rushed into her parents' room and shut the door. Before he took a seat in the bedroom Sammy said to Khye, "Okay, first off bitch, let me tell you something, I was hungry too, and I ain't appreciate how you dissed me for some dick." He expressed himself with his overly animated flair.

"Sammy, you would have done it, too. I didn't mean to skive off on you like that, but really," Khye said, "He gave me three hundred dollars."

"What, bitch?" Sammy replied excitedly.

"Nutters, right?"

Khye pulled out the money and Sammy's eyes lit up.

"So let me make it up to you tomorrow. Let's do something," she said.

"Honey Bun, I'm down," Sammy said, giving Khye a high-five and giggling.

"See, I told you I would make it up to you," said Khye grinning widely.

"You better, bitch."

FIVE

Floyd drove into Brooklyn and made his way toward Canarsie with Khye heavily on his mind. Everything about her seemed perfect. The way she talked, her accent, and her innocence, it got him so excited, he found himself becoming hard as he made his way home. He had "Nasty" by Nas playing in his car and was cruising in the middle of the night. He was tempted to call Khye just to hear her voice, but he decided to wait until the next day. He didn't want to appear desperate. There were so many things he wanted to do with Khye that his mind was about to explode.

He turned right on Rockaway Parkway, almost home. It was a lovely night and the traffic was sparse on his way home. He nodded to Nas and felt good about his life. He was making major moves and felt everything was lined up perfectly. He had money to burn, a nice car, and a nice pad. Most of all, he had respect. Bed-Stuy was his stomping ground, where he made his money and earned his reputation. Canarsie was the place he laid his head every night. It was a working- and middle-class residential and commercial neighborhood in the southeastern portion of Brooklyn. And where Floyd lived, it was quiet.

He rode down Rockaway Parkway with "One Mic" playing. It was one of his favorite songs of all time. He could play it over and over again. Nas was one of his favorite rappers. Floyd had plans. He was from the hood, did things to come up, but he didn't want to stay ghetto. He wanted the perfect lifestyle and needed the perfect bitch to represent him. Khye seemed like she could be the one, but only time could tell.

He made his way toward Avenue N, made a right, and soon approached the condos he lived in near the waters. For $2,200 a month, his place had a balcony overlooking the bay, high ceilings, beautiful original wood floors, three bedrooms, a spacious master bedroom with a long walk-in closet and updated amenities, along with a pool and tennis court. Floyd refused to live any other way. He had grown up poor and underprivileged. His origin was the same cliché: mother on crack, father doing life in prison. The streets raised him, and he found family with the Brooklyn gangs and did things to survive. Looking at him now, he'd come a long way, and he was always the man of the hour—a fly nigga, a get-money nigga—and he yearned to be a paid music mogul. He had a knack for music, and was willing to do or try anything to become the best producer and engineer in the game.

Floyd parked on the shaded Brooklyn street, stepped out of his CL600 with his fresh shelltoes touching the pavement, and walked to his home, hitting the alarm button to secure his ride.

He walked inside to see his girlfriend of two years, Tatianna, sitting on the couch butt-naked, smoking a blunt, and watching late-night TV. Near her feet was an empty bottle of Grey Goose. It was obvious she was tipsy.

"Hey baby, where you been at? It's late?" she asked.

"Another late night in the studio," he lied.

She greeted him with a passionate hug and kisses. She missed her man, and loved him dearly, but the feeling wasn't mutual. Things felt different in his home. Floyd looked at her coolly. Every night it was the same with her; smoking weed, clubbing with her friends till dawn, getting tipsy, and acting a fool. She was a freak and wasn't classy at all. She was exotic and beautiful like Khye, but the many tattoos she decorated her body with was a huge turnoff for Floyd. In his mind, it was like putting graffiti on a Bentley Coupe. She was half black and half Russian, born and raised in Brooklyn like him, and she was hood. Floyd was becoming tired of his live-in girlfriend.

Back in the days, he used to love her—was in love with her. They grew up in the same neighborhood, the same block, knew the same muthafuckas and used to have so much fun together. Tatianna had no ambition, no real goals for her life. All she did was blow his money and look cute. She got lazy and was spoiled by him. The Range Rover she drove was paid for by him and it was in his name. The condo was his, and he paid all the bills. He bought her the best clothes, the best shoes, and the best jewelry and did everything to come up out of the ghetto.

Tatianna didn't have an accent like Khye and she wasn't pure and innocent; she had her trifling past and she never lived abroad like Khye. Floyd instantly found himself comparing Khye and his live-in girlfriend, and of course, Khye had the edge.

He could smell the liquor on Tatianna's breath as she kissed him. He was aloof from her affection. The place was a mess. She rarely cooked or cleaned. She simply wanted to live the high life and not put in her own work, and after a while, Floyd got tired of it.

Tatianna didn't want to remove herself from her man. She kept her arms wrapped around him, smiling flirtatiously in his face, and said, "I wanna fuck." The liquor made her horny and she wanted some dick. She started to fondle with his crotch area, desperately wanting to pull it out and stroke his dick in her hand. Floyd remained distant toward her sexual advances. He had things on his mind.

"Let me suck it," she whispered to him.

As she was about to drop down on her knees to please her man, he politely pushed her away and said, "Nah, not right now."

"Why baby? I want you," she whined.

"It's been a long day, and I'm tired. I just want to get some sleep."

"I can put you to sleep really nice, like I always do, baby," she said, pulling at his jeans, not ready to give up.

Floyd pushed her away again, this time a little rougher. She almost fell over. "I said, chill. I ain't in the mood right now," he said a little more firmly.

Tatianna frowned. "Why you don't want me tonight? Because you out there fuckin' some other bitch?"

"I ain't got time for your nonsense, Tatianna, I'm going to bed," he said, walking away.

"Floyd, don't do me like this. I sat here all night waiting for your ass to come home, and you can't give me no dick!"

He went into the bedroom and shut the door, tuning her out. Tatianna folded her arms across her breasts and scowled. She was upset. She flopped down on the couch and pouted like a two-year-old.

"Fuck you then, nigga!" she exclaimed.

In her gut, she knew she was losing her man, probably to someone else. Tatianna wasn't about to let it happen so easily. If there was another bitch in her man's life, then she was willing to fight for their relationship. They'd had two years together, and had known each other as friends much longer than that. Floyd was her soulmate and she loved him too much to let him go.

Tatianna wanted to charge into the master bedroom and take what was hers, his dick. Her pussy was throbbing and wet, and Floyd was denying her the guilty pleasures she'd been thinking about all night. She continued to sulk in the room and said to herself, "Fuck it!" She reached for her dildo, rolled up another blunt, got high, and fucked herself with the plastic dildo on the couch. If Floyd didn't want to give her some dick, she had her own devices to work with.

There weren't going to be too many nights with her being deprived of sex.

Floyd didn't go to bed right way. He sat at the foot of the bed gazing out the bedroom window. The moonlight came through the window and Floyd's thoughts were stuck on Khye. He was definitely going to contact her sometime tomorrow and set up a date with her. She was something new and different, and the more he thought about Khye, the harder his dick got. He soon found himself jerking off while thinking about her while his girlfriend was in the next room pleasing herself.

SIX

K hye and Sammy hit 125th Street excitedly. Three hundred felt like three thousand dollars to them. As promised, Khye looked out for her friend. They hit the clothing stores with a tight budget; $270 (minus the prepaid minutes for her phone) could only go so far with the clothing boutiques and retail stores on 125th Street. But Sammy was an expert shopper; he knew how to buy the cheap stuff and spice it up with his own flavor. He only needed the right material. So they went shopping up and down the street, going in and out of stores, laughing and having a good time. With $270 to spend, they made off good with many nice items, along with sewing threads and different material for Sammy to work with when they got back home.

They ate at McDonalds and enjoyed the sun drenched day. Off course Sammy caught the fleeting looks and negative stares as he trotted up and down 125th Street with his best friend. Clad in tight bootie jean shorts and a T-shirt that read, *Kiss me before my boyfriend comes back*, he didn't care what people thought of him. He was always himself and living his life.

"So, you heard from Mr. Wonderful yet?" Sammy asked Khye.

"No, he didn't call yet," she said.

"He will."

"I know."

"Look at you, all cocky with it and shit. You ain't fly," Sammy joked.

Khye made sure to put more minutes on her prepaid phone just in case he did call, or if she decided to call him. The last thing she wanted to happen was her time running out during a conversation with Floyd. She wanted him to call. She didn't want to look desperate. Her womanly instincts told her he wasn't going to let her down.

The two walked across the busy Eighth Avenue, also known as Frederick Douglass Blvd, and they walked past the iconic Apollo Theater. Sammy joked around and made Khye laugh. Khye walked around in her colorful short shorts, sandals, and tank-top, and caught some eyes from a few passing males. Some even attempted to try and talk to her, but by their style she knew they were broke niggas not worth her time. They fell in love with her accent, and if a nigga was too aggressive, in her strong English tone, she would say to them, "Piss off!" and they would be blown away.

They spent the entire afternoon shopping on 125th Street and lingering in the stores wishing they had a lot more money to spend. The things Khye wanted to buy were pricey, but she knew every piece of clothing or item she had her eyes on would accentuate her beautiful figure and would make bitches envy her. She just didn't have that type of money to spend. It was a disappointing feeling, but Sammy was always there to cheer her up.

"Khye, I'm gonna make you the perfect outfit this week, and it's gonna explode on you, girl, and then I'll do your hair, and these bitches ain't gonna have shit on you," Sammy said lively.

Khye smiled. "Thanks, Sammy."

"Bitch, we girls, right? I look out for you and you look out for me."

"We always do," Khye replied.

They made their way home via gypsy cab, back to Lincoln Projects on the East Side. They stepped out of the cab with shopping bags and delight displayed across their faces. The corner of 132nd Street and Fifth Avenue was bustling with people and activity. It was Harlem on a sunny day; traffic was far and wide, life going on and on, and the gangbangers and thugs lingered on the street corners and bodegas.

Sammy and Khye seemed to be in their own world as they crossed the busy Fifth Avenue approaching the stack of project buildings. Khye planned on spending the day with Sammy at his place trying on the clothing they bought and spicing it up with different designs.

They walked into the area and immediately Sammy went from happy to bothered and perturbed when he noticed his older brother, Able, and his friends chilling down the block in front of the project building. They were smoking cigarettes and weed openly, along with drinking and gambling on the sidewalk. Music blared from an SUV and they were loud on the block.

"Fuck!" Sammy cursed. "I don't need to put up with his shit right now."

"You'll be fine, Sammy," Khye said.

Sammy sucked his teeth and marched forward. Able took a swig from the Mad Dog 20/20 concealed in a brown paper bag. His right-hand man, The Gun, stood right next to him and looked more intimidating and deadlier every single day. Able was engrossed in the dice game happening with five hundred dollars up for grabs. He was the loudest mouth in the group, talking shit.

"Y'all niggas ready to lose y'all fuckin' paper?" he hollered, shaking the dice in his fist and ready to roll.

"Just roll, nigga, and lose ya fuckin' money," someone said.

"Shut the fuck up, nigga! Just for talkin' shit, I'm takin' all ya money, nigga," Able said.

Both men, Able and The Gun were known for their frosty temperament. Able had a reputation for being icy calm in sticky situations. He stood six feet tall and weighed 190 pounds. He was slim, but dangerous and respected. And he and The Gun were unapologetic for being ruthless, vicious men.

Able rolled the dice and crapped out—1, 2, 3. He hollered, "Yo, fuck that, them dice is rigged."

"Nigga, you lost, give me my fuckin' money," one of his goons said, quickly snatching the five hundred from the concrete.

Able glared at his cohort and felt like punching the man in his face. He hated losing. He clenched his fist and scowled.

"Yo nigga, you gonna give me the chance to win my fuckin' money back?" he asked.

"Nigga, if you wanna keep losin' ya money, that's fine wit' me," the man spat back.

The Gun smoked a cigarette and looked detached from the strong words between Able and Rat. He leaned against the SUV, chilling. He wasn't a gambler. He was strictly a killer. The men were in a circle and anyone passing their way deliberately crossed to the other side of the street, fearing the thugs crowding the sidewalk. Khye and Sammy refused to cross over; they refused to be intimidated by the group.

Sammy marched ahead with his head held high and Khye right by his side.

"Yo, Samuel, what the fuck you got on?" Able shouted.

Sammy rolled his eyes and sucked his teeth. He hated when his brother called him Samuel. It was either Sammy or Sandy. Able didn't care. He knew his brother hated the name, but it was his birth name and Able wasn't going to call his brother by anything else.

"It's called fashion, Able, something you wouldn't know anything about," Sammy quipped back.

"Fashion? Nigga, you look a hot fuckin' mess," Able said.

His friends laughed and looked at Sammy with disgust, but they chose to remain silent. They didn't dare to say anything derogatory toward Sammy. Faggot or not, he was still Able's little brother, and they knew how Able felt about family.

"'Kiss me before my boyfriend comes back,'" Able said, reading Sammy's tight T-shirt, "Nigga, take that shit off!"

"For what? Do one of your friends want one?" Sammy puckered his lips together and threw out an invisible kiss at them.

"Yo, Able, ya brother is disrespecting, son," said one of his goons.

Able approached his brother with intensity showing in his eyes. Khye stood still and quiet next to Sammy. Able stood closely to Sammy and said, "Nigga, you know if you weren't my little brother what these niggas would do to you?"

"But I am," Sammy refuted, "so accept it."

"Go home, Samuel," said Able.

"It's Sammy," he shot back with attitude.

"Moms named you Samuel," he said, knowing calling his name correctly always got under his little brother's skin.

While Sammy and Able were having their sibling moment, all eyes were on Khye and her bootylicious body. The dudes loved everything about Khye, from where she was from, to her sexiness.

"Khye, what's good, beautiful?" Boom said.

"Chilling," Khye simply replied.

"So when we gonna chill together again?"

She slightly smiled and didn't respond to him. It was sad to say, three men in Able's crew already fucked her and the rest wanted to. They heard how good her pussy was and wanted a piece of the pie. She had her whorish moments and she couldn't take back who had fucked her. She was still young and impressionable to the bad boys and the thug life. She had been easily influenced by that lifestyle since she came to the States. Her mum had a more tarnished reputation than she did, and Khye was following right behind her.

"Khye, you ready?" Sammy asked, pivoting in the opposite direction away from his brother and walking away.

"Yeah," Khye said.

Able and his goons watched the odd couple strut away. Able took a final pull from his cigarette, flicked it away, shook his head, and knew he wasn't going to always be there to protect his brother. Sammy's openly gay and flashy lifestyle brought too much negative attention his way. There were plenty of people out there who outright hated everything Sammy stood for and would do anything in their power to hurt and destroy him, even their own father. Despite Able's constant griping about Sammy's overbearing sexuality, he loved his brother and would do anything in his power to keep him safe—even if it meant criticizing him.

Sammy and Khye locked themselves in Sammy's bedroom and started to try on the few things they'd bought, immediately getting to work on altering the clothes to make them stand out more.

Sammy's bedroom was immaculately clean and decorated with posters of shirtless, scantily clad, muscular men. There were many books on fashion design and hair care placed neatly on his desk, his bed was always made, and his closet was filled with clothing that he'd altered himself. Sammy was meticulous when it came to his appearance and his bedroom.

Khye loved Sammy's place because it was quiet and peaceful. It was neat and tidy. He had some food in his fridge, but not too much. It was mainly him and his mother. Able was always gone, hanging out on the streets. There, they could always talk and have their privacy.

Sammy went to work on a few shirts, breaking out his sewing kit and needles. Khye couldn't wait to see what it was going to look like when he was done. Her friend was a master tailor. Sammy taught himself how to sew and over the years became adept with the thread and the needle. They had shirts and shorts displayed on his bed and picked which ones they wanted to work on first.

As they loitered in the bedroom, every so often, Khye would look at her phone, checking to see if she had any missed calls. It had been almost twenty-four hours since she'd met Floyd, and she couldn't stop thinking about him. She wanted to see him again.

"I see you, bitch," Sammy said.

"What?" she uttered sheepishly.

"Don't play stupid, Khye. Looking at your phone, hoping your prince charming calls soon," he joked.

"Shut up, I was just seeing what time it was."

"Yeah, bitch, you need to stop givin' birth to bullshit, because I smell you all the way from over here," Sammy said.

"Whatever . . ."

They continued to chill and talk. It was just them, like it had been for years. They made each other laugh and always had each other's back. They both were promiscuous creatures in the ghetto and shared their stories of lust and love like campfire stories.

Finally the call came to her phone. The 347 number on the caller ID made her heart beat faster. She knew it was Floyd calling. Khye picked up the phone quickly and didn't know what to say. It felt like the governor was calling to pardon her. She took a deep breath and felt like a college player about to be drafted in the NBA. This was her shot.

"Hey, beautiful," Floyd said.

"Hey," Khye replied with joy. She lit up like Independence Day in front of Sammy.

"Aaaah, it must be nice to fall in love," Sammy said facetiously.

Khye waved him off and was ready to curl up on Sammy's bed and talk to Floyd for hours.

"What you doing?" Floyd asked.

"Nothing, just chilling with my friend," Khye said in her accented schoolgirl voice.

"Friend, huh? You sure you don't mean boyfriend?"

"I told you, I'm single."

"Okay. We got sumthin' in common, me too. So how can I change your doing nothing into sumthin'?" he asked.

"I don't know, ask me," she said.

"Okay, tonight, be ready in an hour," Floyd said.

"An hour?"

"Yes. I wanna see you," he said.

"What do you wanna do?"

"We'll figure something out," he said.

She grinned and felt herself becoming giddy just talking to him. It was hard to hide her emotions. She wanted to jump through the phone and be with him.

"I'll pick you up," Floyd said.

"No, I'll meet you," Khye quickly suggested.

"Damn, ya place can't be that bad, ma."

"I'll meet you," she repeated.

"A'ight, I'm not gonna argue wit' you. You can have it your way, beautiful," Floyd said coolly. "So where you wanna meet?"

"Rucker's Park," she mentioned. "You made that place special for me already."

"Oh word? Okay. I'll be there in an hour," he said. "And wear sumthin' sexy."

"Okay, see you in a bit."

"Ooooh, I love the way you talk. See you in a bit, beautiful," Floyd said.

Khye hung up, leaped off of Sammy's bed excitedly, and hollered, "Sammy, you gotta hook me up, he's coming to pick me up in an hour."

"So, bitch, you ready to leave me for him?" Sammy said.

"Sammy, me with Floyd can benefit us both. Think. I got three hundred from him last night. How much you think he'll give me tonight?"

"That's true, slut. Go out there and get your daddy some money," Sammy wisecracked.

He started to go to work on Khye. It was a good thing they had gone shopping. He searched through the items of clothing and said, "Something sexy, but not trashy. You want to leave some things to the imagination."

Khye stripped away her clothing in his bedroom. She felt very comfortable being naked around him. He was one hundred percent homosexual and nothing Khye had made him aroused or got his dick hard.

Khye didn't have time to rush back to her place to get ready. Sammy had everything she needed in his room. She went into his bathroom to wash up. Sammy was hemming her skirt while Khye was freshening up her pussy. She didn't know what tonight might lead to, but she didn't want to take any chances.

An hour later, Khye walked out of the project building feeling and looking like a whole new woman. She wore a short length skirt in a stylish cut. It was beautifully embellished with sequins all over. The halter top she wore painted her juicy tits and showed off her flat, appealing stomach. And she wore flats, because her shoes were worn out.

"Bitch, don't get pregnant tonight," Sammy said to her.

"If I did, you know you my baby's godmother," Khye replied.

"Like a fairy," Sammy joked.

Khye had just enough money to take a cab to Rucker's Park. It was dark and it was late. She rode in the backseat of the gypsy cab thinking about so many things. She hoped Floyd would like her outfit. It was put together in a hurry, but she felt everything had come out fine. It showed off her curvy figure, and it was sexy in her eyes, showing enough skin, but not enough skin to make her look whorish.

She sighed heavily, gazing out the window as the gypsy cab rode up Eighth Avenue, approaching closer to Rucker's Park. She was really nervous.

What if he stood her up?

What if something went wrong?

What if he was a different person?

Khye didn't want to worry, so she tried to stay focused on the positive things. After the cab fare, she would be left with five dollars to her name. If anything went wrong, she would be back to being broke.

The cab came to a stop on the corner of Eighth Avenue/Frederick Douglass and 155th Street. Khye stepped out underneath the underpass and headed toward the park. The area was so still and not busy, without a EBC tournament happening, the place looked dried up, like a ghost town. There were a handful of people in the playground and traffic was so light, the street looked barren.

Khye walked toward the middle of the street and stood around. She felt awkward standing alone and hoped Floyd didn't take too long showing up. It was a nice night with a cloudless sky. She was down to her last cigarette. She lit it up while waiting for him, hoping he didn't do CP time.

Ten minutes later, Khye noticed a pair of bright headlights rounding the corner. She fixed her attention on the car approaching and had a feeling it was him. She could hear music playing. It was rap music. She took a final pull from the cigarette and flicked it into the street. She looked at the car and it was him. Floyd pulled up to where she was standing with the top down to his CL600. Khye was relieved. She couldn't wait to get inside.

Floyd looked impeccable behind the wheel of his convertible. He grinned and said, "I didn't have you waiting too long?"

"No, I just got here myself," she said.

Floyd stepped out of his gleaming car looking energetic about his date with Khye. She smiled, taking in his trendy attire—white and black Gucci ensemble that topped off with a platinum diamond necklace that sparkled in sync with the diamond-filled Rolex on his wrist. He looked great.

He hugged her passionately and the smell of his cologne filling her nostrils made Khye want to melt in his arms.

"Damn, you so soft," Floyd said.

"Like a woman should be," she replied.

He stepped back and took in Khye's outfit for the night. He clapped his hands together and rubbed them jointly and said, "You look so beautiful tonight. I love it."

She blushed. "Thank you."

In Floyd's eyes, she was perfect, everything he dreamed of—no visible tattoos, no excessive piercings, nice body, nice outfit, long, sensuous black hair and a lovely accent. Yes, he could be falling in love so soon.

Floyd escorted Khye to his car and opened the passenger door for her, she glided inside and smiled. He dashed to the driver's side and jumped into his Benz. He couldn't keep his eyes off of Khye. She was golden. She leaned back into the seat and crossed her legs, showing off her thick thighs.

Damn, Floyd thought to himself.

"So, where are we going?" she asked.

"I know someplace nice…this Thai restaurant in midtown. You ever had Thai food before?" he asked.

"No."

"Good, cuz you're gonna love this place," he said.

"Well, I'm bloody ready to try anything different," she said.

Floyd smiled.

He made a U-turn on the street and headed toward Midtown, Manhattan. With the top down, music playing and riding in his first-rate chariot, Khye felt like a queen. She definitely wanted to be seen in his car. She remained humble and kept her overwhelming feelings for Floyd subtle. In fact, she pretended to shun his wealth, which made her more intriguing to Floyd.

Their conversation never stopped or grew exhausting, since he picked her up in uptown, they conversed until Floyd was close to Tao restaurant on 58th Street. It was a stone's throw away from Central Park. Manhattan was never a boring city; the lights, the glitz, the people, the cars, the hip stores and restaurants were abundant. It was definitely the city that never slept. With it being a lovely night, Midtown was flooded with people from block to block. Yellow cabs flooded the area and the noise could be deafening.

Khye smiled the whole time. It was exciting. He was exciting. Being driven around in his Convertible Benz made her feel important. Floyd had a lot to say, especially about the music business, and she listened to every word that came out of his mouth. He knew his shit and he had big plans to succeed.

They parked and walked toward Tao restaurant arm-in-arm. So far, the night was going wonderful. If it was a dream, then she never wanted to wake up.

The enormous, clublike Pan-Asian eatery was known for the giant Buddha centerpiece and its beautiful decor. People talked about the Buddha statue, their sea bass, giant fortune cookie, Asian fusion, and Prix Fixe.

Khye had never been in a place like it before. It was fancy, people were well-dressed, and the service was magnificent. The foreign Thai food she tasted exploded inside of her mouth. There was more to come.

"So, do you like it over here better than London?" Floyd asked.

"I do," Khye responded. "It is truly beautiful over here."

"I think you are beautiful," he said.

"Are you this generous and flattering to every woman you meet?"

"Nah, I'm not, only with the ladies that truly catch my eye, and believe me, I don't impress easily," he said.

"Well I'm glad I was able to impress you."

"You didn't have to try too hard either."

"When it's natural, it's natural," Khye said, grinning with her accent creating a huge smile on his face.

"I can listen to you talk forever," he said.

"You can, eh?"

He nodded. Khye batted her eyes at him.

"I just wanna know everything about you."

"What do you want to know?"

"Everything."

He smiled. She laughed.

"Is it true that police in London don't carry guns?" he asked.

"Well, it's true and it's not true," she said. "Most beat cops don't carry guns in London, but you will see officers during special circumstances have one. In Ireland the police officers carry weapons, but the rest of Great Britain—Scotland, England and Wales—haven't elected to change the law. This is something I'm not opposed to. I hate guns."

"Yo, that's crazy…how they don't carry guns. How they do they job?" Floyd asked, looking astounded by her reply.

"They do their job the same as over here, I guess. Most officers are issued Tasers, cuffs, and a baton."

"Well at least brothers ain't gotta worry about being shot up fifty times over there," he said.

She chuckled.

"But ya really smart, Khye. I like that."

"Thank you."

"I think English women are so fuckin' sexy, and you are the sexiest one."

"You know, you keep this up and you might make me some bloody stalker," she joked.

He laughed. "Shit, I might be the one stalking."

They looked into each other eyes and the attraction and chemistry was so strong, not even winds up to 100 mph could separate them.

She continued talking about London to him, and the more she went on about her old home, the more nostalgic she became. Even though she'd left home at nine years old, there were still memories she endured and friends she missed.

"Do you miss over there?" Floyd asked.

"I left when I was young, and if I never came here, then I would have never met you," she said.

"True that…"

They were able to make each other laugh and smile, and their night together was becoming magical. Time was flying by because they were having too much fun together.

Dinner at Tao restaurant was delicious. Khye never had food like that before. And she was enjoying trying something new, including him.

After the restaurant, Floyd whisked her away in his convertible to the West Side of Central Park, where he romanced her with a horse-and-carriage ride through parts of the sprawling park. She nestled against him and felt so secure with his arms around her.

That night, Khye was in a different world and she continued to play her innocence and shunned his wealth, though she was excited about it. Floyd was feeding into it. He believed everything Khye said, and there was no reason to doubt her.

After the horse-and-carriage ride, they cruised through the city like a gust of wind. The later the night got, the more they got to know each other. They passionately kissed while parked near the George Washington Bridge; the illuminated lights that stretched across Hudson River romantically hypnotized them.

It felt like a Cinderella moment.

Khye walked into her apartment with dawn breaking open the sky. It had been a wonderful date. She couldn't wait to tell Sammy about it. Before she left Floyd, he put five hundred dollars into her hands. It was a small gift from him. It felt like he was trying to buy her love—impress her with his money. At first she put on an act, pretending she didn't want the money, didn't need it. But Floyd insisted. He spent cash like it grew on a tree in his backyard.

"Where you been at, eh?" her father asked. He was up and getting ready for work at the school. He slept off his drunkenness and was ready to function for another day.

"I was out," she told him.

"If you gonna be out all night, you need to bring some cash," he said.

"So, what am I, a bloody prostitute now?"

She wasn't about to tell him about the five hundred dollars on her person. It was her money, her secret.

"You seen your mother?" he asked.

"No, I haven't," she lied.

"Fuckin' bitch doesn't know how to stay her arse home," he griped.

She wanted to tell her father to give her a reason to stay home then. But she didn't. She looked at him with her eyes feeling heavy. "I'm tired. I'm going to bed."

Her father continued to get ready for work, and Khye went into her bedroom and hid the money from her family. Before she went to bed, she texted her best friend:

CALL ME IN THE AFTERNOON, I HAVE A LOT TO TELL YOU. I JUST GOT HOME.

SEVEN

Floyd walked into his condo in the early morning with the sun percolating through the windows. He was tired and horny. Being with Khye all night had gotten him excited. Her soft skin, her soft lips, her speech and English accent, and the way she kissed him, the way she felt, it left a lingering effect on him. He wanted to fuck, but Khye didn't look like a woman that gave it up so easily. And he was willing to wait.

He assumed Tatianna was sleeping, or probably high from smoking all night. She was a weed head. The living room was a mess with clothes and fast food remnants across the coffee table. Tatianna was a sloppy bitch, but he overlooked it for the moment. He didn't feel like complaining. His mind was on something else. He went into the bedroom and his girlfriend was still sleeping on top of the covers, scantily clad in her panties and bra. Floyd eyed her for a moment. Despite what he felt about her, she was still a sexy, black woman with hips and curves, and that gushy pussy.

He undressed and slid into bed next to her, ready to implement his relentless seduction. He was ready to give Tatianna a rude wake up call, or pleasant one, if she wanted his dick or not. He straddled her with his thighs and his masculine instincts took over. His hands caressed the small of her back. He lifted her hips and removed her panties. Tatianna stirred awake, she was definitely high from some potent weed. The tugging of her panties opened her eyes. She didn't even hear Floyd come in.

"Baby, what you doin'?" she asked drowsily.

"What you think I'm doin', just chill, baby. I got this," he said coolly.

He positioned himself between her legs, placing his hard dick at her core and drove himself inside of her in one thrust. She jerked from the rough impact and moaned, feeling his dick suddenly inside of her. Floyd started to work his dick into her, steadily feeling her get wet for him.

"Mmmm," she moaned. "No . . . Yes, wait, wait, Ooooh, don't stop. No…yes."

"Chill baby, I got this," he whispered into her ear, fucking froggy-style, her phat ass pushing against him.

They soon fell into rhythm, a solitary unit of passionate expression. The pussy was good. *Very* good. Floyd held her tight and closed his eyes and continued to thrust himself inside of her. It was no longer Tatianna he thought about, it was Khye. He dreamed this was her he was inside of. He wanted her desperately. He wanted to hear her accent in his ear as he fucked her in every position.

"Baby I missed you. Ooooh, fuck me!" Tatianna cried out.

He was riding high and about to come. He felt the sensation about to hit him like a speeding truck. His body tensed as her wetness coated him. He could tell his orgasm was only minutes away.

"Damn, I fuckin' want you," Floyd exclaimed strongly.

"I want you, too baby," Tatianna replied, thinking he was talking about her. "Fuck this pussy. It's your fuckin' pussy."

It didn't take long for Floyd to reach that satisfying place—that heavy orgasm building up inside of him, and abruptly exploding inside of Tatianna like someone had turned on a garden hose. He quivered against her and exhaled. He collapsed on his back and gazed up at the ceiling with an empty look. She cuddled against him, loving every minute of his sex and his time.

"I love you, baby," she said.

He seemed reluctant in saying it back. He didn't love her, or wasn't in love with her, not anymore. In fact, he lay next to Tatianna and enjoyed a post-coital moment. His mind was on Khye the entire time.

After his nut, he fell asleep.

Several hours later, Floyd was woken up boorishly by having ice cold water thrown on him as he slept. He jumped up and leaped out of bed hysterically. "What the fuck, Tatianna! What the fuck is ya fuckin' problem?"

"Who the fuck is Khye?!" Tatianna yelled madly.

She had dropped the pot and had his cell phone in his hand. She scowled at him, had her hand on her hip and stood naked in the room.

"Why the fuck you goin' through my phone?" he asked.

"Because I got the right to. Now answer my question, who the fuck is Khye and why is this bitch texting you so fuckin' early in the morning?"

Floyd was upset. She had no right.

"This bitch talkin' 'bout she had a nice time wit' you last night, it's been fun," Tatianna added. "You fuckin' this bitch?"

"I fucked you last night, didn't I?"

"That don't mean shit, Floyd. You fuck me three or four times in one night. It's easy for you to get it up. Let me find out you fucked this bitch and then came home and gave me sloppy seconds," she said. "That's nasty!" she screamed.

"Tatianna, you need to fuckin' chill. It was just business. We just met, she's a new singer me and my team are tryin' to sign right now. She got talent."

"You lying, nigga!"

"Yo, you need to calm down," he replied.

Tatianna snapped. She threw his cell phone at him; Floyd ducked, with it barely missing his head. She then charged at him with fury, screaming madly, "Don't fuckin' tell me to calm down!"

She swung at him and missed. Floyd backed up, ready to defend himself. Tatianna had a serious temper with a short fuse, and when she got going, it was hard to calm her down. She was ready to fuck her boyfriend up in the bedroom. Butt-naked, with her tits flapping around, she tried to fight Floyd like he was some stranger. She went at him relentlessly, managing to scratch up his face a little and strike him in the eye. Floyd became so pissed, he cocked his fist, lunged forward, and punched Tatianna so hard, she went flying across the bed. She landed on her side, on the floor, and in pain.

"I told you bitch, don't fuck wit' me!" he screamed, glaring down at Tatianna. "You know what? I don't fuckin' need this shit! I'm out!"

He quickly grabbed his clothes and everything else he needed and hurried out of the bedroom. Tatianna continued to hug the floor, crying her eyes out. "Fuck you, nigga! Leave and don't fuckin' come back! I don't fuckin' need you!" she yelled out heatedly.

She heard the door shut and the tears flooded her eyes. Truth, she did need him, and she did want him to come back. She loved Floyd, but it was clear to her that he was out there cheating. And who was Khye—some new bitch in his life? She didn't believe that she was a singer. Tatianna was ready to confront any woman that put her relationship in jeopardy. Floyd was her heart, and she was ready to kill for him.

***

"So, did you fuck him, bitch?" Sammy asked uncouthly with his smirk aimed at Khye. "Because any bitch that comes home around five in the morning, had to be doing something naughty. So, I need details, give me details." He repeatedly snapped his fingers in the air and looked anxious to hear about it all.

Khye laughed. "Look at you, ready to be all in the business."

"Bitch, you the one that hit me up in the early morning telling me to call, so don't get coy now. You better start snitching."

"No, I didn't fuck him," she said.

"Bullshit! You lie!"

"I'm serious, Sammy. We didn't have sex. We just had fun," she said.

"Fun? And what is your definition of fun?" Sammy asked with a sneer across his face. "Because a nigga just don't give you five hundred dollars for clean, regular fun, okay!"

"Well, this one does," Khye replied.

"Bitch, you think you found you a sugar daddy."

"He's something."

"Well, tell him to sprinkle some sugar my way, I know I'm sweet already, but girl, I'll be a muthafuckin' cavity for his ass," he joked.

"You're crazy."

"I wish I was crazy in love right now. It seems like you found your Prince Charming," he said.

"Sammy, you'll find somebody, too," Khye told him.

"I hope so. Like LL Cool J, I need love, girl."

"We all do."

"And not just love, I need love with some finances, a nice car, nice clothes, jewelry, exotic trips, no baby mama drama, and if it come with some good dick, girl, he gonna have to put a ring on it," Sammy joked.

Khye slapped Sammy a high five and blurted out, "I know that's right."

"I love you, Khye," Sammy said platonically.

"I love you, too, Sammy. And you know I got you, let's go shopping again," she said.

Going shopping always made Sammy smile. "Girlfriend, you read my mind."

She laughed.

Before the pair left the bedroom, there was a knock at the door. "Who?" Khye asked.

"It's me," her mother said.

"Come in."

Sarah came into her daughter's room with a content smile on her face. She was happy about something.

"Hey, Mrs. Sarah," Sammy happily greeted.

"Hello, Sammy," Sarah replied.

"Yeah, Mum?" Khye asked.

"I'm going to Queens this afternoon," Sarah said.

"For what?" Khye asked.

"For my bloody business," Sarah replied. "And if your father asks—"

"I already know, Mum. I got you covered," Khye said.

Sarah smiled. "That's my girl."

She turned around and left the room, leaving Khye and Sammy to talk about her. "Mrs. Sarah, the naughty little whore she is," Sammy joked.

"She's my mum, Sammy," Khye lightheartedly replied.

"And I see the apple doesn't fall too far from the tree," Sammy quipped.

"Oh fuck you," Khye spat back, tossing her pillow at Sammy and playfully striking him in the face.

"Well, at least she's getting some," he said. "And speaking of getting some, when you gonna give Floyd some?"

"In due time. He thinks I'm this innocent little virgin," she said.

"Virgin? Bitch, I know you ain't take it that far. Your pussy ain't that tight."

"No, but it's tight enough," Khye said.

Sammy laughed. "Bitch please, you as tight as the elastic around Monique jeans."

"You ain't right, Sammy."

"That's why you love me," he said.

"Whatever."

***

With fifty dollars in her pocket on a beautiful, sun-drenched day, Sarah didn't mind walking to the A train. Clad in her tightest jeans that accentuated her curvy snowflake figure, a stylish T-shirt that highlighted her tits, and the brand-new white Nikes her retired cop friend bought her recently, she received the fleeting looks and lasting stares on the Harlem streets. Car horns blew at her in passing, catcalling from their windows, and men got whiplash trying to catch a glimpse of her luscious booty.

Sarah ignored it all. The only thing on her mind was taking the trip to Queens and seeing her boo, Marcus. Even though he was a married man with kids, she loved him. He was different from all the other men who came into her life. He treated her like a lady. He was fun to be around, he was smart, and he was paid. Twenty years as a CPA with a top accounting firm, and he had all the toys to play with along with the finer things money could buy—a big house in an affluent community, three luxury cars, nice clothing, and he took his family on lovely vacations abroad. It was the life Sarah dreamed of. It was the life her husband had promised her, but he never delivered.

The sex and romance was amazing with Marcus. Though she was his mistress, she never felt like it. Since they'd met two months ago, the handful of times she spent with him had been magical. Tonight, she was longing to lay by his side naked and dream with him.

Sarah hurried inside of the A train—it was partially crowded on the weekday—and took a seat between a fat lady and a blue-collar working man. She dreamed of the day she would get her own car to get around in. It sucked that her life in New York was the same as in London. One day, her life was going to change. She would do anything for that change.

The trip to Queens took almost an hour. It was dusk when she arrived. She stepped off the train and onto the elevated train platform. She was in Woodhaven. Marcus was supposed to meet her at the train station. She'd called in advance to let him know. Sarah couldn't contain her excitement.

She hurried down the subway platform and instantly searched for Marcus. She didn't see his burgundy Escalade anywhere. He wasn't around yet. Queens was still a foreign place to her; everything was different. It was supposed to be the suburbs, away from the concrete jungle. But it moved a little like Harlem.

With no access to a cell phone, she had no way to contact Marcus, and her only option was to wait on the corner and be patient. Everywhere she went, she attracted attention. Men gawked at her hungrily. She was a beautiful woman; it wasn't a secret that she could have almost any man she wanted, and Sarah wanted Marcus. She wished she was married to him. If a man like him were in her life, then she probably wouldn't cheat.

A half-hour later, he arrived. He was late, but Sarah didn't care. The second she saw him pull up, she hurried over to him, smiling. She hopped into the passenger seat, gleefully saying, "Hey, baby," and hugged and kissed him passionately. He looked stunning in his dark suit and gleaming bald head. He sported a thick goatee, had a very dark complexion, and resembled the actor Djimon Hounsou.

He was fine. And tonight, he was all Sarah's.

"Sorry I'm late. It was a busy day at the office," he said. His voice was deep and brooding. "You look nice."

Sarah smiled. "You look good, baby."

She couldn't wait to taste him. She couldn't wait to spread her legs for him somewhere nice. She wanted to devour his chocolate covered flesh. She wanted to jerk off his big dick in her small fist. He was well endowed—blessed. Naked, he had the body of a gladiator. She wanted to kiss his gleaming bald head while he sucked on her nipples.

"You hungry?" he asked.

"Hungry for you," she replied.

He placed his hand on her thigh and grinned. The little slut that Sarah was, she moved it closer to her pleasing area and placed his touch between her legs. He played with her pussy through her jeans and drove off. They both couldn't wait to have each other.

The hotel suite Marcus reserved was a huge and beautiful room with dark hardwood, a sunken spa tub, and wonderful amenities. It was near the airport and had a picturesque view of the JKF terminal and the runway. Marcus immediately ordered room service. Whatever Sarah wanted, she got. The price wasn't an issue. He had money.

Marcus got comfortable, undoing his tie and removing his suit jacket and tossing it on the bed. His breathtaking physique showed through the material he had on. Not an hour could be wasted. He was a married man; despite his infidelity, he had a family to go home to. And Sarah came there for one thing, and one thing only—to be vigorously fucked by Marcus, and then maybe, afterwards, get some money from him. She wasn't prostituting herself whenever Marcus gave her money. It was something like a donation, and he gave through the kindness of his heart.

Marcus approached his mistress with intensity.

"I fuckin' want you," he growled.

Sarah smiled, but before they could get things started, she politely pushed him away as if she was playing hard to get.

"You know what I want. I don't like when you keep it on. You belong to me right now," she said.

Marcus sighed. "Is it that big of an issue?"

"Yes!"

He held up his hand and started to remove the platinum wedding band on his left hand. It was a beautiful ring signifying his devotion and love to someone else. He placed it on the table and asked, "You happy?"

"Now I am," Sarah said, smiling glibly.

The two wrapped into each other arms and kissed fervently. Marcus was ready to melt his little snowflake. His lust for white women was insatiable, though he'd married an African-American woman. They met by chance, while he was in Harlem on business, in Starbucks on 125th Street. He came out with a latte in his hand and accidentally bumped into Sarah. They both excused each other, but the minute they locked eyes, it was over—an affair at first sight. They exchanged numbers and were fucking each other's brains out in a seedy motel a week later.

The seedy motel upgraded to five stars room and small gifts shortly thereafter. The pussy had him open, and Sarah had him addicted. Marcus loved his family, but he couldn't get enough of Sarah. Whenever he got the chance, he was in her arms and inside of her, knowing it was wrong, but she felt so good.

They stripped away their clothes and kissed. Marcus's muscular thighs were a masterpiece. His arms, his chest, his shoulders were formed to perfection. He had a six-pack of abs that would make any personal trainer proud or jealous. The meat hanging between his legs made Marcus the ideal male for Sarah. He was big and thick, just over eight. His big dick looked as thick as a can of beer and it wasn't even hard yet. It looked like it weighed several pounds, and Sarah couldn't wait to play with it.

Sarah was fingering her throbbing pussy in anticipation.

Marcus was dominating. His dick was fully erect, hard, throbbing, and dripping with precum.

Without any other explanation, Marcus pushed Sarah onto the bed and jumped on top of her. She loved it when he took control, when he had that animalistic look about him. It felt so good to be wanted by a handsome and rich man like Marcus. He gripped the backs of her thighs tightly and rammed his dick in her pussy in one thrust, to the balls. He wanted to feel her raw first, feeling her wetness on his dick. He had condoms in his suit jacket, but there was something about fucking women in the flesh that made it so much more exhilarating.

Her breath was ragged. She could feel his dick cemented into her stomach. He was big. He was good. She panted and howled, half enjoying the pain between her legs.

"Easy, baby . . . easy on your snowflake," Sarah said.

The good pussy had Marcus hypnotized. He gyrated between her legs, fucking her enthusiastically. He grabbed her hair like the reins to a horse and pulled hard.

"Fuck me!" she cried out.

He tossed her into a different position, on her hands and knees, doggy-style. He then shoved his cock into her again, with more force, stabbing her womb with his weapon of flesh. He was about to make her come. Sarah was in the place between pleasure and pain. She had never been fucked so savagely before. She liked being treated so brutally.

"Fuck this nice, white pussy," she would cry out.

Marcus fucked her harder and harder. He shoved his dick in repetitively—pushed, shoved, thrust, smacked her ass, cupped her tits, and rammed his dick until every inch was embedded deep inside of her. Sarah's passionate cries were so loud, they echoed beyond the bedroom walls and into the hallway.

They soon came heavily and all over each other. Sarah could feel him exploding inside of her, and he could feel her juices coating his dick. It was the best sex, and things had just begun. They both were nymphos. Right before they could start round two, room service came knocking at their door. Sarah dined on lobster, shrimp cocktail, and a delicious assortment of fruit before they engaged themselves in nasty sex again.

This was the life for her. Being with Marcus was hard, because she wanted to be with him beyond the bedroom. If only he could leave his wife and his family for her, she wouldn't hesitate to do the same. Sarah knew she was being selfish, but she was falling in love with him, and as she lay against Marcus's strapping bare chest in the hotel room, her mind started to spin with so many things. Why not her? Why couldn't she have a man like Marcus? Adewale was a lie! He was a major disappointment.

He gave her three kids and a life she didn't ask for. Every time she thought about her life now, it angered her.

She only had another hour with him before he got dressed and went to be with his wife and kids. When he would leave, she would cry. She would stop seeing them all, Gino, James, and even her husband, if Marcus gave the word and promised her a brighter future with him. The truth was, he would never leave his ebony, educated wife for a white whore. Yes, he treated her special, but it was only a fling, and the truth was a hard pill to swallow for Sarah. She was scared. She was thirty-five and felt lost. There were so many faults about her, from her gambling, to her laziness, to her addiction to sex, that she seemed only good for one thing, opening her legs and pleasing niggas.

As predicted, before it reached midnight, Marcus pulled himself away from her longing grasp and started to get dressed. He had already spent too long with Sarah and needed to come up with a reasonable explanation to give to his wife as to why he had been out so late.

"You leaving already?" Sarah asked.

"You know I can never stay long," he replied with nonchalance in his tone.

"When I'm gonna see you again?" she asked.

"I'll call you," he replied simply.

Sarah could only look at him and do nothing, knowing nothing she could say or do could keep him. It was a losing battle when she had to compete with his wife of over twenty years.

Marcus reached into his suit jacket, removed his wallet and took out some cash. He peeled off three hundred dollars and dropped it at the foot of the bed for Sarah to take.

"It's been fun," he said. "Take a cab back home, it's on me."

She needed the money, but coming from Marcus, she felt used and empty.

EIGHT

Khye stepped out of Floyd's car dressed fashionably in a sexy dress and a pair of red-bottoms. It was her most expensive outfit yet, courtesy of Floyd. The dress hugged her curvy body perfectly, and Khye felt like a superstar. Her night out with Floyd just started. They had arrived at Spotlight on Fulton Street. It was a spacious Brooklyn club near the downtown area. Tonight, the club had a rap showcase, displaying talent from all over the Tri-State area. Floyd and his crew were promoting the event, and he was delighted to bring Khye along to show her his world.

For the past two weeks, Khye and Floyd had been spending quality time together. When she was with him, nothing else mattered, not family and not even her best friend. She spent less time with Sammy, because Floyd started to become her everything. He took her on expensive shopping sprees in the city, where Khye had access to clothes that she could never have imagined having—Gucci, Prada, Chanel, Donna Karen, Victoria Beckham, and much more. He showered her with cash and gifts, especially jewelry, from diamond tennis bracelets to costly necklaces and earrings. She no longer went hungry thanks to Floyd. She got to see different things, and even spent a few nights with him at Slow Pullz Studio in the city.

Khye loved the attention. She saw herself becoming something that her mother never had been—successful. She did it. She baited herself a baller, a man willing to take care of her. Her parents had never been so proud, and they were dying to meet the wealthy engineer/music producer that had been wining and dining their beautiful daughter. Khye, however, was skeptical. There was no way she would ever allow Floyd to meet her ghetto family. The closest they would get to meeting him was the great stories she told about him.

Khye also didn't share the wealth she was receiving. She stashed the money Floyd would give her and refused to help them out financially. Also, she was learning how to save for a rainy day by continuing to take the subway.

Floyd had always been very particular about his ladies. He loved his women a certain way, classy and stylish. He didn't want them cursing, fighting, or acting ghetto. And he didn't want them embarrassing him. His bitch represented him. Khye was it all, so it seemed. Tatianna was slipping, losing herself, and every day Floyd wrestled with his attraction for her. The tattoos Tatianna had on her body were gaudy, and her constant weed smoking was annoying. The only thing they had was longevity and good sex. So while his girlfriend stayed home and complained to her friends about their crumbling relationship, Floyd was secretly with Khye night and day, enjoying the town with his foreign beauty.

With Floyd, it was all about image—a man's image and his reputation was everything.

Floyd placed his hand on the small of Khye's back and ushered her toward the club entrance. It was lively outside, people in every direction and cars lining the street. It looked like all eyes were on Floyd and Khye. She was ecstatic. She loved the attention and her new clothes. She might as well have been on the red carpet at a Hollywood event.

As they approached the club, everyone made it their business to greet Floyd and show him his respect. They gave dap and glad hands.

"Floyd, what's good, my nigga?"

"Yo, I'm glad you came through."

"What's up?"

"Yo Floyd, I need to holla at you later on."

"My nigga, you always lookin' sharp."

He was bombarded with attention and respect, and secretly, Khye was eating it all up. They had good things to say about the beautiful woman under Floyd's arm with her long eyelashes, appealing smile, and curvaceous figure. Khye wasn't about to mess it up. She stayed focused on what she needed to do to keep him happy. Surprisingly, they had not had sex yet. Her holding out intrigued Floyd even more. It said to him that she wasn't a whore or a slut; that she had respect for herself.

They made their way into the club without paying any entrance fee or being searched by security. Inside, the ultra-modern, sleek space and full bar were the perfect location for the hordes of people jamming to Drake and Lil' Wayne at the highly promoted event. The place boasted state-of-the-art technology with twenty 46-inch LCD flatscreens, and the dance floor was equipped with a customizable LED lighting system, which allowed the club to produce unique lighting themes.

Floyd and Khye were escorted into the VIP area, which was slightly elevated over the main club. Waiting for them were several bottles of pricey champagne and hookahs. The music blared and the place was vibrant like disco lights. Khye sat next to Floyd feeling like Queen Elizabeth.

"You thirsty?" he asked.

She nodded.

He poured her champagne into the flute and Khye took a sip. She sat in her short dress, crossing her legs and posing up. Her facial expression said, "I have him. I have power." She showed a lot of power and attraction.

The VIP area was only occupied with Floyd's crew—Nick, Tommy and Boss—and their ladies. Then there was Carlito, Floyd's best friend and right-hand man. Carlito was a silent figure dressed in black and he looked at Khye as if he didn't trust her already. Each man seated with Floyd in

VIP wore heavy jewelry and looked intimidating with their extravagant tattoos and rough image. They drank from the bottles and made it clear that Bed-Stuy was in the house. However, Floyd was different. He was a thug from Bed-Stuy, too, but he didn't act like one. He was dressed in slacks and shoes, sipped his drink out of a flute like Khye, and he had his tattoos covered.

Khye was the most striking woman in the place, and when she talked with her accent, everyone was floored. Floyd loved showing her off. It was about *his* image. He knew she would be able to fit in perfectly, especially with a little molding and sculpting. He placed his arm around her and smiled.

"You gonna have a good time wit' us," said Floyd.

"I know I will."

The music was jumping, and Khye was ready to dance. Every song played she loved, and it got her hyped. From Beyoncé to Chris Brown, she gingerly danced in her seat and bobbed her head. She wanted to get out there and dance in the crowd. Floyd chose to remain nonchalant and lingered in the VIP area with his boys. He had no interest in joining everyone on the dance floor. He felt comfortable up top with everyone else. He felt it was where he belonged.

Khye wanted to light a cigarette, but Floyd didn't want her to smoke inside the club. So she chose to partake in the flavored hookah and enjoyed that along with the flowing champagne.

"I love your dress," one of the ladies said to Khye.

"Thank you," she said.

"And your shoes are gorgeous," another woman said.

Khye beamed. It was rare that women gave each other compliments, but all night, they kept coming her way. That special feeling filled her head with self-esteem.

"You stick with me, and I'll have you going places, baby," Floyd said.

"I don't plan on going anywhere," she said.

Floyd smiled. She smiled.

When her favorite song came on, "The Worst," by Jhene Aiko, she couldn't help herself and stood up to dance for Floyd.

Floyd sat back, intrigued, as he watched Khye dance to the song. She seemed lost in the music. With her eyes closed and the champagne glass in her hand, she moved smoothly to the beat. The dress looked so great on her, that men couldn't keep their eyes off of her. Everyone felt Floyd was a lucky man to snatch up a woman like Khye.

When the song was done, she sat back down next to Floyd and he whispered to her, "You drive me crazy."

She smiled.

As the night went on, big shots, hustlers, rappers, and a few shady characters came and went from the VIP area. Khye paid attention to it all. Floyd knew everyone, from the good to the bad. Brooklyn and his entire hood were all throughout the club, and it was a party. Everybody got tipsy and were dancing and grinding against each other and making it a fabulous night. Khye had never had so much fun before.

She spent the duration of the party nestled against Floyd, enjoying his company and claiming her territory. She saw other bitches' eyes on him, and she wanted it to be known that he was already taken. No one was about to impede her gravy train. If she had to pull out a weave or two and stomp a bitch out, she didn't care. However, for Floyd, she kept it classy and cool.

When her cell phone rang and she saw it was Sammy, Khye chose to ignore it, sending her best friend to voicemail. Floyd noticed him calling her phone too and he gave Khye a look that said he disapproved of her hanging around with a gay dude. Earlier, he made it clear that she was too good for him.

"It's about image, Khye," he had said. "And if ya seen hanging with a faggot like him, what you think they gonna start thinking about me?"

Khye didn't argue or defend her friend. It felt like Floyd was saying choose him or Sammy. So for now, she chose Floyd. And all night, she had been ignoring Sammy's phone calls. She felt bad, but the feeling passed when Floyd introduced her to some important people.

While other bitches staggered out of the club pissy drunk or tipsy at four in the morning, Khye wasn't either. She wasn't a drinker like that, and it impressed Floyd to see her sober. The entire night, she had two glasses of champagne and smoked the tobacco hookah steadily.

Floyd opened the car door for her and she slid into the CL600. For Khye, the night was still young. She didn't want to go home. Floyd brought the engine alive and lingered around for a moment. It looked like he had something on his mind.

"What's up?" Khye asked.

He looked her way and said, "Why you never want me to come get you from ya crib? You got a man you hiding?"

"What? No."

"I'm sayin', Khye, be real wit' me. I like you. I mean, really like you. But I don't wanna be played for a fool. You feel me?"

"Baby, I do. And I'm single," Khye replied.

She knew he had some nerve. Even though he didn't confess it, her womanly instincts told her he had a bitch at home he wasn't telling her about. She wasn't jealous or worried. It was all part of the plan, and so far everything was still too young to go into effect. She didn't want to tell Floyd about her family, and she didn't want him to come around her way because her mother's reputation was too tarnished and her father was a drunk loser.

She came up with excuse after excuse why she would meet him, and why he couldn't come get her. Floyd became suspicious, but it wasn't enough to doubt Khye's words.

"I promise you, baby, I don't have a man. I'm single. But in due time, I'll tell you why. But right now, it's just too much," she said.

"Just don't lie to me," he said.

"Floyd, I'm falling in love with you," she stated.

She tilted forward, becoming intimately closer to him and pressed her lips against his. Floyd didn't resist her. They started to kiss passionately while still parked near the club. Soon, she felt his hand traveling up her thigh and placing itself between her legs.

"I want you so bad," he said to her.

"You can have me," she let him know with an alluring smile.

They kissed again and then drove away. Tonight was going to be a special night.

✳✳✳

Though she had sucked dick before and was pretty good at it, Khye pretended to gag and choke on Floyd's average size dick and complained about his precum. She would screw up her face and constantly wipe her mouth. She had deep-throated bigger dicks perfectly before, but tonight, it was an act. She had to become something that she wasn't, inept at oral sex.

"It tastes so sour," she griped. "It feels like I'm hurting you."

"You doin' a'ight, baby. It takes practice," he said.

He was laying butt-naked on the bed in the hotel room with his legs spread-eagled and ready for her to continue. Floyd had gotten a nice room at the Marriot in the downtown, Brooklyn area. He wanted Khye to feel comfortable. They became intimate in no time and Floyd initiated the oral sex. When Khye got naked for him, Floyd became so hard, he grew two extra inches. Khye had a wonderful body, and when naked, she was extra alluring. She was stunningly gorgeous, like a painting of a goddess brought to life. She smiled sweetly at him, her eyes sparkling like stars flaunted on the night sky.

She gripped his erection and jerked him off gently. He moaned from her pleasing touch.

"I'm only doing this because I really like you," she said, and then rolled her eyes when he wasn't looking.

If he only knew what she was really capable of doing. With her full, sweet lips if she wanted to, she could have Floyd climbing off the walls and coming so hard he would deflate. She only put up a front because she understood how he liked his women, pure and classy. Khye was a wolf in sheep's clothing—the devil in disguise. She couldn't allow Floyd to find out that she was a whore like her mother.

Floyd was patient with her as she gave him head slowly but surely. Her lips and her touch were soft like cotton. Her flesh made him ready to come already. He wanted to feel the inside of her and kiss her dark, stone-hard nipples. Everything about her was sensational. Floyd couldn't resist her flesh and her beauty. He was ready to penetrate her perfection.

In an instant, he was fucking her senseless from the back. His hard dick devoured her womanhood. She lowered her head, holding onto the headboard and pushed back, he pumped harder inside of her. Every inch of his dick was driven deep inside her, and she adored the sensation.

"Damn, baby . . . you so wet," he said.

Her juices dripped between her legs, and it coated every inch of him as he thrust inside her. He grabbed her hips, she rubbed her clit. He moaned and she groaned. The room filled with moans while the sheets became wrinkled and sweaty underneath them. She came without him missing a beat and he kept fucking her through her orgasm.

"I love you!" Khye found herself uttering.

Floyd didn't respond. He was in a deep trance. They were words pouring out from her during the heat of the moment. Sweat formed on both of them and they grunted and groaned like wild animals. With her English accent in his ear as he fucked her, it made Floyd come inside of her like a gusher. They fucked into the night until they both passed out from pleasure and exhaustion.

The morning came quickly, and sunlight filtered through the hotel windows. Several hours passed and Khye awoke in his arms. It was another beautiful day, and she was with a beautiful man. She still felt weak from the incredible fuck she had gotten. Her pussy still ached and her breasts felt tender, but besides that, it had been a wonderful night—from the club to the Marriot, she felt like a naughty Cinderella after the ball.

Floyd was still asleep. She removed herself from the bed in dire need to use the bathroom. She grabbed her cell phone from the nightstand and took it with her. She sat on the toilet to take a piss and noticed all the missed calls from Sammy. He even sent her text messages. She had ignored him all night.

Khye heaved a sigh, knowing that her best friend was going to be upset with her. She never ignored his phone calls.

She read the text first, and it said:

BITCH, YOU IGNORING ME? I SEE HOW YOU DO, KHYE. YOU DISSING YOUR BEST FRIEND FOR HIS BITCH ASS. BITCH, I HOPE HE'S WORTH IT, BECAUSE HE AIN'T GONNA NEVER HAVE YOUR BACK LIKE I DID. I DON'T NEED THIS SHIT; I'M TOO PRETTY AND FLY TO BE TREATED LIKE THIS. GOODNIGHT!

Khye felt bad. She and Sammy were at odds with each other unexpectedly. But she wasn't about to give up Floyd because Sammy's feelings were hurt.

NINE

Floyd pulled up to his condo with the sun beating him home once again. His night with Khye was unforgettable. He couldn't stop thinking about that sweet pussy. It was only the beginning between him and Khye. He saw a future with her, and it was so bright, he had to wear shades.

It was almost afternoon when he walked inside his place, and the euphoric feeling he felt quickly changed into rage and fury when he discovered the nightmare Tatianna had executed. That bitch had gone crazy. She had ruined his favorite and expensive clothes with bleach and scissors, and everything was piled up on the floor in an appalling display of a woman scorned.

"What the fuck?!" Floyd shouted. "Tatianna!" he screamed.

Tatianna came storming out of the bedroom with more of his clothes in her arms, throwing them at him.

"I'm sick of your shit, Floyd! You cheating muthafucka!" she shouted heatedly.

Floyd was ready to go berserk too. He clenched his fist and scowled in her direction. Tatianna was starting to become a nightmare to deal with. She was dressed in shorts and a T-shirt, her hair in two long braids, and she was ready to attack.

"Where the fuck you been at all night? Huh?" she shouted.

"I was out, in the studio doing business," he lied.

"All fuckin' night, Floyd!" she rebuked.

"It was a long night and I fell asleep."

"And you don't fuckin' call me."

"You know I'm tryin' to finish up this album for my peoples. We putting in a lot of work and got some nice tracks," he said.

"I don't fuckin' believe you," she retorted.

"I don't care what you fuckin' believe, but this shit. . ." He pointed to his clothes destroyed in front of him. "This shit in uncalled for, Tatianna. You gonna pay for everything you fucked up."

"Fuck you!"

"No, fuck you!" he shouted back, approaching her disturbingly close. "I give you every fuckin' thing. I'm the one that takes care of you, buys you nice shit, and got you living nice in this condo. I took you out of the fuckin' projects and I made you, Tatianna. Without me, you wouldn't have shit!"

The tears started to stream from her eyes. She looked at Floyd in so much pain. She didn't know what to do. She wanted to beat him down because her love for him was so strong, but she felt betrayed. She wasn't a fool; she knew there was another woman in his life.

"Who is she?" she asked out of the blue.

"She is no one, because I'm not fuckin' wit' no other bitch. Why can't you get that through your thick fuckin' skull!" he screamed.

"Do you still love me, Floyd?"

He sighed with frustration.

"Answer me!" she yelled.

"I'm the one running shit. I'm the one taking care of you, so don't fuckin' forget. Without me, you wouldn't be shit!" he hollered.

Floyd questioned why he kept her around when he loved someone else. Tatianna was that in-house pussy, and he still liked having sex with her. She gave the best blow jobs and they did have history together, but that was pretty much it.

Tatianna was upset. She knew she was losing the love of her life, and her only means of support to another woman. She was hurt and scared, also very angry. The fact that he kept lying to her was even more frustrating.

"I love you, Floyd," she said expressively.

He didn't reply. The only thing he could say to her was, "Don't ever fuck wit' my shit again, or I swear bitch, you gonna hate me for the rest of your life."

He turned around and stormed out the door. Tatianna simply watched in horror as Floyd left, his threats still lingering in the room. She dropped down to her knees and cried her eyes out.

***

The next evening, Khye sat by her bedroom window quietly and gazed out at the world. The city was a place where you swim or sink, and for a long time, it felt like she was sinking until Floyd jumped into the troubling waters and saved her. Every day she thought about him, and every moment without him, she missed him. She was doing everything with precision, playing her cards right and continuing to manipulate Floyd. The way he looked at her, she knew he was in love, and so was she. Her only precaution was she couldn't allow her promiscuous past to catch up to her. Floyd wanted his woman a certain way, and Khye was determined to become that certain way for him. If that meant lying to him and deceiving him, so be it. She was unwavering with the path she went down. With Floyd in her life, her friend Sammy became an obstacle, and her family became the threat. She needed to keep everyone separate.

Khye hadn't spoken to Sammy in over a week. Their friendship had drifted apart so quickly. They weren't tight anymore. They used to go everywhere together and talk every day, but now it was all about Floyd. Sammy had gotten tired of her bragging about Floyd and his wealth. Khye always talked about Floyd's money and his career, and she wasn't shy in showing off the things he bought her, from jewelry to clothing, and with the promise of her own car soon. Jackpot. She was moving forward, her old life fading in her rearview.

Last week when she called Sammy, he'd gone into a bitch mood, and they had some choice words for each other. Sammy's resentment had been simmering, and Khye was unaware of his seething hate growing toward her.

"Bitch, you fake. Don't talk to me," Sammy had vented.

"Sammy, why can't you be happy for me?" she had asked.

"Because, you get with some cornball who puts a few dollars in your pocket and buys you nice things, and you turn on me faster than fake gold!"

"Are you bloody jealous?"

"Bitch, please . . . of him?"

"Yes. We always talked about finding the man of our dreams, who got money and can take care of us, and now that I found mines, you changed."

"No Khye, you changed. Let me tell you something about your prince charming . . ." he started, his voice flaring up through the phone.

"Tell me what?"

"FYI, bitch, I did some digging on him, because you know me, a bitch can always find the truth. No matter how far you throw it, I'm like a golden retriever and I'll go find it. But to let you know, Khye, he already has a woman that he's living with," Sammy informed her. "So bitch, that nigga is already coming with drama."

It was a fact that Khye already suspected. She wasn't shocked to hear the news. From the hotels and his constant sneaking phone calls, it was obvious. But she didn't care.

"It's not true," Khye said.

"Bitch, he got you brainwashed? Yes it is true, and the bitch's name is Tatianna and they been together for two years," he had stated.

"Why are you telling me this?" Khye had asked.

"What? Ohmygod, Khye, are you that stupid?"

"Don't be an arsehole, Sammy. It's my business, and I don't need you in it."

"You know what, bitch? You is a trip, so have a nice flight. Goodbye," Sammy had said, hanging up on her.

Khye felt bad that she and Sammy didn't see eye to eye. She had her agenda, and she was sticking to it. Khye now felt it was time to make Floyd get leave his past behind and move forward with his future.

Tatianna was about to become history.

***

For once, her room was quiet. Her two little sisters weren't knocking down her door begging to get inside, and her father was at work, and she assumed her mother was somewhere with one of her lovers getting fucked hard. Khye took advantage of being home alone, being able to walk around in her underwear and smoke her weed in peace. It was a balmy afternoon and the Fourth of July holiday was a day away. Floyd had invited her to watch the fireworks in Brooklyn. He made special plans for them that day, and Khye was excited. It would be on the Fourth that she would start to question him about everything.

Khye tilted her head back, took a deep pull from the burning haze between her lips, and exhaled. Getting high was always relaxing. She felt if she leaned back far enough, then she would start falling forever. Khye became extremely lethargic with her eyes seeded. What she was smoking, was very potent. She didn't even notice the door open and her mother walking in.

Sarah looked at her daughter clad in her underwear and said, "Khye, you feel like sharing?"

Khye turned and smiled her mother's way. It was a high smile. She didn't mind. She took another pull from the blunt and outstretched her hand toward Sarah with the blunt at the end of it. They were more like friends than mother and daughter. Sarah took the weed and sat near her daughter with her knees up and placed the blunt to her lips and took a few pulls. It's what they both needed. Sarah exhaled the smoke, placed the back of her head against the bedroom wall, and said to Khye, "So, is he the one?"

Khye didn't answer her mother. She looked out the window attentively watching the sun shine brightly in the clear blue sky.

"Does he love you?" Sarah asked.

"Why do you wanna know?" Khye asked.

"Can a mother have a simple conversation with her daughter about boys?" Sarah replied.

"I suppose."

"You know, I understand why you don't want to bring him around family," said Sarah. "We are far from royalty."

Khye chuckled from her mother's statement. And then she looked at Sarah in agreement.

"You know, I once thought your father was that guy," Sarah started.

"Clearly he wasn't," Khye interjected.

"Don't be so hard on him," Sarah defended. "He once tried—"

"But did he try hard enough for you, Mum?" Khye asked. "Look at us, how we live, him a stupid drunk, and us barely having anything to eat and me always wearing secondhand clothes. I want better."

"I know. I do as well. I think we all do. And I'm not saying I'm an angel—"

"You're not," Khye said quickly.

"You know, you shouldn't be so quick to judge us, Khye," Sarah said.

Khye took another pull from the blunt.

"You should talk," Khye returned sharply.

Her mother was ruining her high.

"Maybe we need to change the subject," Sarah said.

"Maybe we should," Khye agreed.

They shared the blunt, and then Sarah candidly asked, "Has he got a big dick?"

"Wow, inappropriate, for real, Mum," Khye said with a straight face at her mother.

"I'm sorry. But you do look nice, Khye. I see he treats you fairly."

"He does," Khye replied, being short with her mother.

"How did you meet?" Sarah asked.

"By doing what you taught me . . . put it out there well enough, and any man will come sniffing around for a piece. And Floyd, he loves what I'm putting out."

"Floyd, nice name," Sarah said, passing Khye the blunt.

"It is, and he's a nice person, and he's rich. He drives a Benz, runs a music studio, he has lots of money, and he takes care of me," Khye boasted to her mother.

"It must feel good to be taken care of."

"It is. You taught me well, huh, Mum?" Khye said.

"I guess I did."

✳✳✳

The Fourth of July holiday was about to be fireworks in the sky, and the fireworks continued on with Khye and Floyd. Each day together their chemistry and love grew stronger and stronger. It was growing to the point where nothing else mattered but the two of them. They spent the entire day together, starting with lunch at the Blue Cafe in the city and shopping on Fifth Avenue afterwards. Khye was treated to nice shoes and a few evening outfits. Then it was off to Brooklyn, where Floyd had to handle some business and meet with a few people. Khye sat cruising in the passenger seat with the top back, wind flowing through her hair, and one of Floyd's rap artists playing.

They crossed the Brooklyn Bridge and arrived into the downtown area. With the sun shining like a diamond in the sky and it being a warm day, traffic was heavy everywhere. Brooklyn was peppered with towering structures, endless activity, and people everywhere. Floyd was constantly on his cell phone while he navigated through Brooklyn, moving farther away from gentrification to the gritty streets of Bed-Stuy. He seemed more important than the president on his phone. His phone didn't go ten minutes without ringing, and every conversation seemed critical.

They ended up near Marcy Projects to meet with Carlito about something important.

"This only gonna take a minute, baby," Floyd said to her.

"I'm in no rush," she said.

"Tonight is gonna be fun. I promise you," he said.

"I know it will."

With the Fourth of July celebrations happening, fireworks went off on every block and every other household had a barbecue going. Everything seemed peachy and peaceful, but a double homicide that occurred the other night put a slight damper on the holiday. Two men were shot and brutally killed while seated in their car. The streets were hot with cops patrolling the area, and some residents were under certain unrest.

Floyd parked across the street from the projects and killed the ignition. The projects were lively in the early afternoon with burgers, hot dogs, and ribs being cooked on so many grills that the sweet smell of barbecue permeated the air around them. It made Khye's mouth water.

"I'll be right back, baby," Floyd said.

"Okay."

"You'll be fine. Nobody's gonna fuck wit' you out here," he assured her. "I know they won't."

He kissed Khye on her lips and exited his gleaming CL600 that sparkled on the block like one of Bird Man's pinky rings. The convertible Khye sat in caught heavy attention from people passing; their eyes lingered on the car and then her. If a nigga or bitch looked too hard her way, she caught an attitude with them and rolled her eyes. Floyd was right though; they simply looked her way but didn't say a word. She was taken.

She observed Floyd walk toward Carlito and his crew loitering on the urban block. She lit a cigarette in his absence, knowing how much Floyd hated her smoking, but she needed to quickly treat her nicotine craving. Besides, he wasn't looking her way and she would pop an Altoid into her mouth and spray some of her Amber Romance body spray afterwards to camouflage the smell.

Carlito and Floyd greeted each other with glad hands. The two men looked like dons on the street corner. The way they moved, it looked like they were hustlers instead of in the music business. The men around them looked like soldiers and thugs to Khye's eyes. For Floyd to be an engineer and in the music business, he knew a lot of shady-looking characters and he moved like a kingpin. It created some fleeting doubt, but Khye wasn't concerned. She knew he was legit.

Actually, it was none of her business. He was rich. He took care of her, and she believed in him. Every day with him brought her further away from poverty and closer to prosperity.

Her mind was on tonight. They had plans to watch the fireworks together at the Brooklyn Heights Promenade, and then afterwards, commit to some strong lovemaking in a hotel suite Floyd had reserved. They had been fucking like rabbits recently—they couldn't get enough of each other. The sex was like their own personal fireworks show in a contained space—colorful, exciting, and dangerous at the same time.

Khye took a pull from the Newport and patiently waited. Floyd had walked away with Carlito into one of the project buildings, leaving her seated and waiting with the sun in her face. She started puffing on another cigarette to pass the time. She continued to think about tonight. She wanted to step up from his mistress to his main bitch.

When she noticed Floyd had left his cell phone in the car and it started to ring, she was tempted to look and see who was calling.

The temptation won.

She picked up his phone and on the caller ID was the name "Tatianna." Knowing it was his girlfriend calling, she felt the urge to answer it. Khye was curious to hear what she sounded like; curious to know if she was beautiful and exotic-looking like Khye. Who was she? What did she have going on for herself? Why was Floyd still with her? There were so many questions about her that had been on Khye's mind.

Tatianna. The name sounded like ghetto, lowbrow trash. Khye was confident Tatianna couldn't compete with her. She needed to know his truth, though, and she was willing to gamble something tonight so she could become his priority.

Tatianna was calling him again and again, dying for her man's attention. She couldn't have it. The attention Tatianna craved belonged to her. Khye smirked at this bitch calling and with her finger near the answer button, it could be so simple…just one "Hello?" in her English accent and the effect it could create. Hearing another woman's voice answering Floyd's phone could lead to the start of someone's end—some serious drama.

She didn't do it. Khye didn't want to be *that* girl. She didn't want to seem insecure, nosy, or overstep her boundaries. Khye let his cell phone ring and decided to confront Floyd about Tatianna later on.

✳✳✳

From Brooklyn Heights Promenade Park, the fireworks illuminated the skies over the East River. The glorious Brooklyn Bridge served as a backdrop for the sparklers dancing in the sky. Dozens of fireworks were visible from lower Manhattan and parts of Brooklyn.

Khye stood by the railing of the elevated walkway, wrapped up in Floyd's arms, staring up at the fireworks lighting up the night sky. She took in the breathtaking views of the Brooklyn Bridge, the Statue of Liberty, and downtown Manhattan. There were dozens of wide-eyed people enjoying the show on the cloudless night.

Floyd kissed the side of her neck and squeezed her tightly. Right there, at that moment, he wanted her so badly. As the fireworks lit up the sky Floyd touched her in places that made them both aroused.

"You don't want to watch the fireworks?" she said.

"Let's start our own fireworks," he joked.

She giggled. His touch was enticing. His kisses continued.

"Soon, baby . . . soon," she said.

They strolled along the Promenade in Brooklyn Heights, talking and laughing. But the minute the fireworks were over, so was her playful mood. Now she wanted answers from him. While still nestled in his arms, and his touching becoming more sensual, Khye turned around to face him and with an expressionless gaze. "Who's Tatianna?"

Floyd kept cool and responded, "How do you know about her?"

"I saw her calling your phone earlier. There are so many things I don't know about you Floyd, eh. Did you lie to me?"

"It's complicated," he said simply.

"So, can you make it not complicated?"

He removed his arms from around her and started to look like a man who was stuck on a difficult math problem while taking a very important test.

"Who is she, Floyd?" Khye asked again.

Now it was time to rock the boat. She knew exactly what she was doing. She didn't want to be second to anyone. Knowing the way Floyd felt about her after a few weeks, with her good pussy and enticing accent, how could he pick anyone else over her? She was the shiny new model with all the upgrades, and Tatianna was the old, broke-down model.

Floyd looked at her unwavering, and said, "Look, I'm not even gonna lie to you. She's my girl."

"She's your girl!" Khye feigned shock. "You have a girlfriend? All this fuckin' time!"

"Khye, let me explain," he poured out, looking worried.

"Explain what, Floyd? You lied to me."

"We been over, Khye. She just lives wit' me, that's all. We don't even fuck. I haven't touched that bitch in months," he lied.

"I'm falling in love with you, Floyd, and this is the outcome? Why did you lie to me?"

"I didn't lie to you."

"You didn't? Then what do you call it, hey? I feel so dirty and used. I'm no homewrecker, Floyd. I'm not that woman."

Floyd felt she was being too dramatic. He saw his perfect night slipping away from him. He had arranged bottle service and rose petals in the suite. Now it looked like it was about to be a waste of money.

"The bitch is moving out, Khye. She's gone!"

"I can't see you anymore," she said.

"What?"

"You don't share me, so why do I have to share you?"

"Khye, stop playin'—"

"I'm so serious, Floyd. Until she's out of your life, then I can't be in yours." She pivoted on her high heels and walked away from him.

"Khye!" he called out. "Khye, where you going? Khye!"

She continued to ignore him, leaving Floyd standing alone by the railing and looking dumbfounded. She smirked, knowing she had done the right thing and played the right hand. The way he almost begged her to stay, it stirred up a fire inside of her. And it was a chance she was taking. It was a move that could easily backfire on her. Walking away from Floyd and giving him an ultimatum meant her gleaming lifestyle could suddenly come to an end. It was the last thing she wanted to happen. But what reward could come without risk?

TEN

Sarah climbed off James's hard dick after feeling him burst into the condom. He came inside of her like a rocket going off, but the latex barrier prevented any pregnancy or STDs. She had rode James's dick so good that he couldn't stop shaking after his nut. It looked like he was having convulsions. She had that effect on a man. He lay underneath Sarah's spread legs with his protruding gut and hairy chest in view and showed a satisfying smile. His affair with the blue-eyed blonde beauty was the highlight of his life.

"You're the best," he told Sarah. He exhaled again.

She smiled halfheartedly. "I'm glad you enjoyed it."

"I always do."

James had paid her cab fare from Harlem to the Bronx. He was always kind and generous to her. He lived alone. He had been divorced and retired for five years and living off his pension, his life simple and predictable. Sarah became the spicy seasoning in his bland food. To her, the sex was run-of-the-mill, but he was okay company and someone to talk to once in a while.

Clad in only a T-shirt, Sarah went into the bathroom to wash up. She turned on the faucet and splashed some water on her face and thought about Marcus. It had been a week since her sexual rendezvous with him. Every day without seeing him, she missed him more.

Sarah continued gazing at her reflection. Her hair was in disarray after James pulled and ran his hand through it during sex, and she was emotionally fatigued. Every day with her husband became worse, and jumping around from guy to guy to please her sexual desires started to become redundant. The one black man she wanted was taken. She thought about Marcus every day. She tried calling him, but most times he was either too busy with work or his family to answer or return her calls.

She was getting older, and life at thirty-five wasn't what she'd dreamed of.

Thinking about Marcus made her mind whirl away with unruly thoughts; one of them was doing the unexpected and become pregnant by him on purpose. It was a simple way to try and keep him in her life, and even receive child support if push came to shove and he didn't want to leave his wife for her.

Her conversation with Khye the other day sparked a little jealousy inside. Where she had failed, Khye was succeeding—finding a handsome man to take care of her. It was clear that her daughter was doing well for herself. She had attracted a man that was financially well off—and whom Khye kept secret. She was clearly embarrassed to bring him around the family. Sarah couldn't blame her. What was there to bring him around? They were somewhat ghetto trash.

Sarah noticed the changes in her daughter's behavior and style. Khye's hair always done, the jewelry, the outfits, extra cash she had, and much more. Khye was glowing. Sarah wanted to glow too, and the only man able to make her glow like that was Marcus.

James was a fat, retired cop with a lot of spare time on his hands and not much to spend his money on besides her. He had no kids, rarely any family around, and had devoted twenty-five years to being a NYPD detective—fighting crime while his own personal life was in turmoil. He met Sarah through Facebook. He befriended her, she accepted, they gradually started talking via inbox, and eventually they met. He was fifty-two and she was thirty-four at the time.

The attraction was never there, but his willingness to freely and always give was a beautiful thing, and James grew on her. But it would go no further than casual sex and a few favors back and forth.

Now Gino, he was an exciting guy with a big dick. He was a fledgling drug dealer in her neighborhood, and she used to always see him around. Gino was a handsome and physically well-built man, and the second he first laid eyes on Sarah, he wanted her. He was persistent and relentless toward Sarah, always flaunting his body around the hood, and for her, showing off on his motorcycle, popping wheelies and bunny hops in the street and riding his bike like a daredevil.

The sex was good, but Sarah wasn't in love with him. He was a risk. He was something to do and someone close. And when she needed some cash, Gino didn't mind providing. He had the attitude "You do for me, and I'll do for you."

Now Marcus was the complete package, and he was the man she saw the least and who was already taken. He was the man that made her exhale. He was the man that she could be faithful to. He was the man that she would leave her family for. All he needed to do was ask.

"Hey, what you doing in there?" James called out. "You okay?"

"Yes. Give me a minute," she said.

Sarah sighed.

If only she could rewind time, or trade places with her daughter. She wanted to meet Khye's mystery man. The man that had her daughter glowing and in love. She wanted happiness and looked for it in all the wrong places.

"Sarah, come lay with me," James said.

"Okay."

She wiped his sweat away from her body, got herself right, and went back into the bedroom. He was sprawled across his bed naked with the bed sheets barely covering his private parts. Whenever Sarah came around, he lit up like a light bulb. He found so much joy with her. He never wanted her to leave. Sarah went over to him and plopped down beside his hefty frame with a huge smile. He placed his arm around her curvy figure and squeezed her lovingly.

He was very affectionate, but also very needy.

"James, I need a favor from you," she said.

"What kind of favor?"

"I need five hundred dollars," she said.

"Five hundred . . . that's a sizable favor."

"I know, but it's important."

"It's always important."

"James, don't I always treat you right . . . make you come hard and fast, and take care of all you need?"

"Yes you do," he responded.

"So, can I have the money without receiving the third degree?"

James sighed heavily. He looked reluctant to, but he decided to go against his better judgment. "Okay, I'll give it to you."

She smiled. "You are the best."

"I am, huh?"

"Yes."

"If you don't mind me asking, what do you need the money for?"

"I mind you asking," she said.

He used to be a top NYPD detective, so interrogating someone came natural to him. Sometimes he did it without realizing that he was doing it. It became a habit. Lately, Sarah had been hitting him up for cash—a hundred there, three hundred there, but this was the most she'd asked for.

"Is someone in your family in trouble?" James asked with concern.

"No, James," Sarah reacted with some frustration.

"I know you mind me asking, but I worry about you, Sarah," he said.

"There's no need for you to worry about me. I'm a big girl and capable of handling myself."

"I know. But I like you . . . really like you a lot. And I don't know what I would do if anything ever happened to you."

She smiled. It was touching. He was a sweetheart—a big ol' soft teddy bear for her to squeeze when she needed comfort. His huge heart sometimes outshined his sappy appearance. He was one of those men that took his work home with him and became emotionally involved with his cases and the victims involved. If the victims were children or women, James was a detective that couldn't rest until the suspect or suspects were caught and tried. He had a ninety-percent clearance rate in his unit, and when he retired, the city was sad to see him go.

"Sarah, you know you can talk to me about anything. I was cop for over twenty years. I've seen and been through a lot, so nothing surprises me anymore," James stated.

"It's nothing serious, James. Can a woman just borrow money without there being a serious issue attached?"

"Yes, but lately, you've been kind of distant, and—"

"James, I'm okay," she assured him.

He was playing cop again. Retired five years or not, it was still in his blood, being a detective, getting into people's business and wanting to make everything okay. Sarah knew there was only one way to avert his attention, and that was getting him sexually stimulated again. She positioned herself against his stout frame for better grip around his flaccid penis. When she was contentedly in place, she started to jerk him off. She felt him growing hard into her fist. He was moaning softly, closing his eyes, enjoying her womanly touch.

"You know what to do to me, don't you?" he said.

"Just enjoy it."

Up and down, nice and slow, bit by bit increasing her hand movement against his hard flesh. It didn't take long for his hot seed to splash all over her hand. He puffed out with fulfillment and placed his head against the pillow. Sounding winded from the hand job he just received, he said, "The money is in my wallet."

"Thank you," Sarah said, smiling devilishly.

She didn't hesitate to take the five hundred dollars she asked for. James wasn't going to miss it at all. His cop pension made him well off, and living single and alone, he had enough money to go around.

Her sex put James to sleep and she got dressed, feeling she overstayed longer than she wanted to. With the five hundred dollars on her person, Sarah smiled wider than the doorway to Grand Central Station. She needed the money because it was Marcus's birthday next week, and she wanted to buy him something nice. She wanted to impress him and show him how much she appreciated him. Sarah didn't find anything wrong with borrowing from one man to pay for something nice for another man.

Khye wasn't about to be the only one in the family with a rich and fine man taking care of her. Sarah was ready to compete with her daughter. By any means necessary, she was going to get what she always wanted in her life.

ELEVEN

Khye, give me a call back when you get this message. I miss you and I wanna see you. I'm sorry, baby. I'm sorry, and I didn't mean to upset you." Floyd left the message on Khye's voicemail.

It hadn't been a complete twenty-four hours yet, but Floyd was already calling Khye nonstop. Her plan was working, but she wanted to see him sweat a lot more. She refused to take his call anytime soon. She still pretended to be upset about his live-in girlfriend and was ready to carry out the lie until it completely benefited her.

"Khye, this is my fourth time calling you, pick up the fuckin' phone," Floyd had cursed. "Look, I'm sorry I'm about that. I didn't mean to curse at you. I just love you and don't wanna lose you. When you get this, call me back."

She decided to save all of his messages for her personal pleasure. It was exciting to hear him squirm and beg for her to come back. She had Floyd right in the palm of her hand. His pleading messages made her pussy wet. She wanted to take him back, but it was too soon.

"Khye, she's gone. I promise you, Tatianna is out of my life and I only want you in it. Whatever you need from me, it's done." It was his sixth message.

***

Two weeks went by and Floyd was relentless in making contact with

Khye via calling or emotional text messages. He was frantic. He didn't know what to do with himself. He didn't know where Khye lived. He didn't know too much about her. She came into his life and totally captivated him. His only way of looking for her was in Harlem, probably on the East Side where she resided.

"Khye, I'm not giving up on you, you hear me, ma? But listen, I got two tickets to the Jay Z and Beyoncé concert this weekend at the Barclay center. I want you to come with me. I also got backstage passes and VIP access to the after party. I know you don't wanna miss this. It's gonna be the concert and party of a lifetime, and I want you to be there, as my girl . . . the woman I love," Floyd had left on her voicemail.

When Khye heard the message, she was tempted to call him back and give in. Jay Z and Beyoncé concert, backstage passes, and VIP at the after party, it was a dream come true. However, she decided not to go and continued to hold out a little longer. She didn't want it to look like he could buy her love with gifts, even though he could. She had to appear genuinely upset about Tatianna and his lying. A woman with class and self-respect wouldn't be so easily tempted, so she thought.

Two weeks seemed like forever for them both.

Floyd was hurt.

Khye felt she was winning.

***

"Yo, fuck that bitch, Floyd. If she ain't calling you back, then move on, nigga," Carlito said. "I ain't never trust her anyway."

Floyd cut his eyes at his best friend and charged him immediately, grabbing him by his shirt collar and slamming him against his parked car.

"Nigga, watch ya fuckin' mouth about her!" Floyd warned.

"Nigga, you tripping! You barely know her and she got you actin' like this. What, she put that voodoo on you? So what she from London and got that accent, that don't mean she better than an American bitch. I don't like her!"

The two locked eyes. Floyd still had an intense hold on Carlito and had him forced roughly against his CL600. Carlito wasn't a punk and always spoke truth. He pushed Floyd off of him and shouted, "Nigga, get the fuck off me!"

Floyd backed off his friend, but he was still upset with Carlito's harsh mouth about Khye.

"Nigga, I ain't never beat around the bush or sugarcoated a fuckin' thing since the day we met. I don't give a fuck who it offends and I ain't gonna start now, my nigga," Carlito exclaimed.

Floyd frowned.

"We supposed to be about this money, my nigga, and with or without you, I'm gonna still get it. I rather it be wit' you . . . you feel me? Don't let this one shorty stop the show."

Floyd simply stared at his right-hand man.

"She should be chasing you; not the other way around," Carlito said.

Khye had him tripping. He knew Carlito was right. Khye had him going crazy. He didn't know what it was, but it was something about her that had him stir-crazy.

"Yo, you right," Floyd said, relenting.

"I know I am, my nigga."

Carlito passed Floyd the bottle of Henny in his hand and Floyd took a needed sip. They lingered on the Brooklyn corner talking. Carlito was always the one to talk sense into Floyd when he felt himself slipping.

"Anyway, my nigga, the block is hot since that thing the other night," Carlito brought up. "And we need to take this trip to meet wit' the Colombians today, but not before we handle this other thing."

"What other thing?" Floyd asked.

"Nigga, you forgot?"

Floyd had to think back quickly, and then it came to him. "Oh, that other thing," he uttered. "You handled that already?"

"Nigga, when it comes to our money, of course I'm gonna handle it. Niggas out here need to know. And while you was off in Disney World having fun on the rides and shit, I'm holdin' shit down out here," Carlito said.

"Yo, I appreciate that."

"My nigga, we came too far to start slippin' now. You fuckin' *Love Jones* nigga," Carlito joked.

"Fuck you, nigga," Floyd responded lightly.

"Yeah, I ain't one of your bitches, my nigga. You know Tatianna gonna whoop that ass when she finds out you brought another girl into the folds."

"She ain't gonna do shit. I'm 'bout to toss that bitch out soon, anyway."

"Oh word," Carlito responded, looking shocked. "Y'all go way back, and got two years together. Don't tell me you tossing her out because of this new chick?"

"Yeah, and nah. She overstaying her welcome and letting herself go, Carlito. I mean, the excessive tattoos, the smoking, the laziness. She don't do shit but live off of me. I can't even bring her nowhere wit'out her embarrassing me. You feel me?"

Carlito chuckled. "Yeah, I feel you, but you know she gonna act up, she loves you…and c'mon my nigga, you know you gonna miss that good pussy and dope blow jobs you always praised about her."

"Shit gettin' old, Carlito."

"As long as we don't."

The two men laughed. They were like brothers growing up together on the same block, committing the same crimes, and loving the same things. They fought together, got arrested together on a few occasions. They raised up in the drug game year by year, building their empire side by side by murdering, slaughtering, and taking Brooklyn over one block at a time.

Carlito and Floyd became the dynamic duo in the deadly drug game with hopes of succeeding in the music business and one day putting their treacherous past behind them and becoming moguls like their idols Sean Combs, Russell Simmons, and Jay Z. Each man had a knack for music and rhyming, and though they were talented rappers, they found it more lucrative to be behind the scenes; the puppeteer instead of the puppet.

Carlito glanced at his watch and said, "Yo, we gotta go."

"A'ight..."

Floyd downed the last of the Hennessy and tossed the bottle away without any worry that he was littering with beat cops walking around. They climbed into Carlito's money green Yukon with Carlito saying, "This new chick, Khye . . . I mean, do she even know what you really do?"

"She thinks I'm an engineer and music producer," Floyd said, smiling.

Carlito laughed. "Well, at least that's partially true. We are, but . . ."

"I know, my nigga." Floyd interjected.

"You think she would be able to handle the truth if she ever found out about you?"

"I don't know, but she's a strong woman. Classy too."

"At least Tatianna knows what you are. It ain't no hiding it wit' her," said Carlito.

"Yeah, that's true, but it ain't nothin' better than new pussy," Floyd replied.

"Yeah, that new pussy is good pussy, but new pussy can be suicide."

"What you tryin' to say?" Floyd asked with a raised eyebrow at his friend.

"I'm sayin', at least wit' old pussy, you know the mileage on it, especially if you put it there yourself. You know where it's been. New pussy, the shit could look brand new and nice, you ready to get into it and take it for a spin only to find out it's a fuckin' lemon and the shit ain't goin' anywhere," Carlito stated to Floyd.

Floyd laughed. "Whatever. You and your fuckin' parables."

"Simply sayin', stick to what you know."

"Nigga, let's stick to taking care of this business right now," Floyd countered.

"Ain't that what I've been saying?"

Floyd shook his head. Carlito started the engine and drove out of the parking spot. Carlito lit up a cigarette and took a few pulls while he drove. Floyd was quiet, looking out the window and thinking. While on their way to handle business nearby, Khye crept into his mind again like an intoxicating smell. He couldn't wash off her scent no matter what he used or tried. It lingered on him like an odor. He wanted to see her again, but she wasn't answering his calls or calling him back. No woman had ever ignored him the way Khye was ignoring him. It came as a shock, and it was the reason why he wanted her badly.

Fifteen minutes later, Carlito pulled up to a dilapidated storefront on Utica Avenue and they both stepped out of the SUV. Carlito took one final pull from his second cigarette and tossed it away. He looked at Floyd and said, "Let's go in here and remind these niggas what we're about."

Floyd nodded.

Inside the Brooklyn storefront that read "One Stop Deli" on the outside, the owner nodded at his two new customers with recognition. He was a skinny, bald-headed man with aging features and troubling eyes. Floyd and Carlito walked inside like they owned the place and headed straight toward the back of the store, where they were met by one of their soldiers standing guard. The towering thug nodded at his bosses and opened a steel door that led into the basement. They descended down the concrete stairway and entered into a dimly lit concrete room littered with milk crates and expiring consumer goods. Beyond that were five harrowing looking men crowded around three captive men who were masked, gagged, and bound with their hands tied behind them and on their knees in submission. The three men were beaten badly and just about stripped down naked. They whimpered and groaned incoherently under their hoods and the duct tape covering their mouths.

"Yeah, niggas, y'all in for some shit now, muthafuckas!" one of the goons shouted. "You know y'all fucked up!"

When Floyd and Carlito showed their presence, the room quieted down. Floyd immediately glared at the three men kneeled down and subdued in front of him.

"This them, huh?" he said.

"Hells yeah, this is them. Niggas wanna stir up shit in the ranks and think we ain't gonna fuckin' find out," Billy heatedly exclaimed, knocking one of the men upside his head with the bottom of his fist. Billy was one of their loyal soldiers, standing six-three and full of anger and strength.

"Billy, just chill. I got this," Floyd said calmly.

"A'ight, boss," he responded submissively.

"Take off their hoods," Floyd instructed.

Quickly, their hoods were taken off and all three men looked up in fear at Floyd and Carlito scowling down at them. Floyd looked each man in the eye for a moment. He wanted to see them, and he wanted them to see him. Carlito stood by his friend's side with a matching hard look.

It was known that one of their former lieutenants planned on starting a coup d'état inside their organization, overthrowing Floyd and Carlito by killing them. Floyd had ears and eyes everywhere, and the traitor's name was Rash. He had always been a greedy and green-eyed nigga they came up with and one time trusted, but the more money, the more problems.

Rash got into a few workers' ears, brainwashing a few and sweet-talking the others into aiding him in taking down Floyd and Carlito with the promise of a better cut for everyone. Now a civil war had started in their organization, and the bodies started to pile up in Brooklyn, hence the two men killed in their car right before the Fourth of July holiday.

Floyd had a personal hand in that murder.

"Now fellows, let's have a decent talk, okay?" said Floyd with a chilling smile at them. "Where's Rash? First one to speak up gets on my good side."

Floyd motioned toward his men to remove the duct tape from around the captives' mouths. It was torn off and no one had anything useful to say to him.

"We don't know shit," one man shouted. "I swear to you, we ain't wit' that nigga!"

"Well, I hear different, Mike," Floyd spat back. "What I heard, you up that nigga Rash's ass so tight, you can predict his farts. Now I know ya lying to me."

"I swear, Floyd, we weren't on that bullshit! You the man—"

"Shut the fuck up!" Billy shouted, belting the man in his mouth and causing him to spew blood onto the concrete floor.

"I guess no one wants to do me any favors and get on my good side," Floyd said, facetiously.

He removed his nice, clean shirt, not wanting to get any blood on it. Carlito remained quiet, allowing his friend to do the dirty work. Out of the three, two were terrified, but the third; he carried the hardest face and boldly yelled out, "Fuck you, nigga! You don't scare me, Floyd. Rash is gonna be on ya ass, nigga!"

"Oh, is that so? Okay, how about you and me, we have a one to one talk?" said Floyd.

Billy placed a hatchet in Floyd's hand. They untied his arms and outstretched the man's arm for something severely punishing.

"Now, I'm gonna give you a choice, you want short sleeve or long sleeve?" Floyd asked him.

The man struggled, knowing what was coming next. Three men

brutally beat on him and held him down with his right arm lengthened out across the table. Floyd glared at him, raising the hatchet in a threatening method and said, "I repeat, short sleeve or long sleeve?"

"Don't do this . . . don't do this, man!" he frightfully yelled.

He squirmed harder to try and free himself, but he was forcefully held into place for the brutal assault.

"You indecisive huh, so I'll chose for you," Floyd said. Without any hesitation he slammed the hatchet down onto his wrist with a powerful stroke and nearly chopped off the dude's hand. It took two chops before the hand was completely severed from the wrist.

"Aaaaaaaaaaaaaaaaaahhh!!!" the man screamed to the top of his lungs. "You MUTHAFUCKA!!"

Blood was everywhere and he sounded like an abnormal animal be torn apart, as his terrifying screams echoed off the walls.

"Long sleeve then, winter is comin' soon," Floyd said for a laugh.

Clutching his severed arm, the man was in so much pain and agony; he dropped against the floor clutching his injury, curling into the fetal position with tears pouring out of his eyes.

"Nigga, we ain't done yet," said Floyd. "Pick that muthafucka up."

Billy and two other goons roughly grabbed him off the floor and positioned him in front of Floyd, insensitive to his pain and suffering. Floyd came closer and placed the hatchet against his other arm. "Now, where's Rash, or choose again," he said coldly with a stern face.

"Fuck you, man! Fuck you!" he cursed angrily. "You took my hand, man—my hand!"

"And I'm about to take the other one," Floyd callously said.

Floyd nodded to Billy and they stretched out his other arm for dismembering. The dude resisted heavily, but the force against him made it a losing battle. Floyd once again didn't hesitate and swung the hatchet down and cut off the next hand viciously, with more blood spewing and his bloodcurdling screams feeling like they were about to make the walls crumble.

"He ain't gonna talk," Billy said.

Floyd extended his hand for the weapon and Billy placed the .45 into his grip. His victim didn't suffer long. Floyd right away put a bullet into his head, silencing his screaming and ending his torture. The other two captives looked on nervously.

"Now, one down and two to go…and y'all know, there's still time to get on my good side," Floyd said to them humorously.

"We don't know shit, Floyd. I promise you. Please, man, it ain't gotta be like this!" one screamed fearfully.

"Yes it do, cuz y'all fuckin' wit' the wrong muthafucka," Floyd said gruffly.

Half hour later and with three dead bodies in the basement, Floyd wiped the blood off of him and said to Carlito, "I guess these niggas didn't know shit."

"You tried. Maybe you losing your touch, nigga," Carlito responded.

"I ain't losing shit," Floyd shot back. "But when I find this nigga Rash, I'm gonna kill him twice."

"That was ya man, and now he Benedict Arnold out this bitch," Carlito said.

Floyd put his shirt back on, looked at Billy and commanded, "Clean this shit up, and I only want one body found. Disappear the other two."

Billy nodded. "I'm on it, boss."

Looking back to normal and feeling satisfied that they got three traitors off the street, Carlito and Floyd exited the basement and walked back out into the street. Carlito hit the button to deactivate the alarm to his Yukon.

"You hungry?" Carlito asked.

"Yeah, a little something."

"Good, I'm in the mood for Junior's in downtown. We ain't gotta meet the Colombians until tonight," said Carlito.

"Junior's it is then," Floyd said.

Life was good, but for Floyd, it would have been even better if Khye returned his phone calls and if he could see her again.

TWELVE

"Khye, give me a call back when you get this message. I miss you and I wanna see you. I'm sorry, baby. I'm sorry, and I didn't mean to upset you," the message played for Sammy in his bedroom, and he simply shook his head and grinned.

"Girl, you are a hot fuckin' mess. Seriously though, Khye, you better stop playing with that boy's emotions. You already know how these niggas be," he warned her.

"Please, Sammy. I got this nigga so wrapped up on me, he's like a second layer of skin," Khye boasted.

"Whatever, slut, you playing with fire? And I shouldn't even be speaking to you, I'm still upset," he said lightly.

"Whatever, you know you love me and miss me. What would you do without me, Sammy?"

"Be drama-free," he joked.

"You would be so bored."

Sammy threw up his middle finger at her and said, "Bitch, that's how bored I would be."

She laughed.

They were on good terms again and speaking, becoming their old selves around each other. Khye came bearing gifts, buying Sammy something special with the money Floyd had given her over the weeks. Sammy couldn't turn down a free gift, and he did miss her, despite all the shit talking and sarcasm he threw her way. They both had become so tickled listening to Floyd's "I'm sorry" along with his pleading and begging messages on her phone—finding his affliction amusing.

"So you gonna take him back?" Sammy asked.

"Not until he gets rid of that bitch he has staying with him," she said. "He could wait. I'm not coming second for anyone. You understand me, Sammy?"

Sammy looked at her with a change of attitude and Khye picked up on his cautioning gaze.

"What?" she asked.

"I'll tell you what, you got a good thing going, Khye, and I think you're retarded to be gambling with a baller like that."

"Seriously, this from you? You didn't like him at all."

"But look at you. No more cheap or secondhand shit and all blinged out from spending his money? Girl, you looking like a star right now," he said.

His comment made her smile.

"I'm just saying, you taking too many chances by putting him on hold for too long. You know sooner or later, the ice is gonna melt," Sammy added.

It made Khye think for a moment.

Sammy continued with, "I mean, did you at least see the bitch he's staying with?"

"No."

"Well, FYI, I heard she ain't an ugly bitch, Khye. I heard she's biracial, like half Russian and some other shit like that," he said, moving his hand around in the air and crossing his legs femininely.

"So what are you saying to me, Sammy?"

"Look Khye, you think you're something special, but maybe you're not. It's obvious Floyd has a certain type that he really likes, and he sticks to it. He's not a bad-looking guy; in fact, you already know the nigga is fine. Yes, he might be calling you, but don't think the man's lifestyle is monastic. Because you know, bitch, the shoe can easily be on the other foot, and you might be the bitch calling him, and then he starts ignoring you. You know why? Because you might become yesterday's pussy to him," Sammy pronounced in a merciless tone.

Khye didn't respond. She sat silently with Sammy's words weighing down on her heavily, making it look like she was sinking into the chair she sat in. A slight smirk showed on Sammy's face as he told Khye the truth. Secretly, he loved getting under her skin. He was consumed by jealousy all of a sudden. Seeing Khye in her expensive outfits, nice shoes, the jewelry, and her come up, Sammy wanted the same thing in his life. He wanted a nigga that had some good dick and who would take care of him. Yes, his friend broke him off with a few nice garments, but he wanted more. Why couldn't he be happy too?

The look Khye had on her face showed she was thinking about every single word Sammy had said. Sammy loved watching his friend squirm. Yes, they were friends again, but he felt she had changed. Sammy sat there with his legs still crossed and felt that he'd single-handedly broken up the best thing in Khye's life. He told her the truth, and most times, the truth hurts.

"So what you gonna do?" Sammy asked.

"I don't know yet," Khye replied faintly.

"I mean, bitch, you're cute, but we are in New York City, and you know how these bitches are."

"And I thought you were my friend," she replied.

"I am your friend; that's why I'm telling you this," he shot back.

Khye knew what she needed to do. Sammy was right. If she made Floyd wait and suffer too long, then there was the chance he could be gone forever. She couldn't live without him in her life. He had changed her world and made her happy with the expensive gifts, his sex, and his love. So she decided to return his phone calls, but first, she had to make sure Tatianna was completely out of his life.

***

It took a simple text from Khye to get Floyd charged and ready to go. He looked at his phone and was surprised she had texted him.

I miss you, too, but I want to make sure Tatianna is out of your life and I'm in yours for good. No more hotels. I want to spend the night at your place.

His place was still occupied with his live-in girlfriend, but he desperately wanted to see Khye again. So he could no longer prolong the inevitable. Tatianna had to go. Floyd texted back.

She's already gone, and tomorrow night, I'll come get you.

His text made Khye smile.

She texted back: I love you, and I'll call you.

Please do.

That evening, Floyd hurried home to do what Khye had asked him to do. She was the one. He was sure of it. It had been three weeks since he'd last seen her, and knowing that they were about to have something special the very next night got him super excited and feeling great. He just had to do one evil deed—get rid of his old baggage.

Floyd rushed out of his car with a frown as he walked toward his condo. He went inside, and as he'd predicted, the place was a mess. There were dishes piled up in the sink, weed residue was scattered all over his kitchen table, and the house reeked of cigarette smoke and weed. There was loud music playing in the bedroom, and it wasn't a home he liked coming back to. Stank bitch didn't clean or cook. She was able to suck a good dick and fuck like a porn star, but besides that, she was a handicap.

Floyd looked at his unclean apartment and he was fed up. He stormed toward the bedroom knowing it was where Tatianna was going to be. He pushed open the door so hard, that it almost flew off the hinges. He startled Tatianna who was seated on the bed rolling up another blunt to smoke.

"Ohmygod, baby! What the fuck? You scared the shit out of me," she said.

Floyd scowled her way and looked around the bedroom; disorganized, clothes everywhere, music blaring, and his bitch looking trashy.

"You know what? This ain't gonna work, Tatianna. Look at this shit; I'm fuckin' tired of you and your messy ass. Get the fuck out my house!" he exclaimed. He didn't beat around the bush or sugarcoat it.

"What?" Tatianna was taken aback by his harsh reaction toward her so suddenly. "Floyd, you tripping?"

"I just want you gone!"

He thrust opened the closet doors and went berserk, throwing every piece of clothing she owned onto the floor. Tatianna jumped angrily and ran toward him, screaming, "Floyd don't do that. You tryin' to kick me out because of that bitch!"

"Two years, and you still ain't accomplished shit for yourself. You just sit around leaching off me and complain about me cheating, when I fuckin' told you, it ain't about a bitch."

"Fuck you, nigga! Who is she?" Tatianna shouted heatedly.

"I told you, there ain't no other bitch. I'm just tired of ya fuckin' shit," he retorted.

"Fuck you, Floyd! Fuck you! I ain't goin' no-fuckin'-where! Two years together and this is how you treat me?"

Her tears poured out from her eyes like a bathtub overflowing, and she was quickly flooded with emotions. For her, it was hard to accept that Floyd didn't love her anymore, and that he had fallen in love with someone else. Her gut instincts told her that he was lying through his teeth. Within a heartbeat, the man and the world she was used to came crashing down on her. Her clothing and belongings were everywhere. Floyd was acting erratically, like an animal with rabies.

Her heart started to beat rapidly. She had no place to go.

"You can keep all the clothes and the jewelry. I don't give a fuck about any of it. But you are gonna give me the keys to the Range Rover," he said.

"What?"

"You think this shit is a game?" he shouted.

"You know what—" Tatianna exclaimed. She snatched the car keys off the dresser and threw them at Floyd. He ducked. She missed. However the keys weren't the last thing being thrown at him. Tatianna became belligerent, snatching the lamp off the dresser and throwing it at Floyd. It barely missed him too. Next came the TV remote, her cell phone, books, and an assortment of things.

"You want me gone!" she screamed out.

Tatianna showed that she was going to be difficult. She wasn't leaving easily. Scantily clad in her underwear, the rage she felt transformed her into She-Hulk, and she went charging at Floyd, heatedly chanting, "You want me gone! You want me gone! You want me fuckin' gone! For ya next bitch!"

She didn't hold back her punches. She refused to suppress her anger. She never felt so disrespected in her entire life and she only saw violence as her one way to respond. She swung wildly at Floyd, transforming into Mike Tyson in the bedroom. But Floyd wasn't about to become her punching bag. When Tatianna tried to hit him again, he sidestepped, moving right and counterattacking with his right fist striking her in her jaw. The punch was dizzying and staggering, but she was full with rage and adrenaline, ready to go to war.

"Oh, so you wanna hit a bitch?" she said, feeling the blood inside her mouth. "Let's go muthafucka!"

She threw her hands up, ready for battle.

Floyd wasn't shy when it came to putting his hands on a woman. He wasn't going to be disrespected by anyone, not even his own ex-girlfriend.

She attacked, trying to stab Floyd with a pair of scissors she picked up. The look in her eyes was deadly. Floyd took a few steps backwards and placed himself into a defensive stance.

"Don't play wit' me, Tatianna. If you come at me wit' them scissors I'm gonna fuck you up!"

She didn't care for his threats. All she saw was red and hate. She lunged his way with the scissors gripped tightly in her hand and swung wildly at him. She wanted to do him bodily harm because everything inside of her felt broken. Floyd maneuvered like a fly trying to keep itself from being swatted, quickly knocking the weapon out of her hand and he was on her like white on rice, punching her repeatedly. The two quickly went to blows in the bedroom like Ike and Tina.

Lips bleeding, eyes swollen, Floyd and Tatianna were out of breath and looking like they had gone through hell and back. The bedroom was a wreck, and she was even a bigger wreck. Tatianna didn't want to leave. She was ready to fight for her love. With her face hardened with grief and pain, she looked at Floyd like her soul had been ripped away from her.

"Why?" she asked sadly. "Just tell me the truth, Floyd."

"Why? Because we fell apart, that's why. And that's all I gotta say. Look at you—look at us. This ain't love," he replied coldly.

Once again, her tears fell, and her pain was so real, it spread through her heart and soul like a nasty virus and it changed her.

Floyd removed the .9 mm he kept in the closet. It wasn't a threat to Tatianna yet. He kept it pointed at the floor. The look on his face showed that he was as serious as a heart attack if she tried to attack him again. He was done fighting.

"You already know what it is. You proved ya fuckin' point. Now if you ain't out my crib within twenty-four hours, it's gonna get biblical up in this bitch."

She was crushed. There was nothing she could say or do to change his mind. The cold look in Floyd's eyes displayed his callous resolve.

Floyd walked out of the bedroom. Reluctantly, Tatianna started to place her belongings into a few trash bags. She cried and cried. It felt like her tears were never going to stop.

***

"Yo, Tatianna, you don't even need to worry about him, he's a cornball. Fuck him," her sister Kim said. "You better off without him."

Tatianna didn't feel that way. She was devastated. Her eyes were red from crying for hours, and she didn't know what to do with herself. Where would she go, even though her sister offered her a place to stay?

Kim and Tatianna's best friend, Lea, were there to help her move out after she called them hysterical and explained to them what had happened.

Kim and Lea rushed over.

Kim was ready to cut Floyd when she saw her sister's face; it was black and blue, and swollen. She didn't care if Floyd was a big-time drug dealer; once someone put their hands on her younger sister, she was ready to react. She never did like Floyd, and though they all grew up together, Kim would always warn her little sister about men like him.

"Don't worry about him, Tatianna. Niggas like him always get what's coming their way," Lea said.

"They sure do," Kim cosigned.

They talked shit about Floyd as they packed Tatianna's things into the trunk of Kim's Kia. No matter what, they were always going to be there for her.

"He thinks I'm so fuckin' stupid. I know it's another bitch," Tatianna said.

"Of course it's another bitch, Tatianna. And he's a fake-ass nigga who can't even admit it and tell you the truth. See, that's how niggas be—they get some new pussy in their life and forget about the bitch that had their back from day one," Kim proclaimed.

"I know that's right. That's why I don't trust no nigga," Lea chimed.

"Yo, I swear, when I see that bitch, it's on," Tatianna said.

"Yo, all you gotta do is call us, and we gonna fuck that bitch up, you hear me sis?" Kim said.

"Do you know what that bitch looks like?" Lea asked.

"I never saw that bitch. I don't even know her fuckin' name. But if she thinks she can just come up in his life so easily and think everything is gonna be peaches and cream, then that bitch got another thing coming. I'm gonna make it hell for that bitch," Tatianna proclaimed.

"That bitch don't know Brooklyn. Bed-Stuy don't play," Lea said.

Tatianna placed the last of her things into her sister's Kia and then turned around to take one last look at home—what used to be her home. Floyd was away, and she wished she could tell him goodbye before departing. After everything that had happened in the past twenty-four hours, she still yearned to see him again.

"Don't even look back," Lea said to her.

Tatianna sighed, feeling despondent and then climbed into the backseat of the Kia. She had everything out of the condo, but it hurt leaving behind the Range Rover and Floyd. She loved the truck and him so much more.

Kim started the car and pulled away, and the more distance that came between Tatianna and her former home, the more tears that fell from her eyes as she watched it gradually disappear.

THIRTEEN

Sarah walked into her daughter's bedroom with the wrong intentions on her mind. It was early afternoon and quiet in the apartment. Her two youngest daughters were over at their friends' homes for the summer day, her husband was at work, and Khye was somewhere with Sammy. Everyone's absence gave her the opportunity.

Recently, Khye had been showing off too much cash and clothing. She wasn't sharing it with family, and worst of all, she wasn't sharing it with her. Sarah was money hungry. Of the money she had gotten from James, she only had a hundred dollars left. Most of the cash with which she'd meant to buy Marcus a gift had been gambled away in a card game, and now she wanted to make it back some way. The easiest way she saw was taking it from Khye, assuming her daughter had some hidden somewhere in the bedroom.

She went looking around the room, carefully going through her daughter's belongings. First, she went through her drawers, looked underneath the bed, went through her shoe boxes, becoming jealous of the different pairs of nice shoes Khye suddenly had, and then went searching in the closet. Then bingo, she found Khye's cash subtly stashed away in one of her jacket pockets. Sarah lit up like daylight. She took it all—almost three thousand dollars. She placed everything back to make it look like she hadn't been snooping around, like she hadn't even been there, and walked out of the bedroom with all of Khye's money.

***

"The house has twenty-one," the casino dealer shouted out.

"Dammit!" Sarah cursed and banged her fist on the Blackjack table.

"Ma'am, I'm going to ask you not to do that again," the lady dealer said politely.

"I'm sorry," Sarah apologized.

She sighed with frustration. She had already lost twenty-five hundred dollars of Khye's money at the Empire City Casino in Yonkers, New York. She had hoped to triple her money, but with no success. Every minute, every hour she was losing more and more. She spent three hours gambling, feeding her addiction and losing money that wasn't hers to begin with. She didn't see herself as stealing Khye's money; only borrowing it and paying her back when she got the chance. She assumed Khye wouldn't even miss it anytime soon.

Sarah removed herself from the Blackjack table and walked through the busy casino. When she wanted to be alone, it was one of her favorite places to be. She had been on a losing streak lately, and was desperate to win back the money she'd lost. It was a crippling effect, and with five hundred left, she was anxious to make it back—what she stole or borrowed from everyone.

She decided to hit the roulette table. It was blanketed with people placing bets and several people winning on occasion. With five hundred dollars on her, Sarah decided to take her chances with the spinning ball and the wheel. She placed two hundred dollars on black and another hundred on Black 28.

"No more bets," the dealers announced loudly.

He spun the wheel, and the ball went bouncing around like a jumping jack. Sarah watched the ball intently, hoping it stopped on her number, or the color black. It moved around and moved around, gradually slowing until it found a home—Red 14.

"Fuck!" Sarah cursed.

She lost another three hundred in less than a minute. She decided to try her luck again. She placed what she had left on black again. She couldn't lose. What were the odds of the ball landing on red again?

"No more bets!" the dealer announced.

He spun the wheel and dropped the white ball. Once again, Sarah watched it spin intently. Her heart was racing. It moved and moved and— Red 34. Sarah's heart dropped into the pit of her stomach and she flushed with dismay. She had lost everything. She couldn't believe it, now she was completely broke.

She slowly turned away from the table and marched away like a beat-up puppy with its tail between its legs. She had no money and no way to get back home to Harlem. And the worst of it all was that Khye was going to be pissed off and she had no cash to buy Marcus a gift. She felt so stupid.

She hurried outside and lit the last cigarette she had. She took a few needed pulls and held back the tears that started to form in her eyes. Her life sucked! She looked around wishing some miracle would happen, but it was real life and there was no fairy Godmother around. Though she was only thirty-five, she felt too old to start anything from scratch.

"What I'm gonna do?" she asked herself.

Marcus's birthday was fast approaching, and she really wanted to get him something nice. He didn't plan on spending his birthday with his mistress, but they had made arrangements to see each other the day after. Sarah couldn't wait. She really wanted to impress him. She wanted to influence him into thinking that she was a good woman and not some whore who was trying to come between him and his wife and break apart his family—when in actuality, she was. It was the illusion she wanted to show, and he was too much in lust with her to take a closer look behind her veil.

Sarah smoked the Newport until it was almost a butt and flicked it away. The minute she tossed the butt, she heard a man behind her ask, "You look stressed, baby. Bad day?"

Sarah turned around with an attitude on her face. She was having more than a bad day. He smiled in her direction, she didn't smile back. He was a Hispanic male, short, and pudgy looking. And he had a perverted smile about him.

"What do you want?" she asked brusquely.

"I just want to talk," he replied civilly.

"Why?"

"I saw you losing in there, and thought maybe you needed someone to talk to . . . maybe help."

"What are you, stalking me?" she exclaimed.

"No, no. I'm not one of those. I just think that you're a beautiful woman and maybe I can help you out with something," he said.

Sarah wasn't a fool. She read between the lines. She knew what his kind wanted. He was almost certainly the type of man taking advantage of a helpless woman down on her luck and probably giving them a simple proposition. What was it? Did she have it stamped across her forehead— "Will fuck for money"?

"What is it that you want from me?" she asked.

Her accent was exciting to him. He never heard anything like it. She was a snowflake he wanted to lick.

"I can help you with your problem."

She smiled. "My problem?"

Sarah knew he was too timid to come out with his proposition directly, so he beat around the bush, hoping she gave him an offer.

"What, you want me to suck your little dick, huh? That's it? You see me in the casino losing, see me out here crying and desperate and you come to me, thinking I'm some sort of bloody prostitute!" she exclaimed.

He suddenly looked nervous and coughed out, "I didn't mean to offend you."

"Offend me . . . you are *judging* me," Sarah said.

The man turned red and looked embarrassed. There were people around, and when they heard Sarah raise her voice at him, it drew attention that he didn't want.

"I'm sorry to come your way," he said sheepishly.

Sarah needed the money desperately, though. It was like a bizarre miracle coming from some warped angel. He had what she needed.

"How much you have on you?" she asked.

He turned around quickly and quickly said, "Fifty dollars."

She chuckled at the number. Fifty dollars couldn't even get his dick wet with her lips, but tonight, she made an exception. She had to get home, and playing her cards right, maybe she could get much more from him plus a ride home.

Sarah followed him to his Ford Escort. She climbed into the backseat with him, not believing she was about to whore herself out once again. Sarah wasn't doing the unthinkable. She had done worse. He was excited; the size of the parking lot gave them some privacy. He unbuttoned and unzipped his jeans and pulled them down around his ankles. But first, she needed her money. He dropped a fifty-dollar bill into her hand, and she wrapped a condom around his dick. Before she touched him with her breath and lips, Sarah rolled her eyes, wanting to make it quick, and got it started.

She wrapped her sweet lips around his little erection and started to suck him off. He groaned and moaned with his legs spread. Five minutes later, she had him coming into the condom and shaking like a leaf on a windy day. Sarah wiped her lips, propped herself back up into the chair, and was ready to work the man for every penny he had. He didn't stand a chance with her.

Sarah got out of the man's Ford Escort with night blanketing her hood. Just like she'd predicted, she milked him for an extra hundred dollars, always knowing when a man was lying about money. It wasn't what she came to the casino with, nowhere near it, but it was something for now.

She walked toward the lobby, knowing she was going to have to deal with Khye's shit sooner or later, hoping later. She strutted into the building with her six-inch heels echoing against the floor as she walked. Taking the elevator to her floor, she yawned. It had been a long day, and she just wanted to get some sleep. Stepping out onto her floor, Sarah could already hear the commotion going on from inside her apartment. It was Khye's mouth going off, and Sarah knew that Khye had found out that her money had been taken.

She wasn't going to turn away. It was something that she was going to have to deal with. She took a deep breath and heard Khye cursing up a storm inside. The second she opened the door, and before she could fully step inside her apartment, Khye came charging her way like a raging bull and screamed, "You took my money, Mum! I know it was you!"

Adewale had just come home from work and wasn't yet able to drown himself in his liquor. Khye was screaming, upset, and throwing the kind of tantrum that no nineteen-year-old should throw. She tossed things across the room, turned over the chair in the living room, and smashed a small mirror.

"Khye, you need to calm down," said Adewale composedly.

"Don't tell me to calm down. My money is gone, and I know it was this bitch that took it," she heatedly shouted.

Sarah frowned. "I'm your mother; you need to watch your mouth, Khye."

"You're a damn thief!" she countered. "Where is my money?"

"It's gone," Sarah boldly replied.

"Gone?"

"If you knew how to share with the family, then we wouldn't be going through .

this problem, Khye," Sarah said.

"What money?" Adewale asked. He was clueless to all of his family's affairs, and it was the first time they had seen him sober in weeks.

"My money that this bloody *cow* stole from out my room."

"I was borrowing it," Sarah retorted.

"Borrowing?"

"Yes, borrowing," Sarah said.

"You're just jealous of me—all of you," Khye screamed out. "I have a good thing going for me. I have a man who loves me and all you want to do is tear me down."

"What money?" Adewale repeated naively. "And why wasn't I alerted about this?"

"Belt up!" both ladies shouted at Adewale, telling him to shut up in their English slang.

"This is my house," he shouted back. "If there's money in my house, then it goes to bills and family."

"I don't need to be in this dirty bloody house," Khye shot back. "You think I need to be here? I'm leaving!"

"Good!" Sarah shouted.

Eavesdropping from their bedroom doorway were Ava and Maisie. They listened and snickered at Khye being shouted at and chewed out by their parents. They both hated that she was their parents' favorite daughter and got special privileges that they didn't get. So it was entertaining to them. They hoped Khye did move out so they wouldn't have to share a room with their older sister any longer.

Khye continued to curse her parents out, and then she stormed down the hallway, causing Ava and Maisie to jump up and rush into the bedroom.

They quickly got into their beds to pretend like they were sleeping, but Khye knew her annoying sisters were awake. When she marched into the room, she exclaimed, "I know you bad little bitches are awake, so don't pretend like your sleeping."

"We can hear you arguing, Khye," Ava said.

"So what? You two going to have your wish. I'm leaving, and you can finally have this small, ugly room," she told them gruffly.

"Where are you going?" Maisie asked.

"To experience the finer things in life, you hear me, little sister?"

Khye thrust open the closet door and right away started to toss everything into two rolling suitcases. Her sisters watched in silence. She was actually leaving, and they didn't know what to think.

"I'm moving in with my boyfriend," she said.

"I wish I had a boyfriend," Ava said.

"You fix yourself up nicely, Ava, and never take Mum's advice," Khye said.

She continued packing; bustling around the bedroom making sure she didn't forget a thing. She didn't plan on coming back. Since she and Floyd had started talking again, he had invited her to come stay with him at the condo. Khye was ready to move in with him. She was ready to get away from her own family and the ghetto. She couldn't wait to see his condo and be with him night after night, making sweet, passionate love and living the way she always dreamed of—well-off.

Sarah had taken three thousand dollars from her; Khye was confident she would get that back within the week.

Once she had everything packed, she marched out of the bedroom, stormed down the hallway tugging two heavily packed suitcases, and didn't say a word to her parents—not even a goodbye. She didn't need to be welcomed there because she knew she was very welcome someplace else.

Once she was out of the apartment, she called Sammy.

"Hey bitch, what's up?" Sammy asked.

"I need a favor, Sammy," she said.

"What kind of favor?"

"I need a place to crash until tomorrow."

"Bitch, you don't even have to ask, just bring your ass over," Sammy said.

Khye smiled. "You're the best."

"I know."

FOURTEEN

Khye was dumbfounded by Floyd's condo. It was everything she dreamed of and even better—the furnishings, the topnotch sound system with a 70-inch plasma flatscreen, wood floors, three bedrooms, and more. Khye loved the balcony the most. The minute she walked into his place, she made a beeline for the balcony and took a breath of fresh air.

"Ohmygod, I love it out here," she hollered.

Floyd smiled. He stood between the outside and the inside. The scenery wasn't anything new to him, but for a newcomer, the view and the tranquility was breathtaking.

"I could stand out here for hours . . . even make love to you here, baby," she said.

"In due time," he responded.

"Maybe tonight," she teased.

He smiled.

"This place is gorgeous, Floyd. I love it."

"I'm glad you do."

She took a quick tour of the place. The walk-in closet made her want to cream in her panties, and the pool and tennis court were the extra bonus that had her smiling from ear to ear. She couldn't wait to throw on her bikini and show off her curvy figure and then take a dip into the complex pool. Khye loved the water. She loved swimming, and in Harlem, pools were as rare as a solar eclipse.

It was paradise to Khye. Everything about his place was perfect. Floyd had already placed her bags into the master bedroom and he wanted to make her feel at home. Her facial expression said it all, she liked it and she was ready to stay.

"I got another surprise for you," Floyd said.

"You're going to spoil me, eh?"

"You're too sweet to ever spoil," Floyd returned.

She smiled.

It felt like nothing could ever go wrong between them. He always made her laugh and smile, and she was his ideal woman. When he wasn't around her, he yearned to be. When they made love, he wanted to be inside her forever, and he wanted a baby and knew Khye was the perfect candidate to carry his seed. Son or daughter, he felt she would make a great mother.

He tried to have kids with Tatianna, but she wasn't fertile, and after months of trying, Floyd felt that it just wasn't meant to be with her. Beside, her bad habits canceled out any motherly thing he saw in her. He didn't want to become another stereotype, an African-American man with multiple kids by multiple baby mothers. It was never his forte like his friends. Floyd had special plans for whoever got pregnant by him and would carry his child. So far, Khye was winning.

Floyd walked over to Khye and pulled her into his arms. He held her affectionately, with her back against his chest, his arms wrapped around her like a spring jacket. Khye closed her eyes and savored his touch. He was soothing like a long, summer breeze or ice cold water on a hot and humid day. It was a warm and delightful sensation. She could fall against him and spread her wings to his sky.

"Close your eyes and stick out your hand," he said.

"Okay."

She shut her eyes until she saw blackness and stuck out her right hand.

She waited with anticipation to feel what kind of gift he was going to place in the palm of her hand. Whatever it was, it was going to be something special. She felt it coming. She couldn't wait.

Floyd placed his gift into her hand, and she already knew what it was. She didn't even have to open her eyes to tell that they were car keys.

"Floyd! Are you serious?" she said.

He nodded.

They were keys to a Range Rover.

"You bought me a car?"

"It's all yours."

Khye screamed and jumped up and down like she'd won the super bowl. She had never had a car before. She couldn't wait to see it.

"Where is it parked?" she asked energetically.

"It's outside," he said.

Khye was ready to leap from the apartment in a single jump. Her heart raced with excitement. She and Floyd went together to see the truck. When they arrived outside, the 2013 Range Rover stood out across the street. It was black on black with black rims, and shined like it had been freshly waxed. It was a beautiful looking truck.

"I love it! I love it! I bloody love it! It's brilliant!" Khye hollered. She leaped into Floyd's arms and kissed him everywhere. She was overjoyed. He was cool. The smile on her face was fulfillment enough.

"I can't wait till everyone sees me in it," Khye said.

She ran over to the car with the keys in her hand and hit the alarm button. It came fully loaded: leather seats, illuminated dashboard, moon roof, a supercharged 3.0-liter V6 engine, and it was able to deliver up to 340 horsepower. It was the perfect gift—almost better than diamonds.

Khye climbed into the driver's seat, and already she felt like a diva inside of it. It was her style. She wanted to drive in it right away. It came with everything, and she felt secure inside the Range.

Floyd got in on the passenger side. He leaned the seat back and said, "My woman rides around in nothing but the best."

She grinned. "Where do you want me to take you?" she said, ready to start the ignition and take it for her first drive.

He chuckled. "You ready to go now?"

"Yes!"

"A'ight, let's go then."

"Yay!" Khye said, clapping her hands together joyfully.

She didn't have to put the key into the ignition; she just hit the on/off button, and the truck came to life with no trouble.

Khye smiled as she drove, riding south on Rockaway Parkway, heading toward Canarsie Pier. It was filled with fisherman and locals enjoying the pier with the fading day looming above. It was a beautiful evening with the sunset drinking what was left of a hot day to quench its thirst before nightfall. It looked like someone had poured a mixture of orange and red over the sky as the sun went lower and lower.

For a minute, they lingered in the parking lot and talked in her new Range Rover. Everything about the car was lovable, and everything about Floyd was unforgettable. There was this stylishness about Floyd that seemed rare in other men his age. He was a thug, but he seemed so different—well-mannered and so romantic, but there was also a mystique to him. She didn't want the night to ever end.

After the pier, they drove around Brooklyn listening to music and talking. Khye already felt attached to her new ride. She was ready to cross over the bridge and ride all night through Harlem with that attitude, *look at me now.*

Later, the two of them enjoyed a candlelit dinner on the balcony, eating stuffed salmon and drinking champagne. Slow love songs played in the background. It was perfect.

After dinner, it was playtime in the bedroom. She was ready to please her man to the fullest extent. After everything he'd done for her, if he wanted to go anal or give her a golden shower, she would have gone along with it. Earlier, she had sucked his dick and licked him until he came in her mouth. First, she went down on him slow and gentle, teasing Floyd with her lips and tongue, softly sucking his dick until he was moaning in her mouth and dripping with desire. She took no prisoners, licking Floyd from the head of his dick to his asshole and back again, not missing a spot in between.

He was impressed. He remembered the first time she sucked his dick and complained about his precum. Now she seemed like an entirely different woman.

After an intensive pussy licking, making Khye wet with passion, Floyd held her legs up and put them over his shoulder. She lay butt-naked against his silk sheets, ready for Floyd to enter her temple. He lined the head of his dick up with her glorious opening and teased her momentarily, just rubbing the sensitive tip against her smooth pussy lips.

"I want you inside of me," Khye said.

Khye wanted him to fuck her hard and fast.

She grabbed his hips and pulled him closer to her, forcing him to ram his thickness into her. She huffed and gripped him tightly, feeling every inch of his strong, black dick roaming inside of her. She dragged her nails across his back, with her legs spread-eagled on his queen-size mattress. Together, they built up a steady, pounding rhythm. Floyd closed his eyes, thrusting inside her, feeling how good her pussy was, and she took every inch, wanting more and more.

His dick hit bottom, stroking her wet pussy walls, and he could feel the cum in his nuts boiling up before they exploded together with a series of moans.

After their intense sexual experience was over, Khye exhaled more times than Terry McMillan. She lay nestled against Floyd in the calm of his bedroom and had a natural smile about her. The sex was good. He was good, and her new living condition was great. What more could she ask for?

As Floyd slept, she slipped away from his loving hold and stepped out onto the balcony. She lit a cigarette and took a much-needed pull. She exhaled while staring up at the full moon above. It was a gorgeous night, mild and warm with not a single cloud in the sky.

She felt content, because from where she was standing, she didn't see any downfall. Her only goal was to keep her man happy, and she intended on doing that. There was no going back, only pushing forward.

FIFTEEN

Sammy stripped away all of his clothing and became totally nude in his bedroom. For a minute, he gazed at his image in the mirror. He was slim and brown, and he had a big, black dick that any woman would love to have in her life, but it was for men only. He stared at himself with a slight sadness in his eyes. He was lonely. He wanted companionship too. Khye had Floyd, and he had no one. He was different, but he was happy with himself. He wanted to be loved by someone like Khye had, but in Harlem, it was hard. It felt like being gay was a crime, and if it was, then Sammy planned on remaining a felon.

His last boyfriend had been a year ago. His name was Jonathan, and he was the only man Sammy ever loved. Jonathan was handsome, educated, and funny, and the sex between them was amazing. The only problem with Jonathan was that he was still trapped in the closet. Talking about coming out to his friends and family would lead to heated arguments. Jonathan was scared to let everyone know he was gay. Sammy was all out and proud of it, and he hated that he had to go sneaking around just to be with Jonathan. Their relationship lasted eight months, and Jonathan walked away, breaking Sammy's heart.

Sammy puffed out and admired himself. "What man wouldn't want some of this?" he said proudly.

He was picky with his relationships, knowing what he wanted. He also wanted a few surgeries done on himself, and that was money he didn't have. Sammy was desperate to improve his image—a nose job, some butt implants, and a few minor adjustments he felt would make him so much more wanted. But he was so broke, he couldn't pay attention, and selling cheap clothes with his alterations just wasn't cutting it anymore.

While Khye had been led away to live her new life with Floyd, Sammy was still stuck in the ghetto, fighting for his sexuality and looking for the love of his life. Without Khye around, he spent more time in his room sewing and watching TV. On his bed were a few ladies' outfits that he wanted to try on. He pranced around his bedroom putting together the right outfit and altering a few others. He had a few orders to fill, but they were nothing spectacular—just some ghetto hoes who wanted to look more ghetto.

Sammy started to work on a cotton dress that would look striking with one of his designs added to it. He pulled out his sewing kit and material and sat near his bedroom window. Gazing outside, he noticed Able and Jason hanging on the block, smoking, gambling and drinking. They owned the neighborhood and terrorized it with their drug selling, violence, and gang activity. Thinking back, Able had always been his father's favorite. Even when Able thrust himself into a life of heavy crime and regular incarceration, their father still would chose Able over his younger gay son. Able could kill the president, and Sammy could go on and make a career for himself and win the Nobel Peace Prize, but yet he still wouldn't be loved and accepted by his father. The man had such a deep-rooted hatred for homosexuality that it was visceral.

Able was the tough guy—the badass that no one wanted to fight. Growing up, he was a boxer, skilled with his hands, and wasn't known to back down from a fight. If you wanted it, then he brought it, and Able would beat a nigga's ass so bad, they wished they never brought it to him in the first place. By age fifteen, he transitioned to guns and attempted murder, and by age seventeen, he had been in and out of jail so many times, it became a revolving door in his life.

Able always protected Sammy, and Sammy knew that as long as his brother was living, then he could walk anywhere in Harlem and not be fucked with. They could stare, but they couldn't touch him.

Sammy worried as he stared at his brother conversing and hanging around with his friends on the block, because Able lived a hard life and he was known for his gunplay. It would only take one bullet to remove Able from Sammy's life completely, and then what?

While watching his brother and sewing next to his window, Sammy noticed a champagne-colored Crown Vic driving onto the block and two men that he wasn't familiar with getting out of the car. Sammy fixed his eyes on them; they were obliviously not from Harlem. Their hardcore demeanor spoke Brooklyn very loudly. They were clad in sagging jeans, red bandanas, and red beads, indicating their Blood street gang ties. They greeted Able and The Gun with glad hands and everyone knew them. It was odd though; Able wasn't known to make new friends, so seeing the strangers so comfortable around his brother sparked some curiosity in Sammy. He didn't want to get into his brother's business, but it struck him as odd when Able climbed into the Crown Vic and rode off with these two men. In his line of work, Able had always been a cautious man and never fully trusted anyone, except for The Gun, but these two men had Able's undivided trust and attention.

He knew that his brother was up to something big, and he wanted to be nosy.

SIXTEEN

Bedford-Stuyvesant, Brooklyn, was notorious for being the origin and stomping ground for iconic figures Biggie Smalls and Jay-Z. Do or Die, from sunup to sundown, it was a place where the wrong stare or the slightest disrespect could get you killed. It was a violent place, but also a cultural place—where to this day, it is widely known as the black cultural Mecca of Brooklyn, similar to what Harlem is to Manhattan.

For Tatianna, it was an area of Brooklyn she never thought in a million years that she would live in again. The corner of Pulaski Street and Marcy Avenue came to life every day with traffic, the locals moving about, and the corner hustlers.

After two years with Floyd and living in his lavish condo, Tatianna never thought she would be back on the block again. She felt embarrassed and betrayed. She went from rags to riches and back to rags, and with no employment, no education, or any decent work history, her life started to look cruel. Floyd was out of the picture now; she had no support and it angered her. Already, she missed him and thought about him every day. He didn't call or come by to see if she was okay.

Tatianna was staying with her sister and trying to get her life back in order. Without a vehicle, she was walking or borrowing her sister's car to get around. Every day she got high or pissy drunk with her best friend and her old crew. They would linger on the building steps, talking and gossiping, rolling up, and letting the day slip away by doing nothing much.

Tatianna took a much-needed pull from the burning haze that was passed to her. She, Kim, Lea, and two other girls were hanging around on the block and enjoying the Brooklyn evening. It had only been two weeks since she and Floyd had broken up and he kicked her out, but it felt like two weeks of hell, and every day seemed like the longest day of her life. Tatianna placed the burning blunt to her lips, seated on the concrete steps in front of the two-story row houses that stretched the block. Surrounded by her friends, she tried forgetting about Floyd and her predicament by any way possible. Getting high was one way she coped with her newfound situation.

Kim noticed the look on her sister's face, and each day she said to her sister, "Sis, it's gonna be all right."

Tatianna didn't respond. She wanted to enjoy her high and not think about it. When she did, it always angered her.

"You a beautiful woman, Tatianna. Real talk. Any nigga would want a bitch like you," Lea chimed.

The comment made her smile somewhat. She sat against the steps, knees up, leaned back, and took a few more pulls then passed the blunt to her friend Megan. Kim twisted open the cap to a bottle of Grey Goose and Sprite. She placed a plastic cup in her sister's hand and poured everyone a much-needed drink. Smoking and sipping in Brooklyn, it was a regular thing for them. The time and pain passed by much easier.

Megan was running her mouth, talking about a recent fight that happened around the corner the other day.

"Yo, Shakiyla and her sister fucked that bitch up," Megan said.

"Damn, I wished I would have been there. I ain't never liked that bitch," Kim said.

"You and me both," added Lea.

"I know, bitch goin' around fuckin' wit' Shakiyla boyfriend, thinkin' she can't be touched, and Shakiyla touched that bitch real hard," Megan said. "Bitch got her weave snatched out and everything."

Everyone laughed.

Tatianna sat, disconnected from the conversation. She took a sip of Goose and Sprite and chilled. She banged back in her day, and she and Kim were nothing nice to play with. The sisters had a fierce reputation for fighting and cutting, stealing and partying. They had the same father, but different mothers. Tatianna's mother was Russian, born in Moscow, and had come to the States when she was very young girl. Their father was Jake Johnson, one of the biggest drug dealers to ever come out of the Stuy. He met Alina, Tatianna's mother, in a Manhattan club and instantly fell in love with the woman. They had one child together, Tatianna, and Jake Johnson cherished both his daughters by two women.

When Tatianna was eight, Jake Johnson was tried and convicted under the RICO and Conspiracy Act, receiving a life sentence. Her mother died as a result of a drug overdose when she was thirteen, and from then on, Kim and Tatianna raised themselves and became inseparable.

Floyd grew up across the street from her. She was there from the beginning, seeing his come up and being his ride-or-die bitch from day one. She stashed guns and drugs for him, she got arrested for him, she fucked him whenever he was horny, rarely saying no to his sexual advances, and most of all, she never cheated on him. She made her entire life about Floyd, and now he'd kicked her to the curb like yesterday's trash.

The evening continued on. Tatianna was feeling right. Her friends continued talking, gossiping, laughing, and ready to smoke another blunt. Megan continued to run her mouth with news after news, but what came out her mouth next caught Tatianna's attention.

"Yo, I swear I saw your Range the other day, Tatianna," Megan said.

"What?" Tatianna uttered, she saw herself becoming highly upset and wanted to hear more. It was the only piece of news that caught her interest the whole night.

"Matter of fact, I knew it was your old shit, wit' some bitch driving it," she continued.

"Where you saw this at?"

"Over by Atlantic and Rockaway Avenue the other day," Megan told her.

"Was Floyd in the car?" she said.

"I think he was too, chillin' in the passenger seat."

"That lying muthafucka!" Tatianna spat.

Tatianna felt her heart beating faster and her face turning into a deep scowl, knowing Floyd had his new bitch driving her Range Rover and living with him so soon. He'd sworn and promised that their split wasn't over a bitch. He lied. She was furious.

"What you gonna do?" Lea asked.

"I'm gonna fuck that bitch up," Tatianna replied.

"Just say whenever, and we got ya back," Kim said.

She wasn't going out quietly. The news almost brought her to tears in front of everyone, but she kept a stern face and took a sip of liquor to drink away the pain she felt.

It was on!

***

Khye enjoyed a bottle of white wine and a cigarette while seated on the balcony and taking in the sunny day. While Floyd was out on business, she enjoyed her new home from room to room. Earlier, it was soaking in the deep, round tub for hours getting high while listening to some soul music. Then it was relaxing in the master bedroom and arranging her pricey clothing in the walk-in closet. Subsequently, she made a few phone calls and enjoyed some Chinese takeout and a good movie. Now, it was outside on the balcony and smiling proudly and enjoying how far she came up.

As she relaxed, her cell phone rang. The caller I.D let her know it was Floyd calling. She immediately picked up.

"Hey, baby," she answered brightly.

"Hey, what you doing?" he asked.

"Just sitting on the balcony, practically naked, sipping on some wine and waiting for you to come home so we can make a baby together."

He chuckled. "Oh really?"

"Yes, really. I miss you."

"I miss you, too."

"How long until you come home?" she asked.

"Soon."

"Okay, my fanny is waiting for you, baby."

He laughed. "Your fanny?"

"Uh huh . . . my pussy."

"Damn, I love the way you talk. You got me ready to come home now."

"So come."

He laughed. "I gotta take care of some business first."

"Okay. I love you," Khye uttered.

"I love you, too," he replied.

Hearing him say *I love you* was magic to her ears. Rarely would a man of Floyd's status say *I love you* to anyone so soon, and by the sound of his voice, she knew he really meant it. Khye felt she'd cemented her relationship with him, but the one thing that would strengthen them was a baby. Therefore, she was determined to get pregnant by him.

She continued to enjoy her wine and her surroundings.

An hour went by when she heard the doorbell. She rushed up to answer it, flowing in her silk robe.

"Who is it?" she asked nicely.

"Open the fuckin' door, bitch!"

It wasn't the answer she expected. Tatianna hammered on the door harder, demanding Khye open up before she kicked down the door. Khye didn't feel threatened. In fact, she couldn't wait to open the door and finally see for herself if she was prettier than Floyd's last bitch.

Khye swung open the door with her revealing attire. She was face to face with Tatianna, smirking. Khye was taken aback by Tatianna's appearance. She was a beautiful-looking woman, and not anything like she expected. Her flaws were the numerous tattoos that decorated her skin, and her ghetto attitude, but besides that, she was striking like Sophia Loren. Floyd had described her as a Brooklyn thug, so Khye automatically thought she wasn't cute at all.

Both ladies glared at each other, drinking in each other's looks. It was obvious, they both were beautiful ladies. Subsequently, an argument ensued. "You fuckin' my man, bitch!!" Tatianna shouted.

"Bugger off, bitch! Your man? Get it corrected, he's my man," Khye shouted back in her exaggerated English accent.

"You think because you talk wit' that fuckin accent, you better!" Her voice dripped with hatred, as she looked Khye in the eye with a stabbing glare.

"Look at me, I am better," Khye retorted.

They argued at the door. Tatianna took two confident strides toward her enemy looking as fearless as ever, but Khye remained unfazed. Suddenly bursting with an uncontrollable rage, Tatianna threw the first punch, striking Khye in the face, causing her to stagger back. However, Khye wasn't a punk and she was ready to finish it. Khye grabbed Tatianna roughly and threw her into the apartment and charged at her savagely. She went for blood, swinging viciously at Tatianna, every blow connecting, every hit rearranging Tatianna's pretty face. Again and again she attacked her with godlike strength and never seemed to wane.

"You fuckin' bitch!" Khye screamed with a fist full of her enemy's hair.

They tangled against each other brutally, smashing into furniture and fixtures, breaking glass, knocking pictures off the wall from their abrupt force. Khye's pretty white robe flew open, exposing her underwear, but she didn't care. Her main concern was breaking Floyd's ex-girlfriend into pieces and showing she was the better bitch in beauty and at war.

Tatianna didn't expect this kind of savagery and violence from Khye. She was petite, but animalistic like a hyena.

"C'mon bitch!" she shouted.

Tatianna spit blood from her mouth. She wasn't about to give up. She wasn't about to lose to the woman who'd stolen the man she loved all her life. Drenched with rage and jealousy, she picked up a vase and hurled it at Khye's head. Khye barely moved out of the way from it. It grazed her, she hollered. Tatianna saw her chance and lunged at Khye while she was off balance. She wanted to kill that bitch and her frame of mind was insane. Her temper got the better of her and all she saw was red. She snatched up a baseball bat she knew Floyd kept around, and it should have killed Khye. It should have been the final blow. Yet, in a blindingly fast flash, Khye ducked to the side, sending Tatianna stumbling with her own force. Khye grabbed her and grabbed the bat from her hands, catching Tatianna off guard, and in one swift movement, used the weapon that was once a threat to her on Tatianna, striking her in the back and causing her to crumble to the floor wincing in pain.

"You cunt!" Khye shouted.

She kicked Tatianna in the face repeatedly, crippling her, bloodying her image and almost scarring her pretty features. The woman's head swam from pain. She felt her stomach tighten and she threw up. She stayed that way for a bit, on her hands and knees, defeated with her head hanging like a winded horse. She'd underestimated Khye.

With the baseball bat gripped in her hand and Floyd's ex-girlfriend defeated in front of her, Khye felt like hitting her again—scarring her face and proving her point.

But then she heard, "What the fuck is goin' on here?"

Khye spun around, shocked to see Floyd walking inside. He had the look of bewilderment from his ex-girlfriend and his current girlfriend acting out a scene from Kill Bill. He didn't expect to come home to find his place in chaos.

"She attacked me first, baby," Khye explained right away, dropping the baseball bat from her hand.

He didn't know what to think. It was obvious that Khye was the victor. He was shocked to see Tatianna's face badly bruised and bloody. She crawled over to the nearest chair, got a hold of it, and slowly got herself upright. Everything blurred for a minute, then came back into focus again. She locked eyes with Floyd for a moment. It was a surprise to see Tatianna beaten like that, especially by Khye.

"You okay?" he asked her dryly.

His unexpected concern for Tatianna made Khye upset. "You ask if she's okay!" she refuted. "What about me?"

Floyd for a moment gazed at Khye like she was the Antichrist. She had blood on her hands and nearly not a scratch on her. She was breathing heavily and it almost looked like she enjoyed beating up his ex-girlfriend.

When he saw they both were still breathing, his attitude shifted toward his wrecked home. He belted out, "Both of y'all fuck up my place like this!"

"Floyd, she came over here and started with me," Khye said in her defense.

Floyd became very irritated—more so with Khye. He was very particular about his women. He didn't want them cursing, fighting, or acting ghetto. And what he saw tonight was uncalled for and outrageous to him. He lost a small part of affection toward her. It was obvious there was more than met the eye with Khye. She stood there with a hopeless stare.

"We'll talk later," he said to her.

He turned his attention to Tatianna. Once he saw she wasn't completely injured and she was able to stand on her own two feet after Khye's vicious ass-whooping, he screamed, "Bitch, why the fuck you come to my home causing trouble when I made it clear we are done?"

"Floyd, I love you—"

"Tatianna we done!" he screamed.

"You are a fuckin' liar!" she retorted heatedly. "I thought there wasn't another bitch, and as soon as you get rid of me, you move this fuckin' bitch in! And you got her driving my fuckin' car!"

"It ain't ya car no more," he said. "And I ain't got time to argue wit' you."

Floyd charged over and roughly grabbed Tatianna and started to drag her to the door with her kicking and screaming. Khye stood to the side and silently watched her man abuse his ex. He treated her like he was never in love with her.

"Get the fuck off me! Fuck that bitch! Fuck her!" Tatianna screamed.

She tried to fight him off, but she was too weak and battered. Floyd punched her in the stomach, weakening her more, and continued to drag her out of his home. Tears flooded her eyes as she was being mistreated in front of his new bitch. Tatianna felt so violated and embarrassed. Every emotion came pouring out of her at once—rage, jealousy, sadness, distress, and tribulation.

"Get the fuck out my house!" Floyd hollered.

Before he forced her completely out, Tatianna locked eyes with Khye, and there was bitterness and a warning inside of her wide and pleading eyes. "You think you gonna be his only one, bitch? Watch, he's gonna get tired of you and have you replaced the same fuckin' way!"

"Get the fuck out!" Floyd continued his mistreatment toward her.

Khye heard her, but she wasn't listening and didn't feel sorry for her at all. Khye felt she would never become her—never be put in her predicament. Khye smirked Tatianna's way and said, "You ain't me, bitch."

"I'm gonna fuck you up, bitch!" Tatianna screamed madly. "Me and my sister gonna fuck you up, bitch! You better watch ya fuckin' back!"

Khye wasn't scared and showed no concern.

Before Floyd could fully remove his Tatianna from his apartment, she threw heated threats at him too, screaming out, "I'm gonna get some niggas to fuck you up too, Floyd. I swear, they gonna beat you down."

Floyd didn't like being threatened, and with a closed fist, he struck Tatianna against her jaw and kicked her in the stomach like he was some mindless brute. He exclaimed, "Don't threaten me, bitch. I will bury your stupid ass!"

Tatianna was in full-blown tears, and every emotion she had was crushed cruelly. He slammed the door in her face and had no remorse for his actions. Khye stood there in silence. Her special night with her man had been ruined. For a moment, Floyd looked her way sourly. His place was a mess, and he was upset.

He walked toward Khye. She quickly apologized. "Baby, I'm so sorry, she just—"

SLAP!

The hit came out of nowhere; she spun around from the blow and fell to the floor. She was shocked. Floyd hit her so hard that she felt the taste of blood inside of her mouth. She didn't know why she was hit. Why was he was upset with her?

"You are not her," he said.

"What?" Khye was baffled by his words. She dabbed at her bloody lip. He was upset with her for fighting and acting ghetto.

"I don't wanna see that type of behavior from you again," he warned.

He walked away coldly, leaving Khye against the floor in shock and bewilderment. A few tears trickled from her eyes as she picked herself up from the floor and heard the bedroom door slam.

What had just happened?

She wiped the blood away from her lips, dried away her tears, and felt off-course for a moment. Her job was to make Floyd happy, and he wasn't happy with her. She was willing to do whatever to correct her mistake. Tatianna was desperately trying to shake up her happy home, and Khye was determined not to let that happen. Floyd had seen a side of her that she wanted to keep hidden.

From now on, she planned on becoming Little Susie Homemaker—cooking, cleaning, and fucking him whenever; taking care of her man and his home. She didn't want to give him any reason to doubt her. She wanted things to become permanent.

She wanted to become perfect for him.

SEVENTEEN

"Happy Birthday, Marcus!" Sarah shouted happily, as she ran his way and jumped into his arms, kissing him lovingly and dying to give him his birthday gift.

It was the day after his forty-fifth birthday. He didn't look a day over thirty-five. He took care of himself well. He was regular at the gym, and he ate healthy and enjoyed a very active sex life with two women. His wife gave him love and romance, and Sarah gave him the best sex he ever had.

On his birthday yesterday, his wife and kids took him out to dinner at a seafood restaurant in Long Island, he received numerous gifts, had a small birthday party at his firm, and later that night, his wife wore her sexiest lingerie, gave him a subpar blow job and nice sex—one position, missionary. It didn't blow his mind. He loved his wife, but when it came to pleasing a nigga, Sarah got an A+.

Tonight, he'd gotten a room at the prominent Marriot Marquise in Times Square. The hotel had forty-nine floors, nineteen hundred rooms, and fifty-seven suites. Marcus picked out the perfect suite to celebrate his birthday with Sarah.

Like usual, he picked her up from the train station in the city. Sarah welcomed him affectionately, showing off her tight, sexy attire, and she couldn't wait to get the party started. She missed him greatly. She had a special gift for him in the small bag she carried, knowing it wasn't much, but it came from the bottom of her heart.

She climbed into his truck, and they were off to the hotel in the busy Times Square area. During the duration of the ride to the hotel, Sarah repeatedly wished him a happy birthday, and even unzipped his pants and gave him a quick blow job, throwing her lips around his fat dick and sucking him off as they sat in Midtown traffic.

"Now this is a birthday gift," Marcus said with a delighted smile.

With one hand on the steering wheel and the other guiding the back of her head, Marcus didn't want her to stop, but he didn't want to come early either. He could feel himself getting harder and harder inside of her mouth. She didn't even come up for air.

He pulled into the front entrance of the Marriot Marquis and Sarah stopped sucking his dick just in time before the valet came to park his SUV. They both climbed out and walked into the front desk and lobby entrance. It was a place of opulence and grandeur where the distinguished atrium of the hotel featured polished marble, stunning architectural details, and glass high-speed elevators in a column running up the center of the huge hollow space. It was just a trifle dizzying the first time anyone went whizzing up to their room floor.

The behemoth hotel in the middle of Times Square was filled with conventioneers, tourists, and theatergoers. The buzzing atmosphere inside nearly matched the chaos of the streets below.

Marcus quickly checked into the Presidential Suite he'd reserved. It was on the forty-fifth floor, overlooking all of Times Square. The Presidential Suite featured two separate living areas, a spacious master bedroom with master bath, and a separate half-bath, a grand piano, a wet bar, and a dining table that seated up to eight people.

Sarah was immediately floored when she walked into the room. She had never been in anything like it before. It was by far the finest room she ever stayed in. It felt like it was *her* birthday. She went to the huge windows and peered outside at the city. It felt good to be so high and above everyone else. The people so far down below looked like tiny, moving ants from her point of view.

"You like it?" Marcus asked, unbuttoning his suit jacket and getting comfortable.

She smiled brightly. "Yes. I do."

Khye wasn't going to be the only one experiencing the good life. She had her sugar daddy too, and if everything worked as planned, then he would be in her life forever.

Marcus made his way over to the wet bar. He needed a drink. Sarah was ready to get their party started and present her gift to him. Marcus fixed himself some bourbon whisky and gulped it down. Sarah disappeared into the bathroom to get ready for his birthday.

From the oasis of the Presidential Suite bathroom, she had everything she needed for pampering at her fingertips. The master bath had luxurious accents such as marble countertops, sleek faucets, double sinks, dark wood accents, and upgraded amenities.

She started to undress and couldn't wait to adorn her white, curvy figure in the sexy lingerie she bought just for his birthday. She touched up her make-up and fixed her long, blond, hair. She smiled at herself, approving of the sexy outfit she'd put together just for him. Tonight, she wanted to feel every inch of his strong manhood twist and coil inside of her. She wanted to feel his semen travel so deep into her, that it would be impossible for her not to get pregnant. They'd had unprotected sex before, but it always ended with Marcus strapping on a condom for the finale. She wanted to feel his raw flesh all the way to the end, and she had a small gift for him—something to show her love and her feelings.

Sarah stepped out of the bathroom in a pretty periwinkle babydoll and some stripper heels. The material was see-through and it showed she didn't have on any panties. Her pussy was neatly shaved, and her nipples were pressing against the thin fabric. Her flesh looked delectable in the sexy attire.

Marcus looked at her and was stunned. The champagne bottle he had in his hand somehow popped open itself, champagne spilling out like it had a sexual orgasm.

"Shit!" he uttered.

"You like it?"

"Wow. You are truly beautiful," he said.

She smiled and blushed. "I'm ready to give you your gift now. Well, at least one of them."

She walked over to Marcus, looking like a sexy runway model working the catwalk. Her strut was a virtual display of her strong sexuality. She figured she could give him something that his wife couldn't—multiple orgasms and a sexual appetite that surged throughout his body.

Her sensual body fit into his arms, and his lips found the nape of her neck. He kissed her softly. It was like a dream state. His heart was pounding and his breathing was shallow. He wanted to taste her and come inside her until there was no more sperm left inside of him. She was too sexy to share with anyone else, and their meetings together were becoming more intense.

They kissed passionately, their lips locked together stronger than a bank vault, and their tongues were entwined in bliss. Marcus ran his hands across her body and gently gripped her juicy ass. He could have easily scooped her up into his grip, lifting her off her feet with his strength. He wanted to throw her body onto his shoulders and eat out her pussy while she touched the ceiling. He was a tall and mammoth man.

Sarah stepped back and lowered the straps to her babydoll outfit. The dimmed lighting in the room shimmered on her body, making her white skin glow. She lay down on the king size bed and it was all Marcus could do to keep from hyperventilating.

"I want you inside of me. Take me any way you want to on your birthday," she said as she spread her legs and invited him to sexually attack her any way he wanted.

He swallowed hard. He undid the buttons on his shirt. He undid his belt and let his pants fall to the floor. Whatever his wife couldn't do, or refused to do at home—Sarah was ready to comply. She wasn't a lazy woman when it came to sex. It was always her who would carry out the nasty and freakish duties that any wife should almost certainly do for their husband. So what he was missing at home, he got with Sarah.

"I wanna suck your dick so good that you're gonna want to divorce your wife," she said.

He laughed. But she was serious.

Sarah was confident that there was a connection that couldn't be denied. She wanted it to be an affair that had the potential into developing into a relationship. There was an undeniable heat that was smoldering between them.

Leaving his boxer briefs on, Marcus climbed onto the bed and lay on top of Sarah. Her soft skin was like heaven. She wrapped her long, defined legs around him and it felt like he was in a cocoon of sweet femininity. Her touch was enticing. Her smell and kisses were so alluring, it felt like the stars were falling around him, washing him with a high of horniness that was hard to come down from. His dick was hard as a rock, and she was grinding her body against him, making him dizzy with sensations.

She rolled Marcus onto his back and removed the last of his clothing, tossing his boxer briefs on the floor, and was ready to give him a night that he would never forget. His dick was in her sight, and she was ready to give him his birthday blowjob. He groaned as she stroked it, almost gently at first, and then with a firmer grip, making his dick grow harder in her fist in seconds. His breathing was already a bit ragged. She concentrated on sucking the head of his dick. For almost fifteen minutes, she used her lips around the crown, tickling the underside with the tip of her tongue. Marcus squirmed and cooed. He thrust his hips upwards from the pleasurable sensation that inundated him.

"Damn, girl," he said. "You really like this, don't you?"

She didn't answer him, but kept focused on her work. She opened her mouth wide and relaxed her throat and took him all the way inside. She proceeded to demonstrate just how much she wanted his big dick in her mouth.

He groaned and groaned as Sarah took him as deeply as she could into her mouth. She made sure to get him nice and wet, sliding her mouth up and down on him a few times before pulling back to lick him from his balls up to the head, covering that sensitive area with her entire mouth before doing it again. Marcus couldn't keep still, loving every second of his birthday gift. He already had precum at the tip and she lapped it up, looking at him with a grin.

"Does that feel good, baby? You like the way I suck your dick?"

He also responded by grunting his approval and guiding her head down on his dick.

She bobbed her head up and down on him a few more times, following her hand as she stroked him. He placed his hand on the back of her head and he was now shoving his cock into her mouth, saying, "Oh fuck! Oh shit! Jesus! You're going to make me come like that! Oh fuck!"

And then twenty minutes after she started, she was swallowing his bitter, white semen as he groaned from the pleasure.

It wasn't over yet. Things only just began to heat up. Marcus began sucking her hardened nipples. She moaned, grabbing his head in her soft hands and caressing his head. He kissed her body down, licking her tummy and groping every soft piece of her. He stared at her pussy. Her lips opened sensually and seemed to be calling him. Marcus lowered his mouth to her womanhood and began lapping at her flowing juices. His tongue softly licked her sweetness from front to back, tasting her honey and savoring her flavor.

"Ooooh, yes, yes, don't stop," she said.

She was desperate to have him inside her. He took the head of his dick and placed it at her sweet, wet hole. He cupped her tits. The heat traveled up his body and Sarah pulled him to her. He thrust inside of her with her silky walls grabbing him and pulling him deeper. The feeling was bliss. Marcus closed his eyes. He was stroking her hard and she was meeting his thrust with passion. They fucked vigorously with their hot breaths against each other. Perspiration glowed on their bodies and their grunts became animal-like.

"Damn, you feel so fuckin' good. Ooooh, shit, give me that pussy," he said.

They fucked position after position, entangled into each other like tree vines. Marcus braced himself and started working her pussy, hitting every spot at every angle. He was a machine.

His dick felt so good inside of her, Sarah had to prevent herself from screaming out, "I want to have your baby."

She did, though. She wanted to get pregnant by him. Having his baby inside of her meant maybe he would stick around, probably child support and more. She didn't see herself as a home wrecker. She saw herself as an opportunist—and the deeper his thrust, the more likely her chance. So far he hadn't reached for a condom like he usually did. The pussy had him totally absorbed. He placed her legs on his shoulders and gripped her hips tightly. Her soft flesh filled his hands. The head of his dick was hitting bottom, and he couldn't stop his own orgasm from overtaking him.

It was about to happen. She wanted it.

Sarah came all over him. Her body was quivering greatly and her juices were flowing freely. And then the cum in Marcus's nuts boiled up and he exploded inside her as she held him tightly to her body. She could feel his semen moving through her and a small smile showed on her face. If his shit was potent, then her plan could either be the biggest mistake of her life, or a needed blessing.

Half hour later, as they lay nestled against each other, enjoying the relaxing Presidential Suite; Sarah got up and went to present her second gift to him. The mind blowing sex he'd just had was satisfying, but she wanted to give him something tangible that he could take with him—something to remind him of her.

"Here," she said with a smile on her face.

It was a small square box. He took it and opened it. It was a brushed stainless steel thick locket, inside was a picture of her.

"This is nice," he said with normalcy in his voice.

"I want you to take it everywhere with you, so you can always think of me," she said.

He slightly smiled. "I'll keep it somewhere special."

Sarah couldn't tell if he really liked the gift, or if he was just being nice, not wanting to hurt her feelings. It was a cheap gift, cost her thirty dollars, but it came from her heart and she wanted him to cherish it as she cherished him.

"I love you," she proclaimed.

She wanted to hear it back from him. It was farfetched to think he loved her, or was in love with her, but she wanted to dream it. She sighed heavily. When he didn't respond back, she didn't know what to think. He removed himself from the bed and went into the next room to pour himself another glass of bourbon whisky. He remained naked, his big dick swinging and his dark skin still glistening.

Sarah followed behind him, naked too. Seeing him standing there, knowing he wasn't going to stay too long, it just suddenly came out, like a fart in a public area.

"I want you to leave your wife," she said seriously.

He was about to take a sip of bourbon, but hearing her words, he stopped the liquor from entering into his mouth and looked at Sarah as if he hadn't heard her correctly.

"What you say?" he said incredulously.

"Do you love her more than me?"

"She's my wife, Sarah. We've been together for over twenty years. We have three kids together," he stated firmly.

"I know, but you yourself said how you feel about white women."

"And what, I'm supposed to leave my life behind because you're a white woman and you know I have a weakness for them?"

She wanted to say yes, but it would have been a foolish response. She simply said, "We can have a great life together."

"I live a great life now," he countered.

It was obvious she wasn't getting anywhere. Marcus downed his drink, set the glass on the countertop, and walked toward Sarah. He stared at her with some compassion, gently touched the side of her face and said, "Look, what we have, it's great, so let's not ruin a good thing. I get what I want, and you get what you want, and I take care of you from time to time—give you some money, buy you nice things from time to time. So there's no reason to rock the boat, right?"

Sarah looked into his eyes with no response. She was hurt. She held back her tears. What she wanted was the same thing her daughter Khye had—a nigga like Floyd full-time.

"Right?" he repeated again, waiting for the correct answer from her.

Reluctantly, she replied, "Right."

He smiled. "That's my little white snow bunny. It's been a great birthday so far, and I love the gifts, especially the first one."

She smiled halfheartedly.

Marcus took her by her forearm and pulled her naked flesh into his strong, masculine arms. The feel of him always weakened her. His dark, midnight skin was pleasing to her eyes and it was hard to resist him.

"You know what I want," he said.

"What?"

"Some more of you," he said, cupping her juicy ass cheeks with his strong hands and making it clear he wanted some more sex from her.

She smiled.

He scooped her up into his arms and carried Sarah into the bedroom. She kissed him, he touched her freely. And once again, she was on her back with his thick, chocolate and muscular frame climbing between her legs and kissing her stone nipples. He thrust inside of her, once again, without a condom and they fucked. As Marcus was inside of her, Sarah thought, if he didn't want to leave his wife, then maybe a baby might change his mind. Either way, she wasn't about to lose him, knowing men got bored with the same pussy over time and they always needed a reason to stay.

She was desperate to give him that reason, even if he was married. So she worked her hips against him, contracted her pussy walls to his hard flesh, sucked on his lips and milked his big, black dick as it pistoned inside of her. She was a fertile woman, and Marcus was about to find out the hard way.

EIGHTEEN

Khye felt the wind through her hair and the power between her thighs as she held onto Floyd tightly. It was like they were flying through the city streets as Floyd zipped his black motorcycle through Brooklyn like a thoroughbred rider. He even popped a wheelie with her on the back. The Suzuki Hayabusa bike was custom made with chromed detailing, chrome exhaust, and a ten-thousand-dollar paint job. The bike caught attention, but Khye riding on the back of it with her phat butt protruding in the booty shorts she wore caught even more attention.

Floyd was an exciting guy, and the way he handled his bike was more exciting. Khye had her arms wrapped around his waist, her head against his back, she leaned when he leaned, and neither of them wore helmets. The speed and danger were exhilarating, and things felt like they were back to normal; the incident the other night with Tatianna felt like it never happened. Khye forgave Floyd for putting his hands on her. She knew he'd been stressed out.

She was happy, holding on tight to her man and enjoying him, the sex, and his money. They zipped across the Triborough Bridge and made it into Harlem with the sun gradually slipping away, making room for a beautiful warm night. The traffic was thick, people everywhere. They were on their way to the studio uptown—Slow Pullz Studio on the West Side.

Slow Pullz Studio was Floyd's favorite place to be. It was where he spent most of his time, trying to make hit records and become the next music mogul. He and Carlito had invested a lot of time and money in the studio and on talent they believed could take things platinum.

Floyd came to a stop in front of a five-story building on Broadway, a bustling area with shops, people, and traffic. Slow Pullz Studio was on the top floor. He killed the bike's ignition and stepped off, leaving the Suzuki parked near the entrance to the building. Khye followed behind him, excited to see where he worked and made magic. She wanted a tour of the place. They stepped inside, signed in, and took the elevator to the top floor.

Stepping off the elevator, they came to a heavy, soundproof double door—two doors one after the other rather than a single paired set—which had sound locks so that no sound could get into the live room from outside the studio. The first room they walked into was the control room; seated behind a large mixing console was a young white boy, an engineer, who was working on a new track, routing and changing the levels to a song. Floyd greeted him and introduced him to Khye. She smiled and shook his hand, and his eyes said it all: He found Floyd's new girl very attractive.

Behind the control room were a couple of sofas and a coffee table, along with a forty-two-inch flatscreen mounted on the wall. It was the place where musicians, friends, and assistants hung around waiting to be called or just chilling out. The front and the right side of the control room was dominated by the mixing desk—ninety-six channels.

There was a man in the living room. His demeanor was thuggish: sagging jeans, wifebeater, off-center Yankees cap on his bald head, jewelry, and lots of tattoos. He was about to rap. He had on headphones and was close to the pop shield, ready to spit some bars. When he saw Floyd walk into the room, he gave him a respectful head nod. Floyd nodded back.

"You ready to do this?" white boy asked through the microphone.

He nodded. "I'm ready."

The beat played and the man nodded to the track, definitely feeling it. "Who's he?" Khye asked.

"Lavell," white boy said with his attention on the rapper.

She looked at him; he had trouble and talent written all over him. Khye took a seat nearby and crossed her long, beautiful legs. She noticed Lavell's eyes locked on her. She wasn't thrilled about it. Floyd was her man, and she wasn't about to mess up a good thing because a handsome thug made eye contact with her.

The beat playing was clean, melodic, and piano-laced. It had everyone nodding. White boy was a mastermind when it came to producing.

Lavell hardened his face and started to rhyme. "Yo, Yo, Yo, shout out to the BX, red up, we live now, come around wildin' and get shot down, NYPD don't even come around, guns up, we light the night up and bring back the wild, wild west now, gunslinger wit' the mack-ten, shot after shot, bakka—his soul is lost now, twisted nigga, them hot shells got his skin lifting, insides twisting, smoke a nigga like a good spliff, killing got me high now, Lavell on the scene, I'm the live wire, spark up like a fire. . ."

Khye listened to his violent rhyme and figured he probably lived how he rapped. She had been around his type before. His voice was raspy and his flow something like Ghostface Killah's.

As the night went on, Khye observed Floyd taking care of business in the studio. He even got behind the mixer himself and put together two tracks. He seemed like a natural. Watching him work was turning Khye on, and she was ready to suck his dick right there. But she had to restrain herself. She was having a good time with him.

Three hours after they arrived, Floyd spun around in the leather, swivel chair and smiled Khye's way.

"What?" she said, smiling back.

"Go into the booth and cut a song," he said.

"What? No," Khye responded, suddenly becoming shy and afraid.

"C'mon, I know you got skills. Spit a rhyme or something."

"Floyd, I can't sing."

"Wit' that beautiful accent, I know you got some talent."

White boy smiled at her and agreed with Floyd. "Hey, you never know, I'm sure you're working with something special," he agreed.

All of a sudden, Khye found herself on the spot. She couldn't sing or rap, but yet, they were determined to hear something come from out of her because of her beauty and accent. She resisted, but it seemed like Floyd wasn't taking no for an answer. When he attempted to pull her up from her chair and place her into the booth, his cell phone rang out of the blue and it was a call he needed to answer.

"Yo," he spoke.

The caller on the other end was giving him some bad news. "What?" he exclaimed. "What the fuck you talkin' about?"

Whoever it was, Khye was relieved that the focus went from her to something more critical.

"A'ight, I'll be over there in half an hour," he said into the phone.

Khye hoped everything was okay, but by the look on Floyd's face, she knew it wasn't.

"What's wrong, baby?" she asked.

"We gotta go," Floyd said abruptly.

He didn't give anyone any explanation as to why their sudden departure was necessary, but wherever her man went, Khye followed. His mood had changed. He was angry and silent. He climbed onto his motorcycle and started it up. He was ready to hurry off and get back to Brooklyn. Khye was taking too long to climb onto the back of the bike and Floyd suddenly barked at her. "Would you hurry the fuck up? I gotta get back."

He startled her, but she didn't say a word back. She got onto the bike and held on tightly. Floyd took off like a bat flying out of hell. He rode back to Brooklyn faster this time, angrier. It felt like they were going at warp speed. The Suzuki Hayabusa felt like it was flying in the air, and everything went by in a blur.

In no time, they were back in Brooklyn, in Canarsie. Floyd's bike roared in the night like Godzilla screaming out and when he finally got to his block, he came to a stop and jumped off the motorcycle like it was on fire and hurried over to his CL600. The closer he got to the car, the heavier he frowned; it looked like steam came out of his ears. His two front tires were flattened—someone had punctured them with some blade—and the driver's door had been keyed with the words FUCK YOU!!

"What the fuck?!" Floyd hollered.

A neighbor came out of his apartment to talk to Floyd. Khye walked over softly. She was wide-eyed at what she saw. It was a woman's handiwork. It had Tatianna written all over it.

"I'm gonna fuck this bitch up!" she heard Floyd yell out.

Floyd walked around his car, inspecting the damage. He was hurt. He loved his car. He kept it clean and shining. It was his prized possession. Now, it had over seven thousand dollars' worth of damage done to it. The paint job alone was costly.

Floyd wanted retribution. He'd warned Tatianna, and now she had to be taught a lesson. Seeing Khye staring at his car made him upset.

"What the fuck you lookin' at, Khye? Take ya fuckin' ass upstairs! Now!" he barked as if she were a two-year-old.

Khye jumped at the sound of his voice. She didn't want to make him more upset. He was unexpectedly having a bad day, and the last thing she wanted was for him to take it out on her. She did as she was told. While Floyd cussed and ranted, she removed herself from his fury and went into the condo. She made herself a drink and planned to give him a massage and some good loving when he walked through the doors. She wanted to please him, take his mind off his troubles. She wanted to show him she was his ride-or-die bitch, and he'd made the right choice by picking her.

Hearing the sound of his motorcycle start up again, Khye went to the window and saw Floyd on his bike. He sped away, leaving her alone. He most likely wouldn't be back anytime soon. He'd gone looking for Tatianna, and Khye was almost certain he was going to fuck her dumb ass up.

Random, selfish thoughts went through her mind, like, what if he got locked up? Her cozy and lavish way of living would suddenly come to an abrupt stop, and she didn't want it to end. Not now—actually, not ever.

***

Khye and Sammy shared a blunt as they crossed over the Brooklyn Bridge and made their way into the downtown Brooklyn area. It was a sunny and warm day, the perfect day for them to go cruising around in her Range Rover with the music blaring and moon roof back. Sammy couldn't believe his eyes when he first saw Khye pull up in her new toy. He almost came on himself. He was wide-eyed and in disbelief.

"Bitch, what bank did you rob to get his?" he asked.

Khye grinned like the Grinch who stole Christmas. She stepped out of her Range looking fresh to death in her skirt and red bottoms and responded, "I'm a bad bitch, Sammy. Look at me now, eh?"

"I see, I see. Damn girl, you got me ready to become a hater," Sammy joked, but in the back of his mind, he felt jealous and resentful.

"Yo, I'm gonna be that smashing bitch all summer, fall, and in the winter and so on. I love it and I love him," she boasted. "It used to be hers, now it is all mines."

"Bitch, I can't believe he gave you a car."

"Yes, believe it. Because he loves me and I give him this good pussy every night."

Immediately, they jumped into the Range Rover and went driving around Brooklyn and Harlem all day, windows down and music playing, showing off. Sammy loved riding shotgun. It felt good to upgrade from foot patrol to cruising in such an expensive SUV.

Soon, they were in Bed-Stuy, stunting like a number-one stunner, with the car stereo blaring "I'm So Fancy" by Iggy Azalea. It was Khye's favorite song, and together, she and Sammy sang out the lyrics loudly.

Khye cruised around Brooklyn, making sure she was seen by everyone—but mostly she went to the areas that she heard Tatianna frequented. She drove up and down Fulton Street, Bedford Avenue, Throop, made her presence known around Marcy, and then drove down Nostrand Avenue. When they came to a red light on the corner of Nostrand Avenue and Lafayette Avenue, Sammy jumped out of the truck and started twerking and popping his booty in the middle of the street. He immediately caught attention from everyone in the area. Khye laughed and yelled, "Sammy, you are crazy."

"Harlem in the house . . . hey, Harlem in the house, ho!" he screamed.

He put on a quick show, having most in awe and some in disgust. The blue spandex he wore highlighted his booty and crotch area, and with his nails and toes done and hair styled, he was showing everyone that he was a flamboyant, charismatic gay man.

Khye continued to laugh at her friend's crazy antics. They were having a good time, but she was still determined to find Tatianna and taunt her. She had messed with her man's car, and what belonged to Floyd now belonged to her.

"Sammy, get back in the car," Khye hollered, shaking her head, in good spirits at the moment.

Sammy stopped showing off and jumped back into the Range Rover, shouting out to whoever was listening, "Ain't nobody fuckin' with my bitch! Fuck Tatianna!"

"Ooooh girl, you are so bad," Khye said.

"Ain't I? I'm a monster." He grinned.

They drove away. Khye continued her quest to show off her Range Rover—making a crucial statement in Brooklyn that what used to belong to Floyd's ex now belonged to her. Everyone knew the truck, the black-on-black Range Rover with the black rims, and friends of Tatianna's were upset and outraged that Floyd's new bitch would take it that far and be on some petty shit.

The entire afternoon, Khye and Sammy drove around the area, stopping off at places and talking shit. It was reckless talk, and if Khye wasn't Floyd's main bitch, then they would have beaten her and her homo friend down into the ground. For now, she was untouchable—off limits. Floyd had a concrete status in his Brooklyn neighborhood. He was respected and feared.

"That bitch isn't out here. She running scared," Sammy said.

"I know."

They decided to call it quits and head back to Harlem and get something to eat. Khye felt she had made her statement loud and clear to Tatianna's friends and anyone who knew her.

NINETEEN

Floyd and Carlito drove in Carlito's Yukon sharing a cigarette and talking shit, bitches, and business. It was a rainy day, with the rainfall cascading off the truck's window and the windshield wipers going rapidly to give Carlito some vision on the congested road. The cloudy, grayish day didn't stop business; New York was a bustling place in the rain, sleet, or snow.

Carlito drove his truck across the George Washington Bridge, heading for New Jersey. They had a meeting with the Colombians in Fort Lee. Their relationship with a high ranking cartel member named Ruiz Vibora had been going strong for little over a year now. He was their supply, their lifeline. Ruiz's reputation preceded him. He had a strong appetite for money and violence, but his low tolerance and deadly temper made everyone wary of doing business with him. He didn't like or allow mistakes. Carlito and Ruiz took a chance dealing with each other, and so far, it was paying off for both parties handsomely. With Carlito by his side, Floyd flooded the streets with quality cocaine and some heroin. They got rich together and they were building their empire, and making their dreams come through with music.

Almost arriving into New Jersey, where the morning traffic got thicker, Floyd took his final pull from the cancer stick and flicked it out the window. The rain was coming down heavier, and the wonderful view of the city from the G.W. Bridge had been distorted by fog and an overcast day. Floyd exhaled and said to Carlito, "This fuckin' bitch disrespected, yo. I loved that car."

Carlito laughed.

"You find this shit funny?"

"Yeah, I do."

"Fuck you, nigga," Floyd said.

"Nigga, you should have seen this shit coming. I told you that bitch was crazy," said Carlito.

"And when I find Tatianna, I'm gonna show her who's fuckin' crazier."

"If you find her," Carlito uttered.

"She can't hide from me," Floyd said.

"She's doin' a good job so far," Carlito said.

Floyd had nothing else to say about the situation.

Crossing into New Jersey and coming closer to their destination, Carlito, out of the blue said, "Yo, I got a new girl for us."

"What, a mule?"

He chuckled. "Nah, nah, this singer," he mentioned. "She's nice, yo, and talented. I met her in the club the other night."

"Oh word, you fucked her?"

"Nah, my nigga, you know I'm about my business. But her name is Rita, and the bitch can blow."

"She cute?"

"She's gorgeous," replied Carlito.

"And you ain't fuck her?"

"Nigga, you know I don't mix business wit' pleasure. That might be your forte, but I can't deal wit' the headache."

"That's because you ain't me," Floyd said.

"Yeah and where's your CL600 now?"

"Fuck you, nigga."

"Exactly."

Only Carlito could get away with talking to Floyd recklessly. Anyone else would quickly regret saying anything slick and disrespectful. He didn't like to be made fun of or have anyone in his business.

Their conversation went from business to Khye. Carlito asked, "So, how's ya new situation coming along?"

"Damn nigga, what, you Wendy Williams now? You wanna know all the business?" Floyd said.

"I'm ya friend, nigga, don't forget that."

"Yeah, whatever." He laughed. "But she cool. The sex is good, and she's docile, knowing who the fuck is in charge, and I know she got my back."

"What's it's been, two months now?"

"Something like that."

"I give it another month," Carlito said.

"Why you say that?"

"Because I know, Floyd. . ."

"I've been wit' Tatianna for two years."

"That's because you felt you owed her. She never snitched on you. She did your dirty work, and she was a ride-or-die bitch. You kept her around, wifed her up, fell in love, whatever. But this newbie, Khye, c'mon, when shit hits the fan, and I'm not saying it will anytime soon, but you really think she got your back like that? Like Tatianna would have? Yo, all due respect, my nigga, but all any bitch sees is the glitz and glamour, and they get dazzled by it, thinking one thing when it's really something else. And I know you, Floyd," Carlito proclaimed.

"Obviously you don't, because I love this one. Khye has my heart."

"You love her?" Carlito asked with a raised eyebrow.

"Yeah."

"C'mon, you didn't even meet her family yet. You didn't even know where she lived. She always met you somewhere; never had you come around to her peoples. She charmed you wit' her accent and looks. Do you know her history? C'mon, Floyd, I know you smarter than that. A chick moving like that, it's clear that she's hiding something, or don't want you to know something. . . basically, she's looking for a come-up."

"Ain't everyone?"

Floyd thought about it. His friend was right.

Carlito was always the voice of reason. He was smart, ambitious, and always careful. He loved making money, and he wasn't chasing pussy around town like Floyd. He kept a girlfriend or two in the city, but he had grown up thinking that a woman in a man's business was always the start of their downfall. So he kept his business and personal life completely separated. He constantly warned Floyd about Khye; there was something about her that he just didn't like. He didn't trust her at all.

Carlito navigated his Yukon through the streets of Fort Lee, situated atop of the Hudson Palisades. They came to the towering resident buildings on Old Palisade Road. Carlito parked his truck and the two of them approached the lobby. Meeting with Ruiz was always nerve-wracking. He was unpredictable. Someone could walk into his place alive and breathing, but later on be carried out in pieces in a garbage bag. The Colombians were psychopaths.

They got on the elevator and rode it to the 27th floor. Stepping out of the elevator into the carpeted hallway, they walked toward the apartment in silence. Both men took a needed deep breath and knocked. They waited.

"Speak?" they heard a voice say from the other side.

"Carlito and Floyd, here to see Ruiz," Carlito said.

The door opened and a thin, hard-looking Colombian gangster peered at them, unsmiling. The men stepped in. They were searched for any weapons before they walked farther into the apartment. The man gestured for them to have a seat in the living room. The apartment was well furnished and a nice size. There was a 70-inch flatscreen playing soccer—Brazil against Germany. Another one of Ruiz's goons was in the room reading the day's newspaper. Though it looked laid-back and casual, the place was heavily fortified with state-of-the-art security, guns, and murderous goons situated all through the building.

Floyd and Carlito took a seat on the cushy sofa. Ruiz could be seen standing on the balcony that had a picturesque view of the G.W. Bridge, and miles of land stretched beyond it. Ruiz was on his cell phone, speaking in Spanish. He was wearing a white shirt and white shorts, no shoes. He wasn't a tall man, standing five foot seven, but his reputation was tall enough. He had tannish skin and dark hair that swept across his face. He was handsome with a beautiful smile and a soft voice, but it all could change within a heartbeat when he got upset. His eyes could get cold as ice, and his wrath was worse than being caught in a hurricane.

Ruiz curtailed his phone call and stepped into the living room to greet his guests.

"Carlito, Floyd, it is good to see you again," he said.

The men stood up to shake his hand and show him the respect that he deserved.

"It's always a pleasure, Ruiz," Floyd said.

Ruiz oozed power. He was using Floyd and Carlito to get his product into New York, and in their deal Floyd and Carlito were supposed to make sure Ruiz didn't have to worry about the local gangs and getting his money on time. Things had been running smoothly—no difficulties, no interruptions. So many people were jealous of Floyd and Carlito's lucrative deal with the Colombians. Ruiz always received his money on time, and he was content with his two black associates, except for one thing that had him concerned: the negative attention their crew was catching from law enforcement—the bodies and the war with a man named Rash. Ruiz kept his ears to the streets and he seemed to know about everything.

He took a seat opposite of the two men, placed a cigar into his mouth, and lit it. He took a few pulls, enjoying the taste from the expensive Cuban cigar. He wasn't in any rush to speak. He didn't need to hurry for anyone. The odor from the cigar he smoked pervaded the air around them.

"So, business has always been good between us, is that right?" Ruiz finally said.

"Yes, it has," Carlito agreed.

"With that said, I have a hundred kilos coming into town next week, and seventy kilos I will hand over to you two—same arrangement, same prices."

Carlito and Floyd smiled. They were major players in the game and moving seventy kilos was like selling ice cream and bottled water in the summertime. They had established a concrete clientele from Brooklyn to New Jersey, becoming major drug distributors to sixty percent of the city.

"My one problem—who is this Rash that you are having a problem with? I don't like the negative attention that I'm hearing from my sources," Ruiz stated.

Floyd spoke up. "He's nobody. Just a jealous nigga who wants what we have."

"I hear he used to be a friend of yours," Ruiz said.

"Key words, 'used to be,'" Floyd said.

"I don't want any problems. You know I don't like problems, and so far, there haven't been any problems with our business relationship, and because of that, you have earned my respect. But warning: Don't lose it now with this issue going on in Brooklyn. Something you think is small can easily roll out of control and become a big mess, and when it becomes a mess, I will clean it up in a way where there is no more mess leading in my direction. Understand?" Ruiz said.

"Yes. We understand, Ruiz," Carlito chimed.

Ruiz continued to smoke his cigar. His presence was overwhelming. The men spent a half-hour in the apartment discussing business. Ruiz really liked them, but Floyd and Carlito knew that if they became a problem and if the situation couldn't be fixed, they could easily be replaced.

After their meeting with Ruiz, Floyd and Carlito couldn't wait to cross over the G.W. Bridge and be back in New York City. The day was early, the rain continued to come down. They had seventy kilos coming to them next week, but for now, their drug business was put on hold so they could focus on their music careers.

"I want you to meet her," Carlito said.

"Meet who?" Floyd said.

"You forgot already? Rita, the singer I was telling you about. She lives in Washington Heights. I can have her come down to the studio since we're in the area."

"You know what? Do that."

"A'ight."

Carlito made the phone call as he drove. Floyd sat back and gazed out the window, looking at the gloomy weather and thinking about his future. He had plans to one day go legit. They had started their music label and searched for the best talent in the metropolitan area of New York City. He had a few potential talents, but in his eyes, none of them were platinum or commercial selling talent. However the way Carlito talked about Rita, he made it seem like she was Mariah Carey, Whitney Houston, and Beyoncé all put into one woman.

***

She walked into Slow Pullz studio and Floyd was in awe. Rita smiled at him and extended her hand to shake. She was strikingly beautiful— absolutely gorgeous. She was from Brazil and had been in the U.S. for five years. She had tanned skin, a curvy petite figure with C-cup breasts, wide hips, and a plump ass that fit her perfectly. She had short, black hair. Floyd checked her out from head to toe, and he couldn't find a mark, a blemish, or a hair out of place. If she sang as good as she looked, then he felt they found they first major star.

The introductions were made, and Carlito knew by Floyd's reaction that he was already impressed with her.

"I hear you can really blow," Floyd said.

"I do a little something," she replied humbly.

"So, let us hear your little something-something," he said.

She smiled. It took her no time to get started. She went right into her singing, unapologetic about her powerful voice. God gave her a unique and beautiful singing voice, and she couldn't wait for the world to hear her sing.

She started singing a Whitney Houston song, "Saving All My Love for You."

Rita's voice was extraordinary coming from her petite frame. Not too many people could sing a Whitney Houston song and perform it accurately and in tune. But Rita did. Her voice was similar to that of the late pop star. The minute she opened her mouth to sing, everything stopped and everyone wanted to listen. They became transfixed by her voice. It was hypnotic.

"Oh shit," Floyd uttered.

"You like it?" she asked.

"I love it. Damn," he said, blown away.

Rita smiled. The two locked eyes and smiled.

"We definitely need to talk," said Floyd.

"I'm ready to blow, make things happen for myself," she said.

"I told you, my nigga. She can sing," Carlito chimed.

"Let me take you out to eat and we can talk more," Floyd said.

"A girl can always eat."

Carlito stared at his friend and didn't say anything. He already knew what Floyd was leading to. She was a very attractive girl, enticing and sexy. Not a man in the room couldn't take their eyes off of her. She was alluring.

"Yo, we about our business. Right, Floyd?" Carlito said.

Floyd nodded aloofly with his eyes still focused on Rita and he faintly replied, "Yeah, business. We about business."

Carlito was basically trying to tell him discreetly, don't start fucking the talent and make it bad for them. But Floyd's dick was at attention and he wanted her. It almost had him saying, *Khye who?*

***

It was two hours after midnight, and Floyd was just getting home to Khye. He'd had a late night out with Rita and Carlito. They had been talking and drinking, going over business techniques. They didn't want to wait to record Rita and promote her. She was a gift from the heavens. A voice like Rita's only came once in a blue moon, and if executed right, they could make millions off her talent.

Floyd was excited, and he was a little tipsy. He saw his dreams of becoming a successful music mogul getting closer. He was ready to pop champagne with Khye and celebrate. It had been a good day. Their meeting with Ruiz had gone well, and now with Rita in their life, the silver lining was about to show brightly. Floyd loved the game, but he had been selling drugs for a long time and he wanted to become legit soon. The murders, the violence, constantly watching his back from the streets, the stick-up kids, the police and jealous muthafuckas that wanted to take over the throne had become daunting.

He had a bottle of Ace of Spades champagne in his hand, the good and expensive stuff and called Khye's name out as he entered the apartment.

"Baby, where you at?"

He walked into the bedroom and saw his beautiful woman already waiting for his arrival. She was in expensive lingerie, soft and silky. Her smile lit up the bedroom.

"I was waiting for you, baby," she said.

They wrapped into each other's arms and kissed fervently. Being with Rita and thinking about her had made him super horny. He hastily stripped away his clothing to be with Khye. He wanted to take her from the back. He stood behind her and took aim. His dick was rock hard. He rubbed the head of it along her wet slit. He grabbed her hips and thrust himself into her. Khye curved over, face into the pillow and took his dick with her eyes closed. Floyd was intent on ramming every inch of his hard dick inside her. She fucked him back, rubbing her clit, moaning loudly and enjoying how he felt inside of her. It was so good, her legs started shaking and she was about come.

Exhausted, they plunged on the bed in a knot of long legs and flat abs. Khye had a look of profound satisfaction on her face. Floyd held her for a moment, both of them relishing the feeling of a good orgasm.

He then spoke, and what he said was something way out of the blue.

"Why you don't take me around your peoples?" he said. "You hiding something from me?"

Khye didn't expect to hear that, but she had to say something.

"I have nothing to hide."

"Then I wanna meet your peoples."

"Okay, you will."

Khye sighed quietly, but she felt comfortable in her position being his girl. She didn't mind and was no longer afraid to take him around her family and her old neighborhood.

TWENTY

Khye brought the Range Rover to a stop in front of her parents' building in Harlem. Floyd was seated in the passenger seat. It was a cool evening and the neighborhood around the Lincoln Housing Projects seemed quiet. The block was empty, and she didn't see anyone that she knew around, which was good news for her. It had been weeks since she'd last seen her parents and her sisters. She didn't miss them at all. She was enjoying the good life living in Brooklyn with her new ride, the clothes, and the money.

In her mind, she'd come up.

"You ready?" she asked Floyd.

"Yeah."

They both stepped out of the truck looking fresh. Khye was wearing a multicolored Top Shop dress that clung to her breasts and Manolo Blahnik shoes. Floyd sported a red velour suit and white Adidas, with his jewelry gleaming, looking important to the people in the area.

As they approached the lobby, Floyd looked at Khye and said, "You look nervous."

"I'm okay."

"You sure?"

She nodded.

The second they stepped into the lobby, a familiar face appeared. He was exiting out of the elevator. It was Boom, one of Able's thugs. He smiled and eyed Khye excitedly, not having seen her in a long time. He admired her sexy figure in the dress she wore.

"Hey ma, what is good?" he said, sizing Khye up and paying her man no never mind. "I ain't seen you around in a while."

Distantly, Khye replied, "I'm good."

"I see that, lookin' all sexy and shit. What's good, though? You back in the hood?" he said, licking his lips and eyeballing Khye.

"Boom, this is my new boyfriend, Floyd," she quickly introduced.

Boom didn't seem interested in meeting her new boyfriend. He only seemed interested in getting with Khye.

"Oh word, you got a new nigga in ya life now? What's good, my nigga?" he said to Floyd.

Floyd shot a hard stare at him, already not liking what he was seeing. "I was 'bout to ask you the same thing," he shot back.

Boom smiled. "You a lucky nigga, yo. Khye good peoples, fo' real. You took sumthin' good out the hood and wifed it, that's what's up. I ain't hatin' on you, my nigga."

"Look, we gotta go," Khye chimed.

"A'ight, ma. Good to see you again," Boom said, moving closer to hug Khye in his arms. But she immediately stepped backwards, shunning his approach and avoiding him more.

Boom chuckled. "Oh, it's like that now, ma? A nigga can't get a hug from you now?"

"No," she said sharply.

"A'ight, Khye. I see how it is. You take care and enjoy ya new life. It's all good," said Boom casually.

He stepped out of the lobby, laughing and smiling to himself. Khye felt she dodged a bullet. She had fucked Boom on a few occasions and she didn't want that to get out. What would Floyd think if he found out she'd fucked a dirty thug nigga like him?

"Yo, who was that, and what was that about?" Floyd asked.

"He's nobody, just someone that had a crush on me for a very long time," she said.

"You fucked him?"

"No!" Khye flat out lied to him. "I don't even get down like that."

Floyd looked at her disbelievingly, trying to read between the lines. However he had no proof, just suspicion.

"He only likes me, baby," Khye added.

"Okay," he said.

Inside, she was a nervous wreck and couldn't wait to leave her old hood. There was too much dirt on Khye in the streets, and her family was worse. She knew there wasn't any avoiding the inevitable. Floyd was persistent; he wanted to meet her peoples. He wanted to know about the woman he'd brought into his home and made wifey.

Khye stepped out of the elevator, and Floyd followed. She walked down the narrow, graffiti covered hallway. When she arrived at her parents' door, she knocked lightly. It would be a miracle if no one wasn't home, but chances were, someone was always home, especially in the evening in September.

Ava opened the door, and when she saw Khye, she smiled and hugged her big sister. Even though they had their differences in the past, Khye was missed by her two little sisters.

"Khye's back home!" Ava shouted out.

Maisie, the youngest, came running out of the bedroom and joined Ava in hugging Khye. Floyd stood aside, watching the family reunion, almost feeling touched. Her two sisters weren't as beautiful as Khye was. In fact, he didn't believe they were truly related. Did they all three come from the same genes?

Khye pulled herself away from Ava and Maisie and turned to introduce Floyd. "This is my boyfriend, Floyd," she introduced.

"Hello," Ava and Maisie said, smiling, extending out their hands to greet him.

"Hey," Floyd greeted them impassively. He barely shook their small, eager hands.

When he walked into the apartment, he was disgusted by the place right away. It was a mess. It was ghetto. It had roaches and bugs. It had days old dishes piled up in the sink. Floyd didn't even want to take a seat, fearing bed bugs and contamination. But the worst was about to come. When Khye's father walked into the apartment in his dirty work attire, a brown bag containing a bottle of Jack Daniels in his hand and already drunk, Khye expected trouble.

"And who is he?" Adewale asked in a drunken slur.

"This is my new boyfriend," Khye said.

"Boyfriend, huh?"

"Yes."

Adewale looked intently at Floyd and started to size him up. He took a swig from the bottle in his hand and plopped down on the raggedy couch. Already, the introduction was going badly.

"So, here's the bloody fool that took my baby girl away from me," Adewale said. "This nigga, huh? He looks like a tosser. I should tell him to get stuffed!" he ranted.

"Don't mind him, he's legless right now," Ava said, meaning he was hammered—absolutely drunk and embarrassing everyone.

Floyd didn't respond. He was ready to leave. Adewale continued to drink and talk shit to Khye and Floyd. Floyd couldn't believe Khye came from him; he was out of shape, black, and not what he expected at all. Her two sisters tried to make it easier in the room, apologizing for their father's impolite act, but Adewale kept going on and on. Floyd tried keeping his cool. Although he was from the hood, he thought he was better than everyone else. He looked down on Khye's family, especially her father, the drunk, and her two less-than-attractive sisters. It got him thinking how strong her father's genes were. If they had kids, would they come out looking like Khye or her dad? He wanted to have pretty babies. He wanted to be perfect.

"Where's Mum?" Khye asked.

"Not here," Maisie said.

"We need to go," Floyd said abruptly.

"Now?" Khye said.

"Yes."

He hadn't met her mother yet, but he was sure they would meet soon. Floyd had seen enough. He didn't want to stay any longer. His cell phone was ringing; Carlito had been calling him. Khye followed him out the door after only a few short minutes back home. While in the elevator, Khye sheepishly said, "That's the family."

Floyd had no words.

They exited the lobby and walked toward Khye's parked Range Rover in silence. As they walked out the building, another young thug eyeballed Khye and smiled her way. He literally undressed her with his eyes and licked his lips while approaching and not caring she was with her new boyfriend.

"What's up, Khye? Damn, you lookin' good, luv. You back around the way?" he asked.

"No!" Khye replied with an attitude.

"A'ight. . ."

In passing, he made sure to turn around and gaze at her nice ass in the dress she wore. "Damn!" the thug uttered loudly.

Floyd was obviously annoyed by what just happened. Khye looked like she wanted to leave the projects in such a hurry. Her past was catching up to her.

"I'm driving," Floyd said, sticking out his hand for her to give him the keys.

She didn't argue with him. She went into her purse and handed him the keys. Before they could get into the truck, a yellow cab pulled up and Sarah stepped out. Khye hesitated in getting into the passenger seat seeing her mother suddenly arriving. The woman looked like she had spent the night somewhere, having sex, and she was now coming home.

"What you lookin' at?" Floyd said.

"It's my mother."

Sarah strutted over, smiling at her daughter.

"Hey," said Sarah, glancing at her daughter then fixing her eyes on Floyd. "So, this is him. You must be Floyd?"

"I am," he said nonchalantly.

"My, my, my, he is very handsome, Khye," Sarah said. "You do pick them well."

Khye remained cool. Sarah looked at her man like he was a prime steak, and it was quickly making Khye upset.

"We were leaving," Khye said.

"Oh, you were? Did he at least get to meet the family?"

"I did," Floyd chimed with a stone look on his face.

"I know we are not the Cosbys, eh?" said Sarah.

"Definitely not," Floyd responded with a bit of sarcasm.

"But we try."

"We were leaving, Mum," Khye said.

"Leaving, why?" Sarah asked.

"Because this isn't my life anymore," Khye said.

She climbed into the Range Rover with Floyd getting behind the steering wheel. Sarah stared at the black luxury SUV in front of her eyes and immediately, there was jealousy in her expression. Her daughter was riding around in a tank while she was still taking buses, trains, and cabs back and forth. It should have been her life.

"Nice," Sarah uttered.

"I know," Khye replied.

"When are you coming back to visit?" Sarah asked.

"I'll call," she shouted out.

Floyd started the vehicle and put it in drive. He drove away, leaving Sarah standing there looking like a lost soul. When they got to the corner, Sammy was walking toward the corner, and when he saw Khye's Range Rover and her seated in the passenger seat, he smiled and waved.

"Hey, girl," he called out.

Khye looked his way and chose to ignore her best friend. Floyd was in the car, and she knew how he felt about her dealing with homosexuals and how much he wanted to preserve his reputation and hers. So she turned her attention away from him, with Sammy shaking his head and knowing the reason why Khye was shunning him once again.

"This bitch," Sammy muttered underneath his breath.

Before Floyd drove away, Khye quickly looked Sammy's way, imitated like she had a phone to her ear and mouthed the words, "I'll call you."

TWENTY-ONE

Seeing Khye living the golden life made Sarah more desperate to get her own sugar daddy, to be treated like gold, and spend some gold. The only way she saw that happening was to become pregnant by Marcus. For months, the sex between them had intensified. They fucked each other's brains out with no remorse that they were both married, but Sarah had deviously been trying to get pregnant by him. She wanted a bond with Marcus somehow, and naively, she assumed having another baby and him being the father would somehow solidify their affair. Desperate times called for desperate measures.

Her period was a week late.

She picked up a home pregnancy test and locked herself in the bathroom. Pulling down her jeans and panties, she squatted over the toilet, placed the pregnancy test underneath her and peed on it. Afterwards, she left it on the sink and had to wait two minutes for the results. During those two minutes, Adewale came knocking on the bathroom door while Sarah sat on the toilet waiting to see if she was carrying another man's baby.

"Open this damn door! Why is it locked?" Adewale exclaimed with his fist pounding against the door.

"I'm in it!" Sarah shouted.

"Who cares? Open the bloody damn door," he said, acting like an animal on the other side.

Sarah felt he was about to kick the door down if she didn't open it right away. He was loud and sounding belligerent. He had been drinking. He was becoming a nuisance, and Sarah was upset because he'd picked the perfect time to interrupt her when she was doing something important. She could hear her husband kicking the door and trying to force it open. She had no choice but to hide the test and let him in.

Adewale barged his way inside. He was shirtless and his breath reeked of alcohol. She was disgusted by her husband's drinking and his careless actions. She didn't love him anymore, wasn't in love with him, and hadn't been in a very long time. She only tolerated him, but she celebrated Marcus.

"I was using it," said Sarah gruffly.

"I don't care. This is my house, dammit. You are my wife and you gonna start treating me with respect, eh," he exclaimed.

"Respect?" She laughed.

"You find me funny?" he shot back.

He glared at her. She returned the same look. He didn't intimidate her. She found him pathetic and weak. She regretted the years she had with him, the children she gave him, and moving to the States for him, following his empty promises. She was too beautiful to be living in poverty. Now, it was her time to shine, no matter how she shined.

"You can have the bathroom. I was leaving anyway," she said.

She attempted to walk by him, but Adewale forcefully grabbed her arm and prevented her from walking any farther. "Where you going?" he uttered.

"Please let me go," she said.

Though he was drunk and out of shape, he was still strong and he was still a big man. He grabbed her second arm and pushed her against the bathroom wall, making it shake and making Sarah alert.

"You are my woman!" Adewale hollered. His acid breath hit her like a gust of wind.

"Please, get off me," she said.

Adewale stared his whore of a wife in her eyes, and he no longer saw the love for him. It was obvious that her heart belonged to someone else. They hadn't had sex in forever, but for some reason, he was horny and he wanted to be inside of his wife that evening.

He pushed himself against her, her arms still restricted to her sides by his tight grip. He kissed the side of her neck roughly and had her pinned against him and the wall. He slammed the door shut to give them some privacy. Sarah tried to push him off of her, but Adewale was a brute that was drowned in some kind of alcoholic aggression and rage.

She was already loosely dressed from peeing and taking the pregnancy test. He quickly ripped open her shirt, tore off her bra, and continued pinning her to the wall and kissing her lips roughly with his tart breath. Where did this sudden belligerence come from? Why now did he want some pussy from her? She hadn't been sexually attracted to him in years and their sex life was almost nonexistent. So many things spun around in Sarah's head as her husband wasn't taking no for an answer. He cupped her tits and then threw her to the ground with inexplicable force, removing her jeans, spreading her legs, shouting, "You like it rough, you bitch!" and hurriedly unfastening his pants to penetrate his wife forcefully. The pregnancy test she took was in her back pocket. She didn't know the results, but yet, she was about to be violated by the man who she was supposed to have a loyal relationship with.

Why fight it? He was her husband.

So, Sarah closed her eyes and allowed Adewale to remove her jeans to take what he wanted from her, to take what she'd been giving every other man but him. She felt him climbing between her legs eagerly and then penetrating her sharply, grunting as he violated her. She wasn't wet, so it must have felt like sandpaper down below. Adewale didn't care. He was only focused on busting a quick nut.

He moved up and down between her legs, and continued to kiss his wife roughly, from her lips to her neck. It was drunken sex from his end. Yes, he had a big dick, but he might as well been fucking a lifeless doll. Sarah simply laid there on her back, feeling like her husband was going to the bathroom on her. She didn't partake, showed no emotion—she didn't fuck him back.

She closed her eyes and thought about Marcus.

In no less than five minutes, Adewale was coming inside his wife, shuddering from a good nut. Subsequently, he shot up like a rocket going off and went for the toilet, hovering over it and throwing up chunks of vomit inside. Sarah picked herself up from off the floor, pulled up her jeans, and walked out of the bathroom after giving her husband what he wanted. It disgusted her though. She was ready to scrub every piece and smell of him from her skin.

While he was on his knees, praying to the porcelain god, Sarah walked out the bathroom quietly and locked herself in the bedroom. She took a seat at the foot of the bed and removed the pregnancy test from her back pocket. The results were in. She took a deep breath and checked for the outcome.

"Oh shit!" she uttered.

She was pregnant!

A wry smile appeared on her face. *Yes!* It had to be Marcus's baby, because he was the only man she'd had unprotected sex with and allowed to come inside her repeatedly. Now, the only question was, how much would her life change?

TWENTY-TWO

Floyd stood on the balcony of his condo with a drink in his hand and a detached look as he stared out at the lake. It was dusk out, a beautiful evening, quiet for blocks in his neck of the woods. He had a lot on his mind. He had a lot to handle. Slow Pullz Studio was starting to pull in some creative talent, but the street war with Rash was heating up. The other day, two of his soldiers were gunned down in Marcy. Carlito was handling the situation on the streets with gun-toting soldiers while he was running the studio, trying to make their illegal money become legal money. The shipment from Ruiz had been handled smoothly, and they were expecting to receive another seventy to eighty kilos in a few weeks to move from state to state.

Another thing that bothered Floyd was Khye. He turned to look at her as she slept naked across his bed. He had just finished giving her the business, dicking her down until her legs went weak. Now she was sleeping like a baby. Their relationship seemed to be going strong for almost three months now, but there was something about her that swiftly became off. What was more disturbing was that each time they went around her old way in Harlem, he was getting the impression that too many niggas knew Khye, and not in a platonic type of way. He knew the look in a man's eyes when they said hello to her, as if they fucked her and was making fun of him behind his back. He took her out of the ghetto and wifed her, but was it a decision he would regret? She was hiding something. Floyd was determined to find out the truth about the young nineteen-year-old girl he'd fallen in love with.

Standing on the balcony in his birthday suit, he took a few sips of liquor and relaxed for a moment. He took a deep breath and tried to free his mind from the worries, but he couldn't. The one fret on his mind was Khye. Who was she really? She seemed like this innocent, beautiful young woman with an enticing accent, which was starting to get on his nerves too for some reason. Seeing her family, the way they were, and the way she reacted around certain men, speculations came to him and he needed to know the truth before he went any further with their relationship.

Floyd sat his drink down on the table and picked up the cell phone. He dialed Carlito. The phone rang twice before his friend picked up.

"Yo, what's good?" Carlito answered.

"I need you to do me a favor," Floyd said.

"What you need?"

"I need some information. You still cool wit' that retired detective?"

"Yeah, I am. Why?"

"I want him to do a background check on Khye."

"Her shit starting to stink?"

"A little."

"But it shouldn't be nothing, I mean, she a young girl, that should be simple. But real talk, you probably don't even need him. If you wanna know the truth about Khye, then go ask around," said Carlito.

"Got too much on my plate right now."

"I feel you. A'ight, I'll get one of my peoples on it, see if this chick is really who she says she is. . . you know, a good girl. Because I know how you like 'em, Floyd." Carlito laughed.

"What's the deal with that other thing?" Floyd asked.

"Not over the phone. We'll talk in person," Carlito suggested.

"A'ight. One, my nigga."

"One."

He hung up. He turned and looked at Khye. She was still sleeping. Her beauty was extraordinary, but Floyd couldn't help but think there was more than met the eye with his girl. He was thinking she wasn't as innocent and wholesome as he thought; his beauty queen was probably nothing more than a young whore who manipulated people to get what she wanted.

He downed his drink and stepped into his apartment, closing the glass doors behind him. For now, he wouldn't say a word to Khye. He would continue to love her and treat her as he'd been treating her, until he heard different about her.

***

Floyd nodded to the track playing in the studio. He was extremely excited about Rita's voice. When she sang, it was hypnotic. Her soul, the core of her wonderful voice, could grab anyone and pull them in like they were caught in an intense gravity field. You couldn't fight or resist it; you had to go with it. Rita's voice made people want to stop and listen. She could really sing—blow sultry like Anita Baker and soulful like Aretha Franklin.

Floyd was happy that Carlito had discovered her. He couldn't take his eyes off of her as she sang in the recording booth, with the pop shield in front of her, picking up greatness. She was so beautiful and tempting. She smiled his way. He smiled back. It was just them, alone, after midnight in Slow Pullz Studio. They ordered Chinese food and drank wine while putting in another late-night session so Rita could record a few songs that would attract the masses.

Floyd was behind the mixer, doing what he loved best, engineering a beat. He leaned back in the leather swivel chair and jammed to her voice and the song he'd put together for her. It had an upbeat tempo, guitar, and piano laced.

Rita was lively. She didn't just sing, but she danced too, moving her hips and feet, and clapping her hands energetically to her own song. Floyd loved looking at her. Clad in a body clinging outfit, she was eye candy from head to toe.

After recording her song, Rita stepped out of the booth with a wide smile.

"So, how did I do? Did I sound good?" she asked.

"Yo, Funk Master Flex gonna drop bombs over that track, believe that," Floyd told her.

She smiled.

"With your voice, sky's the limit, fo' real. I mean, I never heard anyone like you before. You're beautiful and so talented."

She blushed.

He continued with, "With me by your side, we can go a long way."

"You think?"

"I know, beautiful. Beyoncé and Rihanna, they ain't gonna have shit on you. This here, it's your calling, and we have enough money to promote you diligently and take things platinum."

She continued to smile. Floyd picked up the bottle of white wine and poured them another drink. It was a lovely night. Good music was being made and good conversation was streaming back and forth. They both raised their glasses toward each other and Floyd toasted, "To the next superstar the world is gonna love. . . Rita. We going to the top."

"To the top," she repeated, smiling widely and consuming the wine.

She was so excited. She had come from a small town named Maraba Para in Brazil. Life for her was looking up. She grew up poor, was fluent in Portuguese, and her beauty and figure was striking. Rita felt comfortable around Floyd, maybe a little too comfortable. She gazed into Floyd's eyes and became fascinated by his kindness and his ambition. He was a handsome guy. She wanted to keep it professional between them, but the more time they spent together, in the studio and out, the more she found herself falling for the bad boy. And it was the same for Floyd.

"It's getting late," she said.

"It is."

No one attempted to leave. They stood close and gazed into each other's eyes, their intense look speaking vociferously what their mind and bodies were feeling. The sexual attraction between them was evident.

"You are so beautiful," he said softly, gazing into her lovely brown eyes.

"Thank you."

He wanted her so badly, that the hunger he had for her devoured him internally and it made him want to tear off her skirt. They were alone; it felt like the right time. The lust building inside of him was drowning him. Floyd undressed her with his eyes and what he saw was pure magnificence.

"I want you," he said frankly.

He reached out and pulled her closer into his arms. She didn't resist. Then his hands massaged her breasts through the soft material. She didn't get offended. In fact, she closed her eyes and enjoyed his touch. It felt good. She felt wanted. Floyd kissed her unexpectedly. Their lips pressed together, and their tongues entwined. He reached underneath her skirt while they continued to kiss fervently and he rubbed her clit and felt on her sexy round ass. She made Floyd so hard in his jeans, it felt like he was about to tear through his pants.

"I want you, too," Rita uttered, ready to spread her legs for him and have his manhood thrust into her temple.

He lifted her skirt and ripped off her thin panties. She felt decidedly masculine hands caress the tender flesh of her ass. His hands were kneading her body and gently stroking her thighs and back. They moved their action from the control room into the sofa area. Floyd removed her skirt, quickly undid his jeans, and thrust himself into her warm, massaging place. Every inch of his dick was driven deep inside her, and she adored the sensation. They were beyond the point of rational thought.

He fucked her with passion—fully inside her. Against the couch, on her back, she wrapped her legs around him and pulled him closer. He continued thrusting, feeling her womanly juices cover his dick. Floyd withdrew himself almost completely and then he thrust inside her again.

"Ooooh, fuck me," she cried out.

Passion consumed them and they were meeting each other's bodies, connecting together like Legos. The pussy was good. They were making love now—passionate, hot, sweaty love.

"Ooooh, oh shit, oh god. . . you feel so good," he cried out.

The muscles in his back, thighs, arms, and butt flexed as he worked his dick into Rita's pulsating vagina. They both experienced their own personal heaven. When she came, he came. He collapsed onto her, breathless, feeling nice and satisfied.

With Khye out of his mind for the moment, he comforted Rita with whispers of prosperity and sweet, soft kisses on her face and lips. They were an item now, and his masculine character felt that he needed to protect and help her.

He didn't want to let her go. He gazed into her eyes and said, "When you're wit' me, you get the best. I promise you that."

Rita grinned.

***

Carlito smoked his cigarette while gazing out at the illuminated streets of Brooklyn from the rooftop of one of the project buildings. It was a clear and warm night. Business had been good, but complications in their organization had surfaced, and certain things were becoming a headache. He took a long pull from the burning cancer stick clutched between his fingers and pressed between his lips and exhaled. The solitude was a bit comforting as he waited for Floyd to show up. He looked at the city with an entrenched feeling of ambiguity; Brooklyn had been good to him over the years. It made him rich and it made him respected. But it felt like things were starting to heat up on the ground he walked on.

Between him and Floyd, they had a résumé of ten bodies on their hands. They were dangerous men. They were killers, but reasonable and intelligent men when it came to business and expanding. Working with Ruiz made their portfolio a lot more notorious, but dealing with a heavy-hitter like Ruiz directly was also challenging. One mess-up and it could end them—which was why Carlito had been extra careful with moving the drug shipments and tightening security and their distribution.

Carlito continued smoking and thinking. He exhaled. He stepped closer to the side and peered over. The dizzying heights didn't scare him, neither did the fall. The only fall he feared was falling from the drug game and being outsmarted and losing his respect and his authority.

The metal door opened behind him and Floyd stepped onto the rooftop. He was alone. They gave each other dap and respect.

"Damn, I ain't been up here in a while," Floyd said.

"You miss it?"

"Nah, not really."

"We used to always chill up here, plot and shit. And I got my first piece of pussy on this rooftop," Carlito stated.

Floyd chortled at the comment. "Explains a lot," he joked.

"Fuck you, nigga," Carlito spat back lightheartedly.

"But what's good?" Floyd asked, knowing he hadn't met with Carlito on the project rooftop to reminisce about the old days.

"We got hit tonight," Carlito mentioned.

"What?"

"Nothing big; two kilos and a few thousand in cash."

"Nothing big, nigga, I don't give a fuck if it was a gram we got hit for, that's a problem."

"I know."

"Who hit us?" Floyd asked.

"You already know. Rash."

"This nigga is becoming a fuckin' headache, fo' real," Floyd blurted out. "And we still can't find this nigga?"

"Word is, he got down wit' some heavy hitters from Harlem. He feelin' mighty protected out there."

"Harlem? Who the fuck he know in Harlem?"

"We don't know yet, but we gonna find out."

"I always thought that asshole ate, shit, and lived Brooklyn. He reachin' out like that, niggas in Harlem too, that means he's desperate. The nigga is like a fuckin' mouse scurrying around scared and shit, hard to catch. Yo, set the traps on this nigga."

"We are. And that other thing you asked me about," Carlito brought up.

"Yeah, what about it?"

Carlito grinned. "Ya good girl, is everything but that."

Floyd looked at Carlito impassively. He was ready to hear the not so good news about Khye.

"She's an around-the-way skeezer—a hood-rat," Carlito happily mentioned. "She fucked mad local niggas. Her and her moms get down on some grimy shit."

"And you know this how?"

"I had my people ask around, showed her picture and they knew exactly who she was."

Floyd was listening. He was taking in the information calmly.

"So you sayin' she fucked mad niggas, huh?"

"Word is, she gets around," Carlito said. "What you gonna do wit' that bitch?"

"Let me think."

"Let you think. Yo, she played you. Had you bragging about how she don't know how to suck dick and can't take your big dick cause her pussy so untouched. Please, you should want to stomp a mud hole in that ass," Carlito said disparagingly about Khye.

Floyd didn't say anything. He heard it from Carlito, but now he needed to hear it from Khye's own mouth. Oddly, he wanted to give her a chance to explain herself. Quickly, he changed the subject.

"Yo, Rita, she's goin' to work out really fine. She got talent," Floyd said out of the blue.

Carlito snickered and then asked, "You fucked her?"

Floyd looked at his friend blankly. He then forthrightly answered, "Yeah."

Carlito shook his head and replied, "You just had to go there, right?"

"Shit happens, my nigga."

"Yeah, I bet it do. Where you fucked her, in the studio?"

"Like I said, shit just happens."

Carlito sighed. "Man, slow it down."

"Nigga, you know I'm high speed all the way."

"That's what I'm afraid of," Carlito said.

TWENTY-THREE

Khye was enjoying the warm shower that cascaded off her fair skin. She closed her eyes and ran her hand between her wet thighs and lowered her head. The warm droplets formed steam as she stood there without moving at all. The hot water stream collided into her skin, releasing some tension. Khye kept her eyes closed and the hot haze enveloped her body. She breathed out and thoroughly cleansed herself from top to the bottom, making sure every inch of her was fresh for when Floyd came home.

She stepped out of the shower and toweled off. Looking into the bathroom mirror, she smiled. Life was good, despite the minor ups and downs. It was early October and in a week, Floyd had promised to take her to the Hamptons in Long Island. She was excited about the trip. She'd heard so much about the Hamptons, the place where many celebrities traveled and had summer homes. It was an affluent place far away from the city, and Khye couldn't wait to go. She was ready to go on a shopping spree and rub elbows with a few celebrities, maybe get a few autographs and some connects.

Hearing the front door slam shut, she assumed Floyd was home. She finished drying off in the bathroom and walked into the hallway clad in a blue towel. When she came across Floyd in the hallway, he merely looked at her with no emotion.

"Hey baby," Khye greeted with her gracious smile. She was ready to hug him closely and lose the towel, giving her boyfriend a special treat.

Every moment he was away, she missed him.

Floyd slightly scowled at her.

"I want the truth from you," Floyd flat-out said, not beating around the bush.

Khye was confused. "The truth?"

"How many niggas you fucked in Harlem?" he asked sharply.

"What? Where is this coming from, baby?" she asked, looking taken aback by his sudden statement.

"I knew sumthin' was up that day when we went to see ya peoples and the way niggas was lookin' at you; fuckin' you wit' their eyes, smirking and shit."

"Baby, I'm not that girl," she said.

"Don't lie to me!" he shouted.

"I'm not lying to you. Where is all this coming from?"

"I asked around about you, and heard a lot of unflattering shit about you and your moms."

"Whatever you heard about me, it isn't true!" she denied vehemently.

"I don't know what is true wit' you anymore."

"What is true? I tell you what is true, I love you so much, baby, and I would never lie to you, or hurt you," she proclaimed. "Now that's the truth."

Khye approached him with a soft stare, hoping things didn't get too heated with him and he believed her. Floyd stood there as Khye attempted to appease his resentment, but at the moment, he didn't want anything to do with her. He couldn't prove the rumors at the moment, but hearing them already changed him.

Khye tried to reach for his zipper, thinking the only way to make him veer off the subject was to seduce him. Floyd remained expressionless. The look in his eyes was cold toward Khye. Before she could go any further with her seduction, Floyd cynically shouted, "You fuckin' whore!" and his rant was followed by a backhanded slap to her face. Khye lifted off her feet and fell to the floor. It felt like her cheek was on fire.

Without any remorse about striking her, he turned around and decided to leave.

"Baby, where are you going?" Khye called out, believing it was her fault that he had to hit her.

He ignored her. He kept walking, leaving the apartment and jumping on his bike. Khye hurried behind him clad in her towel, racing to grab him like she was trying to catch the city bus, but Floyd moved fast. She watched him take off on his motorcycle, leaving her dumbfounded. She didn't care that he was abusive and she was in a towel and a few neighbors saw her nearly naked body. She wanted Floyd to come back. Something was going on, and she felt him slipping away.

***

Rita's smile was able to light up any room, her talented voice could soothe and warm any cold space, and Floyd couldn't help himself. He wanted to spend every minute and every day with her. Over the next few weeks, he showered her with gifts, took her on expensive shopping sprees, rode her around New York City in his drop-top Benz, and took her to see the Hamptons, a trip that he had promised Khye but reneged on. Rita became his new queen, as they spent day and night in the studio, recording and talking, touring the town, having fun, and really getting to know each other.

Besides the studio time, Floyd and Rita fucked their brains out crazily. Floyd saw something in Rita that he hadn't seen in any other woman— unlimited talent, success, and loyalty. His feelings for Khye were gradually fading, and as the fall went on with the changing of the leaves, so did his heart change. He saw less and less of Khye and started to dislike her.

Rita was steadily becoming his priority, and, Khye—she was becoming an option.

Khye started to realize the sudden disinterest with her from her man as they hadn't fucked in almost a month. Almost overnight, the passion stopped. The gifts dried up, and his time became more valuable elsewhere.

With it being a cool, fall evening, Khye decided to take a ride somewhere. She had been blowing up Floyd's phone all day, but he wasn't answering or returning her phone calls. She was tired of staying home alone. She had her hair done, nails done, and a new outfit to show off, plus her Range Rover was washed, waxed, and gleaming outside. She picked up her keys and strutted outside. She climbed into her Range and drove off with Rihanna's "Diamonds" blaring.

She wanted to be happy. She wanted to shine like a diamond for her man to see. She was doing everything she could, but it felt like she wasn't shining bright enough for him, like when they first met. When did her light go out?

Getting on the Jackie Robinson Parkway and heading toward the Grand Central, Khye picked up her cell phone and dialed Sammy to tell him that she was on her way to Harlem. She sped over the Triborough Bridge and shortly arrived back home.

Parking her Range Rover across the street from Lincoln, Khye lingered behind the steering wheel smoking a cigarette while gazing across the street at what used to be her home. She puffed out. Someone had been in Floyd's ears about her reputation, and she sat looking afoul about the whole incident with Floyd. She'd tried her best to keep her past hidden, her promiscuous ways buried deeply like dinosaur fossils, but somehow, it all came to the light and Floyd was looking into her window clearly and already judging her. He wasn't trying to let her explain. His mind was already set with the preconceived notion that she was a slut and that she had lied and manipulated him. True, she had, but her plan was supposed to be flawless.

Khye took one last pull from the Newport and flicked her cigarette out the window. She locked up her truck and stepped out. She crossed the street with a "me against the world" attitude, her wedges striding against the stretching, cracked pavement as she walked by her old building and headed toward Sammy's. She didn't miss her home at all. It was quiet in the projects, and the streets were still. She didn't run into any old boyfriends or family. In fact, the area looked like a ghost town. She wished it had been a ghost town when she was with Floyd a few weeks back. But she didn't have that kind of luck. It seemed like the moment she showed up with Floyd, every nigga she'd ever been with decided to show up out of the woodwork and flirt with her. It frustrated Khye that niggas had no respect for her at all. She did her best to keep her cool and keep things restrained, though she knew Floyd wasn't a stupid man.

Khye strutted into the lobby and took the pissy elevator to Sammy's floor, hoping to have a long talk with him. She did miss her friend, but honestly, she had been somewhat standoffish with family and friends as she transitioned into the middle-class lifestyle. She was willing to step on anyone just to get to the top.

It had been weeks since she and Sammy spoke and hung out. She never called, even though she said she would. When Sammy called her phone, it was always at a bad time; she was around Floyd or it was some important business that had her distracted. Khye did everything to appease Floyd, but her everything wasn't enough. Sometimes he could become a complicated man. He could also become an abusive and violent man, and Khye experienced his wrath firsthand on a few unfortunate occasions.

She wondered when things became so difficult in their relationship and why Floyd was suddenly so out of touch with her. It had to be another woman. The only explanation she could come up with was he was fucking the next bitch. Ironically, she found herself now in Tatianna's shoes, feeling misplaced, unloved, and scared.

Khye knocked loudly and waited. Sammy's apartment was quiet; it was always quiet. The only time Sammy's place livened up was when Able came by with his crew, and they smoked, drank, and played loud rap music in the living room. Tonight, Able wasn't around, leaving Sammy home alone with his mother working the graveyard shift. Khye knocked a few times, and Sammy answered the door in some jeans shorts and a belly T-shirt. When he saw Khye, he didn't give her the pleasant welcome greeting like usual. He caught a slight attitude and said, "Oh, so I see you finally decided to come by and check a bitch. What, you got some beef with your boo now?"

"Hey, Sammy," Khye greeted humbly.

"Don't 'hey' me, bitch. Why this sudden visit from the almighty queen?"

"Can I come in?"

Sammy stared at her for a moment and sighed, then said, dryly, "Come in."

He opened the door wider and stepped to the side to allow Khye into the apartment. They went into his bedroom to chill and talk. He shut the door, giving them privacy. Khye came with a simple peace offering, a bottle of Peach Cîroc, some Sprite to chase it down with, and a pack of fresh cigarettes. Sammy sat at the foot of his bed and leaned back, looking at Khye clothed in her highend gear.

"You look cute," he said.

"Thank you."

There was some minor tension between them, so it was going to take the Cîroc to even things out between them. Sammy got some cups from the kitchen and Khye poured them both a drink. They both lit a cigarette to relax. Sammy sat on his bed, took a few pulls from the cancer stick, looked at Khye without a smile, and dryly said, "So, what's going on with you, bitch? Since you don't have the time to call anybody, return phone calls, or come around because you too busy. I'm your best friend, and look how you treat me over some dick."

"Like you don't go crazy over some dick yourself," Khye said.

"Bitch, this ain't about me, my problems, or my sex life. You the one over here in my room," he said with attitude.

"I know."

"You should know. I'm the one that always got your back and forgiving your trifling ass," Sammy said, flaring up with his hand gestures and slick talk.

"And I will always owe you," Khye replied, trying to smile.

"Yes, you will. Owe me like the U.S. debt."

"Which is why I brought this." She held up the Cîroc.

"You trying to get me drunk and take advantage of me?" said Sammy lightly.

She managed to laugh.

Khye poured herself another drink and downed it like it was water. She had a lot on her mind. She had a lot to say, or confess, and Sammy was the only person she could talk to. She was grateful that he didn't shun her like she had him on a few occasions. She was grateful that he was home and wasn't being an asshole to her. Sammy had always been a great friend to her, but she couldn't say the same for herself.

Sammy took a swig of Cîroc. "Okay bitch, tell mama what the problem is."

Khye sighed heavily and said, "I think I'm losing him."

"Why do you think that?"

"Because, things aren't the same. We haven't fucked in almost a month. He always gone, leaving me home alone. He's changed, Sammy. He's more aloof toward me. And it's only been three months."

"I'll tell you your fuckin' problem, bitch. Any cute face and some good pussy can *get* a rich nigga, but you know what…it takes a real bitch to *keep* a rich nigga."

"So what you saying? I'm not real?"

"You met the nigga on lies and on some fake shit," Sammy said bluntly. "I'm just saying, bitch, niggas like Floyd get bored easily. Yeah, he was feeling your English accent and you a pretty bitch, but what else you got the nigga intrigued on?"

"I cook and shit."

Sammy laughed. "You cook?"

"Yes!"

Chuckling, he replied, "Seeing is believing."

"I'm a bloody damn good woman to him, Sammy."

"Yes, but what else you got going on? Do you speak any languages? Have a trade? Play piano? Have some type of talent? A degree?" Sammy was being facetious to his frenemy.

"Well, I know niggas like Floyd, and all they want is eye candy on their arms. I'm pretty and I stand out always as soon as I open my mouth," Khye spat back.

"Bitch, what you saying? Obviously that ain't keeping your man home at night."

"That's why I'm here, Sammy. I need your help."

"So you think your man is fuckin' the next bitch, huh?" Sammy said.

"He ain't been fuckin' me lately."

"Truth be told, I don't put it past any nigga, feel me bitch? A ho is a ho, and your man, yes, he's a ho. If it walks like a duck, talks like a duck, then chances are, it's a fuckin' duck," Sammy proclaimed.

"Floyd ain't no duck—"

"Bitch, stop being so fuckin' naïve. And I bet you still think he's an audio engineer and he's legit, running a studio and got his hands clean."

"My man is legit," she defended him.

"Dummy, open your eyes and see the light. You acting more blind than Stevie Wonder. From what I heard, your nigga is into everything from Brooklyn to Baltimore, moving that serious yayo, and he got bodies on his conscience, girl. His hands are so dirty, he bleeds mud."

"I know my man, and he's a good dude, Sammy. Yes, he got his ways, we all do. I don't know where you got your information, but it's wrong."

Sammy shook his head at her denial. "Girl, that dick must got you going stupid. Where do you think he get his money from?"

Khye didn't answer him. She refused to believe what she was hearing. It sounded like hate was coming out of Sammy's mouth. She had told Sammy everything about Floyd, and she regretted telling him anything. Sammy was her best friend, and what girl didn't tell her best friend everything? But it was too late. He knew about the studio, the condo, Tatianna, and how Khye had gotten with Floyd.

"He's your business, not mines," Sammy said pointedly.

They continued to drink and talk. Sammy was able to take Khye's mind away from her troubles with his colorful attitude, raw humor, and blunt talk, though it was temporary.

As they were about to finish off the Cîroc Peach, they heard the front door slam and a bunch of men suddenly in the living room. Khye jumped up and asked, "You got company?"

Sammy waved it off, saying, "That's just Able and his gang that can't shoot right, taking over shit like they always do."

But they could shoot right. They were cold-blooded killers.

Khye, being curious, walked to the bedroom door and slowly opened it. She peered around the corner and into the living room and saw at least five thugs occupying the small space in her friend's apartment. They were loud and vulgar, playing rap music, and she could already smell the weed burning.

"What are they up to?" Khye asked Sammy.

"I don't be in my brother's business like that. But they got something big brewing. Lately, I've been seeing some Brooklyn niggas come through here and meet with my brother. You know how Able is, always plotting something, trying to get that money. I wouldn't be surprised if someone was about to get murdered," Sammy said.

"Your brother, he's an issue."

"I know. But let his bitch-ass do whatever, because a bitch like me, I don't have time for it," Sammy said.

Khye stood by the door, eavesdropping, hoping to hear what Able had planned. She didn't know why she was doing it, but she was. It was nosiness. But her nosiness was brief when she saw Able coming her way. She quickly ducked back into the bedroom and pretended to be cool. Able walked into the bedroom without knocking or announcing himself. It angered Sammy. He went off, saying, "Nigga, you don't fuckin' knock. I mean, I could have been naked or sucking dick in here."

"Samuel, don't fuck wit' me, you ain't though," Able said.

"I can't believe we come from the same DNA. You're so fuckin' barbaric."

"Fuck you!"

"No, fuck you!" Sammy retorted.

"Anyway, I came to let you know we gonna be up in here fo' a minute."

"Why?"

"Because we can, nigga. I got shit to take care of," Able said.

Sammy sighed with annoyance. Khye sat silently. Able looked her way and said, "Hey Khye."

"Hey," Khye returned dryly.

The look in Able's eyes gave Khye a chill. He was a scary dude and sometimes made her uncomfortable.

"I heard you fuckin' wit' some nigga from Brooklyn," Able said.

"Yes, and he's none of your business," Sammy said, quickly speaking for her.

"Ain't nobody talkin' to you, little brother."

"Well, I'm talking to you," Sammy shot back.

Khye was ready to leave. With Able in the apartment, she and Sammy weren't about to get any more peace. It was already looking chaotic, their moms at work, niggas filling the apartment, drinking and smoking—Khye being the only female, it was definitely unsettling. Her intuition told her to get up and leave immediately.

"I'll talk to you later, Sammy." Khye stood up and grabbed her purse.

"You leaving already, ma?" Able asked, looking boisterous.

"Yeah, busy day tomorrow."

Khye told Sammy goodbye, pivoted on her wedges, exited the bedroom, and walked through the valley of wolves in the living room. Heavy weed smoke saturated the air, and a thug was lounging around in every direction. Those who had fucked Khye already yearned for her sex again, and everyone else wanted sloppy seconds. They heard she had a man now, but they didn't care. A slut like Khye, in their eyes, was always going to be the skeezer of the town.

Khye was able to leave the apartment without an incident. The wolves had showed their sharp teeth, but somehow, she was able to back them down. She hurried out into the street and moved toward her vehicle. The emptiness of the night sprawled from block to block. She hit the alarm button to her Range, deactivating the loud siren, and as she stepped closer, she heard, "Khye!"

She turned around to see Sarah staring at her. Sarah stabbed a smile at her daughter. Khye, however, didn't look too sociable. She looked expressionless—burning to get away. Her mother was looking for something, some friendliness, a word or two. However, Khye gave her nothing, just sour narcissism and a blank gaze. She turned away from her mother and climbed into her truck. Sarah was bowled over and wordless by her daughter's hurtful action. Khye started the ignition and drove away without so much as a wave. It almost felt like she was giving her mother her ass to kiss—and after everything she had done for her. Sarah almost cried.

TWENTY-FOUR

Sarah was pregnant, and she was confident it was Marcus's and was sure he would do the right thing and take care of her and his unborn baby. She missed him. She hadn't spoken to Marcus in over three weeks. It seemed like he had fallen off the face of the earth. Using her prepaid cell phone, she'd blow up his phone night and day, melting away her minutes. He either was ignoring her or something had happened. Was it something tragic? Had his wife found out about their affair and threatened divorce? She had no way of knowing. Sarah had no other way to reach him, no Facebook page, no email address, no home address, or any idea where he worked. He came and went like a burglar in the night.

She lingered in the bedroom, and for the past week she kept to herself, needing some solitude. Everyone in the apartment came and went, but Sarah stayed home, gradually falling into depression. She had a new baby growing inside of her, and without any support, life looked gloomy. Briefly seeing Khye again the other night had made her sad and a little jealous. The Range Rover her daughter was cruising around in was the best gift any woman could get from a man, second from diamonds and cash. Every day she thought about taking her shit to the next level with who and how. Though she was pregnant, she lit up a cigarette and took a few sips of vodka. She took a pull from the cancer stick and stared out the bedroom window. The cold fall had made its way through the area, blanketing the last week of October with freezing rain and a few premature snow flurries.

The nicotine eased her mind, the alcohol calmed her nerves. Depression weighed down heavily on her as life felt like it was becoming a burden. She was dead broke. Her life was a sad country strong. To cheer herself up, she got naked and donned a long trench coat and some high heels. If she couldn't see Marcus, then there were other niggas that were vying for her time.

Out the door she went, up the stairway and knocking on Gino's door. He would never turn her away. Gino always loved him a snow-white beauty with that liquid paradise between her legs. Though it had been a while since they'd fucked, there was no way he could resist any of her good loving.

"Yo, who that?" Gino called out.

"It's me," she said.

Hearing the accent and seeing her through the peephole, he smirked. The door opened, and Gino appeared in the doorway shirtless, gun tucked into his waistband. He seemed hesitant to let her inside. She could hear Rick Ross in the background and smell the weed burning from the hallway. Gino took extra notice of Sarah in her trench coat and heels and said, "What's good, ma? You up this way on some late-night shit, huh?"

"You know why. Let me in," she said.

"Now is not a good time, ma."

"Why not?"

"It's just not," he said, not caring to explain himself.

Hearing the rejection made Sarah upset. She wanted some dick and she needed to borrow some cash from him. Out of all people, she didn't think Gino would turn her away. His dick was always hard and ready for her.

She wasn't about to be rejected by some low-level gangbanger. She didn't like hearing the word no. Immediately, she assumed he had some other bitch in the apartment. She had no right to get jealous—

they weren't an item—but there was something about coming second to some other hood rat that was unsettling. She needed him right now. Her mind had been trampled with thoughts of Marcus and the baby, and his whereabouts, and she needed to fuck the next nigga to try and escape the emotions.

"Come back tomorrow, ma, and we could have some fun." He smiled, she didn't.

"Tomorrow!" she exclaimed. "If I leave right now, I'm not coming back."

"Stop being like that. I got serious business right now."

"Serious business. What bitch you got in there that's more serious business than me?" she said.

"Making that money."

She didn't believe him. Her emotions were running on high. Running on impulse, she suddenly shoved by him and pushed open the door wider, gazing inside his place. To her surprise, there wasn't another naked bitch in his apartment, just gun-toting goons smoking, cleaning guns and looking ready for a war. Sarah stared into the gun-filled room like a deer caught in headlights.

"Oh." she uttered faintly.

"Damn, ma, I told you I'm fuckin' busy right now," Gino shouted.

"I'm sorry."

"Damn, Gino, you got bitches charging up in the spot like they police," one of the seated thugs said.

"She leaving," said Gino. "My bad."

"Yo nigga, control ya ho," another thug added.

Gino quickly grabbed Sarah and pulled her out into the hallway. What Sarah caught a glimpse of, was Able, The Gun, and several other killers becoming locked, stocked, and loaded. They had more guns in the apartment than a small armory.

"What was that about?" Sarah asked.

Closing the door behind him, and stepping into the hallway, he frowned Sarah's way and said, "That right there ain't ya business."

"I didn't mean—"

"Just go," Gino said rudely.

Sarah tightened the straps to her trench coat, covering her nudeness completely underneath, and pivoted on her heels. She started to fade away from what she saw. Gino looked her way for a moment and then slid back into his apartment. She screwed up. She was lucky they didn't take the incident too serious and punish her.

Sarah was about to take the stairway back down to her apartment, but before she could enter the stairwell, she was shocked to see Sammy stepping off the elevator on Gino's floor. Taken aback by his presence, before she could speak, Sammy said, "You know me, Ms. Sarah, I'm everywhere and I gotta get my high on."

"You don't have to explain yourself to me."

He looked her up and down, taking in the trench coat and heels, and said, "And you don't have to explain yourself either."

She faintly grinned, and they both went their separate ways.

***

Sarah lifted her T-shirt up to her tits, showing her stomach in the mirror from the side view and imagined what it would look and feel like being pregnant again. Her slim figure was impressive for her age. She wasn't showing yet. She blew air out of her mouth. She was six weeks pregnant, and still no word from Marcus. It had been a long time since she'd last given birth. Maisie, her youngest, was thirteen now. She'd had all three of her kids at a very young age with the same man. Now, carrying another man's baby, she had a choice to make: to keep it or get rid of it. Not hearing from Marcus at all, her decision was leaning toward an abortion. There was no way she was going to raise a baby alone, in poverty and fatherless. She wanted to use the baby growing inside of her as an instrument for trapping a man for his wealth—the same cliché: snare a rich nigga for child support. Her plan was backfiring on her, though. If she couldn't contact Marcus, how could she give him the good news?

She lingered in front of the mirror, contemplating her next move. She breathed out, feeling stressed out. She lowered her shirt and turned away from her reflection. An abortion was expensive. Five hundred dollars. She didn't have the money now, and the later she waited to have the procedure done, the higher the cost. She was still indecisive.

Lying across her bed, staring up at the ceiling, her cell phone rang out of the blue. It was near her reach, but she hesitated to answer it. It could be anyone calling. Sarah wasn't in the mood to converse with anyone. Her mind was in a haze of worry and apprehension. She let it ring and go to her voicemail. Seconds later, it rang again. This time, she looked at the caller ID indifferently and her eyes sprung open abruptly with excitement. It was Marcus calling her, finally! She immediately answered.

"Hello," she couldn't hide the thrill in her voice, expressing how good it was to hear from him.

"Hey, beautiful," he said.

"Ohmygod, I've been trying to call you for weeks now. Where have you been?"

"Out of the country, on business," he said.

She wanted to jump through the phone line and see him. She knew why he was calling—he wanted some pussy.

"You got time for me?" he said.

"Yes!" her answer jumped out like a fast pitch going 99 mph.

"Okay, an hour from now, where do you want me to come get you?"

"Harlem, pick me up from my building."

It was different than their regular rendezvous. Marcus wasn't expecting her to say that. "Your building?" he said, sounding surprised.

"Yes."

"What about your husband? Your family?"

"They're not around."

"You sure about this?"

"I am. I miss you so much," she said.

"I miss you, too, and my dick misses you even more," he said.

It was all about sex—always about sex. Their relationship was one-dimensional, but Sarah was about to drop the bomb on him. She didn't want to give him the news through the phone. She wanted to tell him in person, see his reaction, and make it clear to him, she was carrying his baby and she was going to keep it. Now was her chance to make something happen for herself.

Hanging up, she quickly searched for the perfect and sexiest outfit. She decided on a skirt, a midriff-baring turtleneck, her high heels, and a fall jacket. She looked absolutely amazing. She was ready under the hour and strutted out her apartment door with a wide smile on her face.

Marcus turned the corner in his burgundy Escalade and came to a stop in front of the building where Sarah was patiently waiting. She strutted to his truck feeling healthy with happiness. She quickly got in the passenger seat and kissed him on the lips.

He smiled at her and said, "You look great."

"Thank you. You look good, too, baby."

She eyed his sharp attire—a signature grey two-button wool pleated suit. It was obvious he had just come from work. His cologne made her nostrils buzz, smelling fresh and clean. The gold Rolex he wore thinly showed through the cuffs of his shirt. He was always subtle with fashion and jewelry.

The sight of him made the place between her legs start to prickle. She couldn't take her eyes off of him. Three weeks was too long of a time to go without him. She felt like a heroin junkie who needed her fix. She couldn't wait to fuck him and tell him the good news, or tell him the good news, and then fuck him. The order didn't matter, as long as she was in his presence again. Sarah was ready to whip out his dick and throw her lips around it.

"So, you live here," he said.

She wasn't proud of it. She could only imagine the house he lived in with his family, probably three times the size of her tiny apartment and more the space—backyard, in-ground pool, long porch, circle driveway, two car garage, and the latest amenities. She wanted to see it.

"Don't remind me," Sarah said.

Marcus put the truck in drive and slowly moved away from the curb. Sarah wished her daughter could see her now, so she could prove to Khye she wasn't the only one who could snatch up a baller.

Marcus drove through Harlem and came to a stop at the Aloft hotel on Frederick Douglas Boulevard. This time, they found a location closer to her home. She stepped out, gazing up at the new hotel in Harlem, right across the street from the Magic Johnson Theater.

They quickly got a room—a loft inspired area with an oversized shower and plush platform beds. Marcus was ready to sexually ravage his mistress. He looked at her like a well cooked meal and immediately started to undress himself. Sarah didn't know how she was going to tell him the news. But it had to be today. There was no telling when she was going to see him again.

"Come here, baby," Marcus called out to her with his arms slightly spread open, indicating he wanted her to fall into them. He had his shirt unbuttoned, revealing the muscular six-pack that rippled across his stomach.

"You missed me?" he said.

"You know I did."

"Show me how much," he said with a lecherous grin for her to see, now rubbing his crotch and growing hard for her.

She had so many questions to ask him, like where did he go abroad? Did he go alone or with his wife and family? Why no contact? Why now? She wanted him badly, but something suddenly made her hesitate to undress and take his dick the way he liked it—freakish.

She sighed, knowing it was best to tell him first before she gave him the goodies and the business.

He wanted sex and made it clear he didn't have any time for a decent conversation. It was clear to anyone that Sarah was a world-class slut of epic proportions. But since finding out about her pregnancy, the one she deliberately made happen, she started to look at life differently. She was afraid. Marcus stared at her like a sex-crazed bloodhound. He pulled out his big dick and started masturbating, waiting for her to help him finish. Sarah wanted and needed to feel desirable. All her life, she had an intense, deep seeded need to feel sexy, and that led to late-night sexing with different men to fulfill her need to feel wanted. It was her compulsion. She wallowed in immoral sexual behavior night and day, always looking for "love". Nevertheless, at thirty-five years old, it was suddenly getting old and she had nothing to show for her promiscuous behavior but three kids, ghetto living, and not a dollar to her name.

Marcus was in full stride, jerking his big dick in front of her, anticipating her company. "You gonna make me handle this big dick alone, or you coming to help?"

She managed to smile. She stepped closer, slowly undressing for him and wanting to feel him inside of her. But she needed him to know. And before things became too hot and heavy between them, she looked Marcus squarely in his eyes and uttered the words, "I'm pregnant!"

He stopped mid-stroke, like he had been hit with a freeze machine.

"What?" he simply uttered.

"I said, I'm pregnant, and it's yours."

"You pregnant," he repeated in an incredulous tone.

She nodded.

"You have to get rid of it," he said coldly.

"What? Why?" Sarah was shocked by his words.

"I'm too old to be having babies, and besides, I'm married with three kids already."

"But this is our baby."

"And I don't want any more kids, especially from my mistress. How would that fuckin' look?" he exclaimed.

"Are you bloody serious?"

"Yes!"

Suddenly, the passion and fire in the room had been put out by the abrupt tension between them. Sarah didn't think the outcome would turn out like this. They had known each other for months, he always treated her well, but now, Marcus had distorted into some cold, uncaring man.

"I'm keeping it." She stood her ground, hoping it would change his mind.

"We'll see about that," he threatened.

He put his dick back into his pants and fastened them. It was clear no one was fucking tonight. They started arguing. He belittled her, called her a nasty whore and a lot more unflattering things. Sarah was nothing more than a fuck toy to him, a thing to be used. Why had she been so naïve?

"You know what, I liked you, thought we could continue this for a very long time and satisfy each other," he said, quickly getting dressed. "Obviously, I was fuckin' wrong about you. You ruined a good thing, Sarah—a very good thing. You know how many bitches would love to be in your position?"

Sarah was fuming while watching Marcus rashly throw his suit back together, but looking more imperfect than before.

"I'm no baby daddy, and definitely not yours," he spewed out.

What did he think what was going to happen when he went inside her raw repeatedly and came?

Once Marcus was fully dressed, he spun to make his exit, but not before saying, "I don't want any part of you or that baby. Lose my fuckin' number, because I damn sure will lose yours."

He walked away, but with a sudden afterthought, he turned back around. Sarah hoped he changed his mind. He reached into his suit jacket and pulled out the thick locket she gave him for his birthday. She was amazed to see that he had it on him.

"I don't need or want this. It was a cheap gift from a cheap whore," he exclaimed, tossing it in her direction. It fell to her feet and her teary eyes looked at it.

Marcus left.

Sarah dropped to her knees, now in full-blown tears. She felt sick to her stomach. What now? What was she going to do now? Her hopes and dreams about coming up like Khye walked out of the door, and she knew he wasn't coming back.

TWENTY-FIVE

The month of October came and went like a tropical storm. It had been rough for Khye, up and down, but she was still in the game and playing hard. She tried and did everything to get back into her man's good graces. She was on her best behavior, reforming, changing her entire act—cooking, cleaning, sexing her man down nonstop, and she even stopped smoking for him. For a moment, it seemed it was all working in her favor. Floyd was loving her again, paying her some attention, treating her like she was his girl. If he was still fooling around with the next bitch, she couldn't tell.

On a good night, her mind would be awash with waves of lust. His dick was being good to her. Her head game became the bomb; she would engulf his dick with her mouth and take him all the way in. She became his personal sex slave, whatever he wanted to do, or try, she was down.

And tonight, the sudden and unexpected attack on his dick as he slept surprised Floyd and his hands quickly went to her head. The feel of her brown tresses with his fingers through her silky, long hair was smooth as her head bobbed back and forth, swallowing his dick, wanting him to come inside her mouth. She worked his dick inside her mouth, coiling her tongue around the mushroom tip, stroking it up and down with her soft, manicured hands. He squirmed in her sensual grasp, feeling her warm, wet mouth appease him.

"Oh, baby," his lips released faintly.

She was his baby, and Khye wasn't about to let him forget it.

She sucked his dick with no plan on slowing down until he came in her mouth.

Floyd breathed out like a deflating balloon. He looked down at her as she stared up at him. She then rose up from her position, her hands sliding across his chest as she rose. She wanted to nestle against him for a moment; enjoy his body and maybe have some pillow talk. He was visibly satisfied.

Sooner than expected, he was fast asleep again, nestled in Khye's arms.

The next morning, Floyd woke up early, got dressed, and was out the door before Khye would awake. He had somewhere to be, and it was urgent he get there. The forecast called for cold and light rain on the November day. Thanksgiving was right around the corner. He'd promised to spend it with Khye, but he really wanted to take Rita away somewhere special. She still factored heavily into his life, and he felt he loved her.

Floyd walked out the front door, hurried down the stairway with his car keys in hand, and moved toward his Benz. He jumped inside, slightly leaned his seat back, changed the music, and took off, not even giving his passionate night with Khye a second thought.

He drove to the Bronx and knocked on Rita's door. She answered, clad in a black silk kimono robe. Her smile was radiant. He lit up every time he saw her. They hugged, and then kissed passionately. He walked inside and the door closed behind him.

Her lips, her tongue, her saliva were all just as sweet as the nectar that she was leaking from below. Floyd could not get enough of her, as his tongue probed deeper and her succulent lips became more insistent to keep him close to her. Floyd wanted nothing more than to kiss Rita and never stop. One of her hands slid between them and began to caress his raging lust.

"I want you inside me, Floyd," she purred, using her other hand to press on his chest and break their steamy kiss.

Floyd was ready to fulfill her promise. Since they'd met, they had felt inseparable.

"I love you," he sincerely proclaimed.

"I love you, too."

They kissed again, undressing each other. Her voice oozed sex. His eyes flared with a hungry lust, as Rita reached into his jeans and grabbed his hardening manhood. He moaned as she fondled him.

They made passionate, strong love that morning, that afternoon, and all throughout the evening. When his cell phone rang, seeing it was Khye calling, he ignored it. Though he was in love with Rita, he had a bad habit of keeping two women around in his life—and he always felt the new chick more strongly than his previous one. Khye was fading from his heart. Rita was the successor. He was ready to commit to her fully.

The following week, it was about Rita. In fact, he was so sure about her, as he cruised in his CL600, he made a phone call to his personal jeweler in the diamond district, Gabriel.

"Floyd, my man," Gabriel greeted happily.

"What's good, Gab," as he called his jeweler.

"Making money, making shines," Gabriel said. "You looking to come through, cop another piece?"

"Yeah, in due time. Looking for sumthin' special to show off for the holidays."

"You know I got you."

"I know."

"When you coming by?" Gabriel asked.

"Around the holidays, and I want the back room."

"The back room," Gabriel replied, sounding off guard and surprised.

"Yeah, the back room," Floyd repeated.

"Okay, this one, she must be very special."

"She is," Floyd said.

He hung up and proceeded home.

When he arrived at the condo, Khye had cooked a full meal for him and was waiting for him in her sexiest, most revealing outfit. She greeted her man with hugs and kisses, and the smell of a home cooked-meal plagued his nostrils. She had outdone herself, but Floyd wasn't moved or touched by her sexy and good deed. His mind was elsewhere.

Kissing him lovingly, while wrapping her arms around him, Khye said, "We still on for Thanksgiving, dinner at Mr. Chow, right?"

Floyd barely listened. He nodded aloofly and removed himself from her welcoming touch.

"Yeah," he dryly replied.

Khye smiled.

"I know you are hungry, baby."

"Actually, I'm not."

"But I made your favorite—mashed potatoes and lamb."

"I'll eat it later. I'm tired. I'm going to bed," he said.

Khye sighed heavily, feeling she wasted her time slaving in the kitchen and looking nice for her man. She watched him walk into the bedroom and shut the door. She didn't know if she should be pissed off or worried. With Thanksgiving a few days away, nothing felt cheery or thankful in her house. With her romantic dinner being wasted, she dumped everything into the trash and shut everything down, trying to hold back the tears. She hadn't smoked in weeks, but tonight, she needed a cigarette. While Floyd was in the bedroom, doing whatever, Khye left the apartment and went to the nearest bodega to grab a pack of Newports and she nearly went through an entire pack that night, feeling stressed out.

✳✳✳

Floyd and Khye rode to Harlem in complete silence. Lately, their conversation and communication had been sparse. Their chemistry was frizzling out, and the sex becoming dry and almost nonexistent again. It was the day before Thanksgiving, and they were on their way to her old neighborhood because Sammy called her phone earlier and told her that her mother had been sick. Although they had their differences, Sarah was still her mother, and the way Sammy made it sound, she was really ill. So Khye wanted to check up on her before they went to Times Square to catch a Broadway play. Floyd had two tickets to *Of Mice and Men,* and then tomorrow, a fine dinner at Mr. Chow—one of the most beautiful and successful restaurants in New York City.

There was no way Floyd was going to spend Thanksgiving in the hood. He was too good for that.

The black on black Range Rover came to a stop in front of the project building on 132nd Street. Floyd was driving. It was a cold day, so they both were wrapped up in stylish mink coats and in their finest attire—looking like a power couple.

"I'll be right back, okay, baby?" Khye said, leaning toward Floyd to give him a kiss on the lips. He seemed somewhat reserved, but kissed her anyway.

He didn't want to go inside. He didn't want to be around her family. He didn't like any of them at all.

"Don't take long. Ten minutes, tops," he instructed.

She nodded.

Lingering in front of the building were three men, and they were all familiar with Khye and her former reputation. The minute she jumped out of the Range Rover, all eyes were on her. She strolled their way looking like perfection, more dressed up than Beyoncé at an award show. Her red bottoms click-clacked against the cracked pavement as she tried to avoid eye contact.

As she walked by them innocently, one of the goons grinned and said, "Hey, Khye," and as she went by him, he tapped her on her ass just for fun. Floyd observed the disrespect and quickly became troubled by what he saw. He didn't waste any time in confronting the issue. He grabbed his pistol from underneath the seat and jumped out of the truck scowling like a maniac. Khye couldn't even get a word out, as Floyd was on the young goon like stink on shit, pistol-whipping him in front of his friends. The butt of the .9mm crashed against his skull repeatedly, spewing blood and crippling him to the concrete.

Khye was shocked. The young dude was harmless. She had fucked him a few times, but it was a while back. She barely remembered his dick. Floyd beat him down to a bloody pulp then pointed the gun at his friends and shouted, "What, y'all niggas want some too!"

They took a step back from the gun and threw up their hands up to show they weren't a threat to him.

"Nah, my dude. We good, ain't no beef," one said.

Floyd then turned his anger toward Khye and shouted, "You fucked this nigga, too?"

Khye was taken aback by the assault. It happened so quickly. She didn't answer him right away. He shouted again, "Bitch, you fucked him?"

"It was a while back, baby. I was a different person before I met you," she admitted.

"You lying, cheating, manipulative fuckin' whore!" he shouted. "I'm fuckin' done wit' you!"

"What?" Khye said.

The incident was the straw that broke the camel's back—in this case, Floyd's back. He was so angry, it looked like he had transformed into the Incredible Hulk. He almost killed the young hoodlum. The gun was covered in his blood, and his friends were helpless to aid him. Floyd became a lunatic.

"You know what, I want you gone, bitch! I want your shit out of my crib," he said.

"Baby, no! Don't do this to me. Please, baby, I love you," she pleaded.

She ran toward him, grabbing onto him as if he was the Messiah leaving her out of heaven. Her manicured nails dug into his mink coat like talons from a hawk snatching up prey from the ground. Floyd pushed Khye away from him with brute force, knocking her to the ground, embarrassing her in front of the growing crowd that heard the commotion.

"Fuck you!" he cursed. "Get ya shit, and get the fuck out my crib. I never wanna see you again."

He hurried to the Range and jumped inside, rapidly throwing it into drive and sped off, tires screeching. Khye quickly picked herself up, her pants torn from the fall, her tears streaking her face, and her pride crushed. She chased after Floyd as he drove away, leaving her in the projects.

"Floyd, no! Please! I'm sorry! Baby, come back, don't do this to me!" she shrieked in horror.

She fell to her knees in the middle of the street, crying hysterically, and watched the Range Rover—her truck—disappear into the night. She didn't know what to do. Everyone stood around her, watching, whispering, and some snickering at her humiliation. It was a nightmare. She wanted it to be a nightmare she could wake up from. But it wasn't. Everything was real. Floyd was gone.

TWENTY-SIX

Floyd was hell-bent on kicking Khye out of his condo. He was taking the truck, the jewelry, and leaving her with nothing. To add insult to injury, he was ready to move Rita in right away. Khye found herself in the same predicament she'd put Tatianna in a few months back. The shoe was now on the other foot, and it cut her deep to the core.

Floyd decided to make moves, first calling Gabriel again and heading to the diamond district in the late hour. He was unaware that he was being closely followed. A dark blue Ford Taurus went where he went, scoping his every movement, trying to scope out his key locations from Harlem to Brooklyn. So far, they knew about the studio in the Heights, Rita's apartment in the Bronx, and a few other significant locations around the city he frequented. The one place they didn't know about was where he laid his head at nights—his condo in Brooklyn.

Floyd was so agitated, he didn't pick up on the tail behind him. He continued driving to the Diamond District in the city and was about to meet with Gabriel, after asking him to stay late.

He stepped into the jewelry shop nestled between numerous boutiques in the middle of the block, and shook hands with Gabriel. He was a thin, very well-dressed Jewish man, wearing a tight yarmulke on his head and a rich smile.

"Floyd, you are looking healthy. To what do I owe the pleasure?"

"I'm looking for an engagement ring," Floyd said flatly.

"You came to the right place, my friend," Gabriel said, smiling.

He lifted his hand, indicating for them to head into a private back room where he would be able to display an assortment of expensive diamond rings while they sat secluded from the public.

Both men were very familiar with each other. Floyd had been doing business with Gabriel for nearly two years, and in total, he spent nearly a quarter of a million dollars in the store—purchasing everything from custom-made diamond pendants to tennis bracelets and pinky rings.

Floyd followed behind Gabriel into a concealed room. Inside, security cameras were strategically situated above. It was soundproof and furnished with a long, mahogany table with several high-back leather chairs, empty black walls, and a few beverages and snacks for the customers' enjoyment. Gabriel removed a black briefcase from a steel vault, sat opposite Floyd, and presented him with a healthy choice of rings.

"Here is nothing but the best for you, my friend," said Gabriel.

Floyd smiled. Every ring was flawless and made a statement. He leaned closer, inspecting the merchandise. Gabriel knew a lot about diamonds—the color, the stones, how to detect if they were real or not. He had his jeweler's loupe to inspect the diamonds. Gabriel had been selling and buying diamonds for over twenty years. Floyd spent fifteen minutes in the room. He finally picked out the perfect ring—a flawless, brilliant-cut center diamond engagement ring that cost nearly twenty thousand dollars.

"This is it," he said.

The ring cost $20K, but Floyd only had ten stacks on him. He wanted the ring tonight. Knowing Floyd was good for it; Gabriel took the ten thousand as down payment and allowed Floyd to take the ring with the promise to pay the full balance by tomorrow evening.

"I know your money is good, my friend. Tomorrow evening, same time, come by and we'll settle what you owe. Now go, and make her a very happy woman," Gabriel said.

"You good peoples, my nigga," Floyd said. "Rita's gonna love this ring."

He left the shop with the ring in a velvet ring box and climbed back into the Range Rover. He called Rita to find out she was at the studio recording. It's what he loved about her; she was ambitious and always working. She was ready to make a name for herself, and Floyd needed a woman like her around.

He was excited.

Though he hadn't known her for too long, he immediately knew Rita was the one for him. She was smart, talented, and innocent, and she was about to become a superstar. He just hoped she accepted his proposal.

As he made his way to the studio, he called Carlito to tell him the good news.

"What's good, my nigga?" Carlito answered.

"Everything. That bitch is out of my life," he said, referring to Khye.

"About time."

"And I'm about to pop the question."

"What?"

"Yeah," he said.

"Rita?"

"She the only one I love."

Carlito laughed. "Boy, you a trip."

"She the one for me, Carlito," Floyd said.

"If you say so," he returned, sounding doubtful. "But if you're happy, then I'm happy."

"Oh, I'm very happy. And I'm gonna be more happy when she says yes, and when we get this label and studio popping and start making this legit money."

"I feel you. But look, you got that forty stashed nicely right?" Carlito said about the drug shipment they received from Ruiz on consignment.

"Yeah, I got it secured," Floyd let known.

"Cool, cuz we got people waiting on delivery."

"I know."

Floyd got onto the West Side Highway and did 60 mph northbound, hurrying toward Washington Heights and yearning to be with his lady. He felt good and excited. He was making money and in love, once again, and felt nothing could go wrong in his life. There were minor issues to deal with—warring with Rash, and Khye—but he was confident it would all work out.

It was a clear and cool night on the West Side. Traffic was flowing, and with lights blazing from every skyscraper and the vague bridge outline in the background, New York was definitely holding true to its nickname—The City that Never Sleeps. Neither did Floyd. He and the Big Apple coexisted.

He arrived at Slow Pullz Studio late that night. He parked his truck around the corner from the entrance and walked into the studio feeling a little bit of uneasiness. He was never nervous, but proposing to Rita had his heart fluttering. However, tonight felt like the perfect night to do it. It was a full moon, and he was about to get rid of Khye and move on. He walked through the lobby, took the elevator to the studio floor, and stepped into the control room just in time as Rita was ending her session in the booth. White boy was in the room, seated behind the mixing console and creating some of the hottest beats. Floyd greeted him with glad hands and smiled at his beauty on the other side of the glass. She matched his smile, clearly excited that he showed up.

"How she do?" he asked white boy.

"She did her thing, Floyd. I mean, she got a phenomenal voice."

Floyd smiled. "That's my girl."

Rita couldn't hurry out of the recording booth fast enough to greet her man with a loving hug and some heated kisses. She threw her arms around him and kissed him with passion. Floyd embraced onto her softness like he never wanted to let her go.

"I missed you," she announced.

"I missed you, too."

As they embraced, Floyd's cell phone rang. He looked; it was Khye. He sent her call to voicemail. Soon, he was about to block all of her calls. She was becoming nothing but a past affair and an insignificant memory to him.

"Who's that?" Rita asked.

"Nobody important," he explained astutely. "You're the only one important in my life baby."

"Aaaah, you mean it?"

He nodded. "In fact, I'm about to show you how much I mean it."

He took her by her hands and led her away from white boy and the control room. They went toward the back of the studio, into a private room where he planned on popping the question. Floyd felt a little giddy. The feeling was new to him. He didn't want to let go of her soft hands. He couldn't stop gazing into her eyes. With Rita, he didn't mind showing her some public affection. In one motion, he dropped down on one knee and slid the velvet ring box from his mink coat pocket. Rita became wide-eyed, knowing what was about to come next.

"Ohmygod!" she uttered, throwing her hand over her mouth, looking down at Floyd in wonderment.

Floyd opened the ring box to reveal the large diamond engagement ring inside. She was astounded by it. It was the biggest rock she had ever seen in her life.

"Baby, you know I love you so much, and I know you're the one for me. So, will you marry me?"

There was a moment of hesitation from her end, and then she gladly said, "Yes!"

She dropped to his level and hugged him so tightly; it felt like his eyeballs were about to pop out of his socket. He was thrilled though. They kissed fervently. Floyd was changing his life, or trying to, and when she became a number one pop star, he was going to be the reason why she shined.

Everything was going perfectly. White boy was putting the finishing touches on a few tracks, off in his own world as Floyd and Rita had their privacy, enjoying their intimate moment.

There was a buzz from the security door. White boy glanced at the security camera overseeing the area and noticed a police officer outside, flashing his badge, waiting to be buzzed inside. He simply pushed the button to allow the cop inside, having respect for the law and not knowing what was about to come next.

The door to the studio opened and suddenly, three masked gunmen came charging inside wildly with their guns showing and screaming. Before white boy could react, he was shot in the head and collapsed face down on the mixing console, his blood spilling over the machine.

Hearing the gunshot, Floyd raced toward the door and saw the gunmen approaching the room. Rita was in a panic, shrieking when she heard the shot, instantly giving away their position.

"Shit!" he uttered.

He was defenseless, having left his pistol in the truck outside. He tried to think fast, shutting the door and locking it, this being his only line of defense. He frantically searched the room to find a weapon to protect himself and Rita, but their options were limited. There was nothing sharp or useful, just recording equipment and a few chairs.

"What's happening?" Rita cried out, her face flushed with fear.

"Just be cool," Floyd said, trying to follow his own advice.

Abruptly, the door to the restricted room was kicked open forcefully, the glass shattering, and three masked gunmen came flying into the room like wild monkeys. Floyd swiftly came from behind the door, charging and tackling one of the gunmen like a linebacker drilling a quarterback from the blindside. He was ready to fight for his life and tried disarming one of the gunmen. It was a clean shoulder to shoulder hit, throwing his attacker to the ground, gun clattering from his hand. Floyd kept coming, smashing his elbow into the man's skull, trying to take him out. But it was a losing battle as soon as it started. He was outnumbered. As he struggled with one, the second gunman fired a shot from behind him.

Boc!

The bullet tore through Floyd's back and pushed him forward. Rita screamed.

Boc! Boc!

Two more bullets tore through Floyd's body, and he fell to his knees.

"Yeah, muthafucka!" one of the gunmen shouted.

Floyd stumbled near Rita, his breathing becoming labored and his shirt turning crimson under the mink coat from the three gunshot wounds in his back. He was on his knees, knowing this was his end. His face was ashen and his eyes manifested defeat. The third gunman stormed his way with an intense scowl under the mask, and thrust the .45 to the back of his head and fired, blowing Floyd's brains out. It was unnecessary. He was already dead.

Rita screamed so loud, it was piercing.

"Shut up, bitch!" The gunman stretched his arm her way with the same .45 that had just shot her fiancé, and he fired.

The bullet ripped through her front skull, and she dropped like a sack of potatoes, collapsing over Floyd's body. The gunmen stood over their gruesome work, admiring their kill like it was artwork. One gunman, with a keen eye, snatched the huge sparkling diamond ring off Rita's finger.

"Let's go!" he shouted.

No hesitation—they fled the crime scene, succeeding in what they had come to do: kill a drug kingpin. The two innocent causalities were something extra, not planned. They didn't care; it was all part of the game.

TWENTY-SEVEN

Khye was in shock. Everything had happened so fast that it was still hard to register in her mind that Floyd ended their relationship and left her stranded in Harlem like a two-dollar whore. She had never seen him so upset. She saw it in his eyes, that he meant every word he said. He wanted her out of his apartment. She didn't want to leave. She didn't want to go back to her parents' place. How could she go back to the hood, humiliated? They would talk about her and mock her.

She rushed home via cab, and he wasn't there. She was hoping he would be, but he wasn't. She was still devastated about everything. It was all falling apart. One incident and her masquerade was coming undone at the seams.

She called Floyd relentlessly, but he wasn't answering his phone. Each and every one of her calls went to voicemail. She left him countless messages, apologizing, begging and pleading, wanting a second chance. She cried for hours, not giving up, ready to fight.

Floyd wasn't picking up, but Sammy did. Heartbroken and feeling dejected, she poured out her emotions to her friend, and she and Sammy talked for hours. He was the one person able to console her and talk to her.

"Girl, be strong, he'll come back," Sammy said.

"I love him so much, Sammy. I can't go on without him."

"Yes you can, Khye. He ain't air, bitch. You can breathe without him.

Shit happens. If he comes back, good, I think. And if he don't, bitch, you're stronger than that. Don't let some dick cripple your well-being," Sammy bluntly told her.

She heard him talk, but she really wasn't listening. She was anguished with worry and distress. She locked herself in the bedroom and folded into the fetal position, thinking that she would beg on her hands and knees to be forgiven before she would allow him to kick her out.

***

She cried herself to sleep that night. She couldn't stop thinking about him. All night, Khye laid in the fetal position on his bed, curled up like a ball with the phone in her hand. She woke up to her cell phone ringing. It sparked her fully awake suddenly, hoping it was Floyd calling. He wasn't home yet, and she was becoming worried.

Her bags were already packed and were placed by the door, but there was still a glimmer of hope that they could rekindle things—maybe she could convince him to allow her to stay. Giving up wasn't in her blood.

Hearing her phone ring in the late morning, she felt that hope had come alive and Floyd was finally returning her numerous phone calls. She quickly answered, anticipating hearing his voice. "Hello?"

"Khye, it's Sammy," he said.

Her hope deflated quickly like a balloon being popped.

"What?"

"Are you watching the news?" he said quickly.

"No."

"Turn on the news now! Hurry up!" The sound of his voice was as demanding as a drill sergeant.

Khye hurried out of bed, not knowing what was going on. She wormed her hand through the sheets searching for the remote control, finding it by the foot of the bed and immediately hit the power button to the 42-inch flatscreen in the room. The TV came alive with a daytime talk show; she turned to the news and there it was, Floyd's place—Slow Pullz Studio.

Khye perked up, her eyes glued to the TV and seeing the horror happening right in front of her eyes. The broadcast reported, "Three brutally murdered in Washington Heights Studio." The news flashed police cars in front of the studio and a body being carried out the building and placed into a white coroner's van. Khye's heart sank into the pit of her stomach.

She turned it up and heard the report. It was still unclear what and why it happened, but the facts were: three dead, two males and one female. The media weren't releasing any names at the moment, but in her heart, Khye knew Floyd was one of the murdered victims.

She couldn't think. Her eyes were flooded with tears. It felt like she was having a panic attack. Sammy was still on the phone, in her ear, asking her too many questions that she didn't have any answers to. It was too much. She hung up on him and clicked off the TV like it would erase the pain. She climbed back into bed and cried her eyes out. Her sobs echoed so loudly, in the now quiet and still apartment.

Several hours later, she woke up with the bedroom sheets stained with her tears and hoped it was all a terrible dream. But with Floyd's absence from her side and the stillness in the bedroom, her heart hastily took her back to that awful feeling. It wasn't a dream. It was all real. The news media was all over the story, especially after the names of the victims had been released. Every news station was swarming outside of Slow Pullz Studio, cameras flicking away, with live coverage of every square inch outside the building, and looky-loos standing outside the crime scene.

The news of Floyd being murdered traveled so fast through the Tri-State area, like lightning speed, that Khye's phone started to blow up. She refused to talk to anyone. She was devastated.

Sammy continued to call her phone. She only picked up for him. She sounded drained and defeated.

"Khye, I'm coming over there, and I'm not taking no for an answer," he said. "You don't need to be alone right now."

She didn't refute him. She just sat there in a zombielike state and huffed, staring blankly at the bedroom walls. How was she going to cope with the loss of him? She missed him already. For a brief moment, she felt suicidal, yearning to be with the man she loved. She refused to get out of bed, not wanting to eat or do anything. Khye fell into a deep shock, her eyes soaked with tears and her pain feeling endless.

Three hours later, she heard knocking at the front door. Knowing it was Sammy arriving, she didn't want to get out of bed to let her friend in. She didn't want to do anything but mourn and think about Floyd. She could hear his loud voice, shouting, "Khye, open this door, I know you're in there. I didn't come all the way from Harlem, by train, in the damn cold to stand outside your door. I know your ass is mourning, but don't let me get stupid out here."

He knocked repeatedly and was ghetto loud outside her door.

Khye finally answered the door, looking a hot mess with a tear stained face and her hair in disarray. Sammy stood in front of her with his hand on his hip, wearing a sideways trucker hat, black lip-liner, pinkish eye-shadow, a tight woman's top, and skinny jeans under a faux fur.

Sammy made his way inside, carrying a gift—a bottle of Johnnie Walker and a dime bag of weed.

"Girl, I'm here for you and we gonna drink, smoke, and get better. I'm here for you, Khye. You know this. I'm not going anywhere. You need me, so I'm gonna be Doctor Phil for the day," he said.

She managed to smile. Sammy went to work on her, fixing her a drink, rolling up the weed, and being there for her. He was animated while Khye sat there looking and feeling reprehensible.

"I should have stayed with him. I shouldn't have left his side. If we hadn't gone back to my parents' place, then none of this would have happened," she said dejectedly.

"Khye, listen, none of this is your fault. Floyd left you there because he was upset, and besides, you didn't really know that man."

"Yes, I did."

"Whatever. Look, this will pass like gas, girl."

Khye sighed loudly. Sammy handed her a glass and she barely took it. For an hour, they talked and smoked weed. Sammy had become her crutch. If it wasn't for him being there, she didn't know what might have happened—suicide, something crazy.

"At least you're still here, enjoying what he left behind," said Sammy, not knowing he triggered a thought in Khye's mind.

It abruptly dawned on Khye, slowly seeing the silver lining; she realized that she dodged a bullet. With Floyd dead, he couldn't kick her out, which possibly meant that the apartment, the truck, his car, and whatever else, it was all hers, right? Who was coming for his things? He didn't have any family that he spoke of, did he? And as for Tatianna—Khye wished the bitch would try coming back to reclaim his things! She would suffer from another beatdown much worse than before.

With Sammy comforting her, she dried her tears and took a deep breath. She needed to come up with some type of plan. With Floyd gone, Khye had to think about her own survival.

***

It was War of Worlds in the New York hoods. Floyd's murder created tension in the streets. People pointing fingers, soldiers ready to carry out revenge, eyes leaking, blood boiling, and people were talking, saying Rash was behind Floyd's demise. Brooklyn and Harlem were in conflict, the grounds were shaky, and the heat was turned up to fiery hell levels. Everyone in the game was on edge.

Carlito went berserk after hearing about the shooting at the studio. Floyd was his best friend, his brother. He destroyed his own pad, turning over furniture, punching holes in the walls, smashing anything he could get his hands on. Ultimately he fell to his knees in deep grief after hearing about Floyd's murder. He felt angry and violated. Who had the audacity to kill his friend? It all pointed to Rash, and the streets talking about Harlem niggas helping the traitor with setting up his friend.

Carlito immediately was ready to avenge his friend's death. He wanted to round up his soldiers to strike back right away, but cops were probing everywhere, and everyone was on high alert. The media coverage of the murders was everywhere, and as long as the story was live and running, his revenge was on hold. Besides, Carlito had another huge problem to worry about. Floyd had stashed forty kilos of cocaine, and he needed to find out where, because they were still on the hook with the Colombians for the product.

TWENTY-EIGHT

It was hard to identify his body, but Khye did so at the city morgue. It was an unbearable place to be—in the bowels of the city building. The smell of the dead mixed with the clean air in the room, and the pathologist looked something like a mad doctor. Floyd's body was on the stainless-steel operating table in the center of the room covered with a white sheet. He was toe-tagged, which was disturbing. Khye and Sammy stood in a separate area, peering into the refrigerated room through a large glass window. The coroner lifted the sheet from the body fully and Khye caught a good view of Floyd.

It was him.

She burst into tears and fell into Sammy's arms, grieving. He consoled her with his arms wrapped around her. She needed to leave right away. The uninviting and foul atmosphere was crushing her. Her breathing became sparse, and it felt like the room was trapping her. Sammy was right behind her, and the second Khye exited the building, she hooked over from a sudden pain and cramping inside her stomach and threw up chunks of gunk. She purged herself from the sudden illness that seeped into her body.

Sammy stood over her, patting her back lightly and trying to ease her pain.

"You okay?" he asked.

"I'll be fine," she said faintly.

It took Khye a few minutes to compose herself. She wiped her mouth with a tissue handed to her by Sammy and took a deep, needed breath. She dried her tears once more and said, "He's really gone."

"Don't worry, they're going to catch the assholes that did this," Sammy assured her.

The culprits who murdered her boyfriend weren't even on her mind. How was she going to move forward? What now? And whoever killed Floyd, would they come after her, too?

***

A week went by, and Sammy had fully moved into the condo with Khye. She didn't mind it. She needed the company. When she was alone, the horror and nightmares plagued her. Her friend was optimistic, though, helping Khye take her mind away from the pain by any means—talking and smoking weed into the wee hours of the night, sipping on alcohol, and watching movies.

Sammy loved living in the building, away from Harlem, enjoying the Brooklyn suburb. He felt fabulous in the condo. It was a major step up from the cramped project building he'd called home for too long. In the condo, he truly became Sandy, coming and going from the building in skinny, tight jeans, or a black kilt, gold doo-rags, and hoop earrings. His lip gloss and eyeshadow became brighter, and he began dressing more risqué than a stripper. None of his behavior went unnoticed. The building residents loathed his actions and antics.

He smoked his cigarette and sipped his drink on the balcony, shirtless and in a gold thong, eyeing and smiling at the male neighbors in passing. The tranquility around him was a breath of fresh air. It was sad to say, but Sammy was exhilarated that Floyd was gone. He took delight in knowing that Floyd would be rolling over in his grave double time if he knew Sammy took up occupancy at his beloved condo. It was no secret that Floyd hated gays and despised him. Sammy didn't lose any sleep over his death. He was only there to console Khye, but he felt nothing for the man at all.

***

With his funeral approaching, Khye tried to ease her mind by smoking weed and having her solitude from everyone, except for Sammy. While the streets were going crazy over Floyd's assassination, with buzz of retaliation and war spreading around, Khye and Sammy tried to stay away and out of the drama. Not too many people knew where Floyd lived, so currently, no one came around.

While Sammy was out with some new play-toy of his for the evening, Khye lingered in the bedroom, blowing trees and thinking about her future. She lounged across her bed, relaxing. Everything was quiet, until she heard someone at her door.

Donning a long, black silk robe and placing her feet into some fuzzy slippers, Khye dowsed the weed, curious to see who was knocking. Company was rare, and Khye became alert, not knowing what to expect. She slipped a .22 handgun into her robe pocket and went to the door.

Peeping outside, the first face she saw was Tatianna's, and standing behind that bitch, three other ladies Khye was not familiar with. Not knowing what was going on, Khye thought the worst: that Tatianna had brought her friends by to beat her down and ransack Floyd's place, thinking she was vulnerable. She wasn't about to let it go down like that.

"Bitch, open the fuckin' door," Tatianna yelled out.

"Why, so you and your friends can jump me?" Khye said. "It's not happening, Tatianna."

Khye wished Sammy was home to have her back. But she was alone and fearing for her life.

"You stupid bitch, it's Floyd's mother and sisters standing out here. Shows how much you know," Tatianna said.

Khye looked through the peephole again. One woman looked much older than the rest. She looked sophisticated and was well-dressed. *His mother?* She thought it could have been a ruse, but her gut feeling told her it wasn't. Slowly, she opened the door, her hand astutely in her robe pocket, fingers on the pistol, and she fixed her eyes on the oldest woman. Immediately, Khye saw the resemblance in her features. Floyd definitely looked like her.

"Mrs. Simpson, I'm sorry for your loss," Khye said.

"Call me Judith," she said.

Tatianna stood close to the three ladies with her arms folded across her chest and scowling at Khye. It looked like she wanted to leap at Khye, but she restrained herself. Khye glared back, daring the bitch to try something. She was ready for her. After everything she'd been through, Khye was ready to take her frustration out on Tatianna.

"Can we come in?" Judith politely asked.

Khye showed a moment of hesitation. *What is all this about?* She nodded and stepped to the side, allowing all four ladies into the place but staying watchful with her hand still in her pocket. Judith looked around, taking in the décor. She was a classy and beautiful looking woman, wearing a trench coat, riding boots, long black hair, and diamond earrings. She introduced her two daughters, Victoria and Jacqueline, Floyd's older sisters. The two looked elegant and posh—and they were extremely beautiful. *What was going on?* Khye had a preconceived notion about Floyd's family, thinking since he was from Bed-Stuy—the hood—that his family was ghetto, but nothing like this. It contradicted everything she believed.

But then, Floyd had never spoken about his family to her, and seeing Tatianna with them, looking comfortable and cool, Khye became jealous that Tatianna knew about them and she was left out in the cold.

"Floyd never mentioned his family," Khye said.

"Of course he didn't," Judith said, suddenly sounding snooty. "He didn't need to."

Tatianna stood behind Judith, smirking at Khye. Khye knew something was up; they hadn't come to console her, ask her how she was doing, and make friends. She wasn't stupid—a minute ago, she hadn't even known they existed.

Judith walked farther into the apartment like she owned the place, looking around. Before she could say a word, like her knight in shining armor, Sammy showed up and looked foully at the unexpected company in the living room.

"Um, hello, and who are you bitches?" he greeted sassily. "And why are they in our home?"

His wardrobe stood out like Elton John—orange skinny jeans with untied Timberland boots, a muscle shirt with a lace bowtie, earrings, a tote bag in his hand, and over his extreme wardrobe, a quilted Burberry jacket.

All eyes were on him, and it was clear that the ladies disapproved of his way of life and style, staring at Sammy and then Khye as if they were parasites. Sammy went and stood by Khye's side, indicating he had her back if something was about to go wrong.

"He stays here, too?" Judith asked.

"Um, and why is that your business?" Sammy asked with an attitude.

Khye quickly updated Sammy who the woman was. "This is Floyd's mother."

"Oh, I'm so sorry for your loss," Sammy said, changing his tone.

Neither Judith nor her daughters were moved by the homosexual giving his condolences. They stood, looking stone-faced and apathetic. It felt like they were in a standoff. Judith looked cynically at Khye and said, "I'm giving you one week."

"One week for what?" Sammy chimed.

"To vacate my son's place," Judith said composedly.

"Our brother never owned this place. Our mother did," Victoria spoke up.

It was sudden news to Khye, and Sammy. "He didn't?"

"Yes."

It all came to light; Judith and her rich husband owned the condo. It turned out that Floyd's family was wealthy and lived in Connecticut. His mother's husband, who wasn't Floyd's biological father, was a very, very rich man. Judith had all her three kids by one man long ago, and they had lived poor and in Brooklyn. But after divorcing her kids' father and moving on, she met Patrick, an investment banker who was making millions. Floyd always felt resentful about his real father, who was a bum, a nobody, so he set out to make his own way and make his own money.

The news came as a shock to Khye. She was dumbfounded. She had no idea who the man she loved really was. She was embarrassed that she had to meet his family on such malicious terms. Meanwhile, Tatianna stood in the background, smirking and loving it all. Khye wanted to rip her face off.

"Look, where is she going to go?" Sammy exclaimed, standing up for his friend.

"I don't care, but she can't stay here," Judith said. "She can take whatever she wants with her, and whatever she doesn't take is going to be donated to charity. We have no use for it."

"What?" Tatianna suddenly blurted out, furious. "How she gonna pick and choose what she can take from here? I was wit' your son for two years, and we grew up together, so I should be the one taking his things."

"He was with me, not you, Tatianna," Khye spat back. "He loved me! So you need to belt up and bugger off, you bitch!"

"Bitch, you is a fuckin' homewrecker! That's what you are!"

Sammy stepped up, ready to confront Tatianna with his hands flaring and said, "You better step the fuck back, bitch!"

"I'm supposed be scared of this faggot?!"

"I'll show you a fuckin' faggot," Sammy retorted.

"Enough!" Judith screamed out.

She and her daughters were annoyed at the bickering right in front of her face, over her son's belongings.

"My son isn't even buried yet, and you two are arguing over his things," she exclaimed.

Everyone stood around and stayed quiet.

She continued with, "My son is dead because of his poor choices in friends and in his women. I always warned him."

It was a clear shot at Khye. Khye didn't pick up on her comment, or she didn't care. She had other things on her mind. Tatianna was still fussing, and Khye threw it out there, saying, "For all I know, that bloody bitch behind you could have had him murdered. She was always jealous of me, and he dumped her."

Hearing that accusation, Tatianna went off like a volcano, and the arguing started back up, but Judith stepped in between the two warring parties and made it clear, everyone had to leave. She came and said what she needed to say, now it was time to go, and Tatianna was going with her.

"Take what you need to take and leave in a week," Judith repeated.

When the door slammed, and her unwelcome company left, Khye plopped down on the couch and released a stressful sigh.

Sammy sat right beside her, put his arms around Khye, and said, "Don't worry, girl. Everything's gonna be okay."

Was it, though?

TWENTY-NINE

It was the day she dreaded, and she felt she didn't have the strength to go through it, but she had to—Floyd's funeral. It was going to be a hard day. Outside, the sky was rapidly graying, looking like it was about to rain soon. It was breezy, and the weather matched her mood.

As Khye got dressed in the bedroom, her cell phone rang. She didn't know the number calling, but the minute she answered, the caller asked, "Is this Floyd's fiancée?"

"Fiancée?" She wished she was getting married to Floyd, that he was alive and well, and still in love with her. "No, I'm not," she said.

"I know he's deceased, but I'm calling in the matter of an engagement ring that he was to make a final payment on."

"Engagement ring?" Khye was lost. What ring? What engagement?

"Yes, my name's Gabriel, and he bought the ring right before his death."

Assuming Floyd had gotten the ring for her, she became happy, thinking his rage toward her was all an act so he could fully surprise her with the engagement. He was going to propose. Khye couldn't believe it.

"He never got the chance to propose to me, so I have no idea where the ring is," she said.

"What do you mean? I know he did," Gabriel said, believing Khye was lying to him. "He was meeting you that night."

"I haven't seen Floyd since our argument, and how did you get this number?"

He seemed frustrated on the other end. Gabriel didn't want to lose out on the money that was owed to him or risk not getting the ring back. He sounded desperate.

"It was an expensive ring, and I do not want to involve the police—"

"I don't have it!" she exclaimed.

"Listen, your name is Rita, right?"

"Rita?" Khye said, taken aback by the name. "No, my name is Khye."

Gabriel was dumbfounded. Khye didn't understand, but then it all made sense.

"Was he proposing to another fuckin' woman?" She already knew the answer to her own question.

She heard a terse, "I'm sorry," from Gabriel.

It was obvious to him that she had no idea what was going on and she was clueless about the ring. He was reaching a dead end and hung up, accepting the ten-thousand-dollar loss.

Khye sat at the edge of her bed, feeling the acrimony swelling up inside of her. It was the ultimate betrayal. How could he? She felt angry and sad. The tears started to trickle down her face and she felt her heart sink lower and lower, like she was about to shit it out. She called Sammy.

"You're not gonna believe what I'm about to say."

"What now, bitch?"

"Floyd—" Khye could barely say the words. "Floyd apparently bought a ring and proposed to some bitch named Rita!"

"Rita?" Sammy repeated. "The dead girl?"

Khye was clueless. "You mean from the studio?"

"Well what other Rita is there, right? I mean, the news has been saying her name and showing her picture since the incident. And now that I think about it, she is his type of chick."

"And what type of chick is that?!"

"You know, fair skin, soft hair, nice shape. The only thing that separates

Rita from you and Tatianna is that I heard she had talent. I heard that bitch could really blow."

Khye exploded. "You think I give a fuck about some autotuned bum bitch! We don't know that it's her."

Behind the scenes, Sammy snickered. He loved getting Khye's pressure up. And with Floyd murdered, it was just too easy.

"Look, calm down, bitch. The bright side of this scenario is whoever Rita is, she ain't getting married. At least not to Floyd. So if I were you, I would be laughing my ass off cause there's an unmarried Rita either living or on the other side thinking *'what the fuck just happened'*."

"Sammy I don't feel like laughing because shit ain't funny, understand? And I can't take any more snarky remarks—not now. Not while I'm grieving."

"Okay, bitch, I get it and I'm sorry. You going through a lot, and believe me I'm really only trying to cheer you up in my own way. I may not use tact, but believe that I love you."

"I love you, too."

Khye hung up. She was drained. Floyd was proposing to someone else? And was finding this out hours before his funeral. She really didn't know Floyd at all. But how could she judge him, thinking about herself? He didn't know her either, the true her. And it seemed like they had both schemed each other.

***

Khye climbed out of the black Benz beneath the graying sky and began to make her way across the cemetery. Dozens of leaves crackled loudly under her high heels as she walked slowly to the burial plot. Dozens of people were standing around the dark brushed-bronze casket with bronze finish and premium velvet interior. It was about to be lowered into the ground.

His family, mother and sisters, stood with their eyes glued to the casket, looking stoic through the entire funeral, and now his burial. Dark shades covered their eyes and they were completely dressed in black. At the funeral home on Atlantic Avenue, hundreds of people came to pay their respects to Floyd. He was well-liked and very popular. His name rang out. His reputation was notorious.

Carlito was front and center with his goons at his friend and brother's homegoing. He dressed sharply in a black three-piece suit, keeping his cool until it wasn't time to keep his cool. He looked sorrowful, but kept his emotions under control. He locked eyes briefly with Khye. At that moment, he had nothing to say to her.

During the viewing of the body, Tatianna was the one that put on a show, crying out hysterically and clawing at Floyd's body in the casket.

"I love you, baby! I love you so much! Why him? Oh god, why? Why!" she screamed and ranted.

It took several people to pull her away from the casket and drag her outside into the foyer.

Khye stood in the back of the room, refusing to view the body. She was still angry at the information from earlier, and she felt the tension in the room. She hid her eyes and her emotions behind mirror shades and looked blank throughout the entire service. She only had Sammy by her side.

At the gravesite, Khye and Carlito looked at each other silently, as the preacher said a few words to the casket being lowered into the ground.

"I am the resurrection and the life, saith the Lord; he that believeth in me, though he were dead, yet shall he live; and whosoever liveth and believeth in me shall never die," said the pastor. "For none of us liveth to himself and no man dieth to himself. For if we live, we live unto the Lord. And if we die, we die unto the Lord. Whether we live, therefore or die, we are the Lord's."

Carlito frowned and said without caring, "Oh, there's gonna be plenty of people dying, amen to that."

Khye heard his statement and didn't budge. She didn't know if the comment was directed toward her, or if he was speaking in general. The crowd around the casket was heard weeping and moaning. With Floyd finally in the ground, the crowd started to disperse, going in different directions.

Khye walked off with Sammy by her side. She suddenly heard her name called out brashly, "Khye!" She turned to see Carlito approaching her way with a steely glare. He was alone. His goons were elsewhere throughout the cemetery.

Sammy frowned at the man, and said, "I got your back, girl. What he want?"

"I don't know," she said.

Carlito approached the two and looked at Sammy; he chuckled lightly at her friend's gaudy appearance. He then looked at Khye and said, "Can I have a word with you, alone?"

She looked at Sammy and said, "I'll be okay."

"You sure?"

She nodded.

"Girl, I'm over here if you need me," he said.

She nodded.

Sammy slowly walked away, but not before staring intently at Carlito and saying to him with his eyes, *I'm watching you.* Carlito didn't see Sammy as a threat, but a joke. Once Sammy was out of earshot, and away, Carlito said to Khye, "Did Floyd ever tell you everything?"

"What do you mean?"

"I mean, he was no ordinary guy. He wasn't just an audio engineer," said Carlito, spilling the beans.

"Then what was he?"

"You can't be that naïve, Khye."

Khye simply looked at him.

"Look, let me be frank wit' you. Floyd and I, we were one of the biggest drug distributors in this fuckin' city, and he didn't work at Slow Pullz Studio, he owned it. The studio started out as front, along with a few other businesses to wash and launder our drug money. Things started to take off, and Floyd wanted to go legit, to make a good impression on his family. Now, here's my dilemma. There's a matter of forty kilos Floyd had in his possession. Forty kilos from the Colombians on consignment that I need to get back. Because with him dead or not, I'm still on the hook for it," Carlito proclaimed.

"I have no idea what you're talking about."

"I'm sure you don't. But listen here, tomorrow morning, I'll be by the condo and I'll check for myself."

"No you won't."

He laughed. "You must have this confused wit' it being a choice."

The look on Carlito's face was contemptuous. He was cool, though, not trying to raise his voice and argue with a woman he felt was inferior to him. She had no idea who he really was.

"Listen, you little bitch, you don't know who you're fuckin' wit'," he warned through clenched teeth.

"And you have no idea who you're fuckin' with," Khye retorted.

He smiled wickedly. The bitch was being stubborn. Khye pivoted on her heels and headed Sammy's way while Carlito looked at her, fuming on the inside.

"C'mon, let's go," she said.

"What did he say to you?"

"Nothing important. Everything out of his mouth was irrelevant."

But she knew it wasn't. What Sammy suspected about Floyd was confirmed. He was a murdering thug and drug distributor who had plans to go legit. He had more bodies under his belt than a cemetery, and he was living not a double life, but a triple life with so many different personas.

Khye hurried back to the condo while Sammy was on his way to Harlem to check on his mother.

Alone, Khye now knew something was hidden inside the apartment, and she had to react quickly. Her gut feeling told her Floyd left something valuable behind and she needed to find it before Carlito came over with his goons.

She started in the bedroom, ransacking everything, finding nothing. She went to the second bedroom, going through everything. Nothing. Khye went through the entire apartment with a fine-toothed comb, nothing. Then she inadvertently triggered a mechanism in the bathroom—the medicine cabinet had a false back, and behind it was tons of cash. Khye was in awe. She removed the bundles of cash and placed them in the bedroom. Her search continued.

She found more cash in a shoe box in the closet and a drug ledger and more extra cash inside the kitchen cabinets—revealed only when the shelves were taken out. The more money she found, the more nervous she became. What came next was the mother lode. Why she'd thought about the couch, she had no idea, but something was telling her to rip the couch apart. She did, realizing that under the custom couch was a flat compartment and inside, forty kilos of cocaine wrapped tightly and hidden. Khye was wide-eyed and afraid at the same time. She had never seen so much money and drugs in her entire life. She didn't know what to do or who to call. The only person who came to mind was Sammy.

Two hours went by while she waited for Sammy to come over. She counted the money: in total, two hundred thousand dollars. She took a deep breath. What was her next move? She wasn't sticking around the condo, that was for sure. She needed to leave immediately.

When Sammy finally showed up, he was taken aback by everything.

"Bitch, you Tony Montana all of a sudden," he wisecracked.

"It's Floyd's," she said.

"Obviously."

"I'm scared, Sammy. I don't know what to do with it."

"That is a lot of drugs and a lot of cash."

"I know."

Sammy looked like he was ready to swim in the cash. There was so much they could do with it, the things he could buy, and the places he could go.

"How much cash?" he asked.

"I counted it…two hundred thousand."

"Whoa…"

"I know."

"Okay, I know somebody that can help us with the drugs," he said.

"Who?"

"This might sound crazy, but my brother."

"Able?"

"Girl, he's the only drug dealer I know that could handle something like this. We can sell it to him."

Khye looked unsure. She was worried. Carlito came into her mind, knowing someone like him would kill for this. She didn't care about his debt to the Colombians, but only about what he would do if he found out she had the drugs. Money and drugs like this were an opportunity that she couldn't pass up.

"Khye, Able might be many things, but he's still my brother and he knows you. My brother won't allow anything to happen to you, believe me."

Khye thought about it. She really didn't have a choice but to trust Sammy and Able. Forty kilos of drugs was nothing to sneeze at.

"We need to go. I mean, pack our shit and leave this place for good," Khye said.

Sammy agreed.

They got no rest that night. Khye packed up every single thing she owned, hid the cash in a book bag and the forty kilos in several large garbage bags, and in the middle of the night, she loaded everything into the truck. They left Floyd's condo ransacked and destroyed. It was a gift to Floyd's family and Carlito.

They got a hotel room near the city and stayed there for a few nights, trying to come up with a faultless plan. They were also trying to find a new place to live—someplace safe, comfortable, and up to her speed. With two hundred thousand dollars in possession, Khye had a variety of choices, and she knew she had to move fast. That morning and one pregnancy test later, she had gotten the news of her life—she was pregnant. And it was Floyd's baby.

THIRTY

Sarah walked into the abortion clinic on 149th Street in the Bronx. It was early morning and she had no idea what she was doing there. She was scared and upset. Marcus was completely out of her life. He wasn't calling her, and when she tried to call him, his number had been changed. It devastated her. She loved him and thought that by getting pregnant, she could make him stay with her forever. It was a stupid plan, and she felt like a stupid woman.

Sarah cried and cried for several days. She was heartbroken and devastated. She wanted to be alone. She wanted something different in her life, but got the same status-quo. She despised her drunken husband, her mediocre younger daughters, and Khye, a younger version of her who seemed to be doing everything right while she was doing everything wrong.

Inside the clinic, there were many women of different ethnicities, seated around, all looking despondent and thinking they were correcting a mistake. There were many pamphlets given out about unplanned parenthood and abortion. It felt like a ghastly place where majority of the women, young from old, looked ambivalent about their choice.

The mounted TV above the room entertained the ladies to some extent with daytime talk shows. It looked like any normal clinic with doctors, a receptionist, and staff, but behind the doors, deep in some undisclosed room, some called it murder and some called it unplanned parenthood. Either way, a baby was being disposed of.

Sarah filled out the information needed and took a seat among the others. Her expression was blank. The shades she wore covered her eyes and she was still unsure if she was doing the right thing. She was carrying his baby, and wanted to hit Marcus with child support. She dreamed about receiving two thousand, maybe five thousand a month from him. Cash like that on a monthly basis, it would've set her life up for good. Definitely put her into a new place to live, finance a nice car, some nice clothes—her baby was supposed to be her cash cow, but the child growing inside of her was becoming a burden.

Of course Marcus would proclaim it wasn't his, ask for a DNA test, most likely get lawyers involved, and put her through the grinder and probably deny the baby until the day he died.

Sarah sat there, thinking, feeling hopeless. She was a thirty-five-year-old woman who was pregnant. She had nothing to her name and a past so sordid she carried a stigma with her like a bad omen. She was tired of her life. She had failed. She had become her worst nightmare—old, broke, used, and abused.

Sarah quietly got up, placed the clipboard and information on her chair, and walked out of the clinic with her eyes leaking water. She felt trapped. Why? She was beautiful, but unlucky.

It was a cold day, but she decided to walk—to where, she had no idea. She walked aimlessly with the December cold nipping at her skin and feeling invisible to the world.

THIRTY-ONE

With the money, Khye was able to move into her own apartment, a two bedroom rental in the heart of NYC. It was up to her speed, sunny and furnished with a private terrace—top of line with an 11 foot ceiling and a block from Columbus Circle and Central Park. It was three thousand, five hundred dollars a month, but with the two hundred thousand and the forty kilos, Khye was sure she could afford the place for a long while.

Sammy moved in with her. They became the best of roommates, but for the one problem: Khye was pregnant and Sammy wasn't too thrilled about it. He didn't want their new lifestyle to get overshadowed and crowded by a baby.

"You keeping it?" Sammy had asked, when she told him.

"I don't know," she had replied.

"Khye, a baby is the last thing you need in your life right now. You know how crazy it's gonna get, especially with no baby father in your life and this thing with Carlito and whoever. You really wanna put an infant through that?"

Khye was skeptical. The fetus growing inside of her was her last connection to Floyd. It was his baby. Boy or girl, she was already growing attached to it. But Sammy kept trying to convince her to get an abortion.

"We hook up with my brother, and we'll be making tons of money, so much, you'll be bleeding green blood, bitch. Think about it, Khye, you wanna be pregnant and in that life? You think anyone is going to respect a pregnant woman? You think that's going to be healthy for a baby?"

He had Khye thinking about it. Reluctantly, she agreed. Two days later, they went to the abortion clinic and she had the procedure performed. Afterwards, she felt sick to her stomach. She locked herself in her bedroom for the entire day, crying and crying; knowing a part of Floyd—his baby, was gone from her forever.

Several weeks went by, and Sammy and Khye still contemplated their next step. They had to be cautious. Able was willing to meet with them and talk. They agreed to meet in the city, Central Park in the mid afternoon, in public.

Khye and Sammy sat on the park bench, bundled up in their winter coats, bearing the December cold. They waited for a half hour, until Able and The Gun showed up, alone, looking like two cold-hearted gangsters. Khye clutched a book bag with a kilo inside it. It was to show to Able that she was for real.

"This better be important, Sammy," Able said to his little brother, smoking a cigarette and already looking agitated. "You know I don't fuck wit' the city like that."

"I know, but believe me, this is really important," Sammy said.

The Gun was quiet while standing behind Able. He was Able's muscle, the killer. While Sammy and Able talked, The Gun locked eyes with Khye with a stone-cold expression. He was a handsome man, standing six-one and muscular with a narrow face and intense eyes, and when he talked, his voice was deep and raspy.

Khye's eyes lingered on The Gun, also known as Jason. She hadn't realized how handsome he was until recently. There was something about him that was intriguing—something that Khye picked up on while they met in the park.

"So what you got to show me?" Able asked.

Sammy looked at Khye, signaling her to show his brother what was inside the bag. Khye stepped forward and unzipped it. Able glanced inside, his eyes smiled at the large kilo of cocaine in their possession. He whistled. "Damn!"

"We got your attention?" Sammy asked, looking smug.

"And where did a homo and a pretty thang like Khye get something like that?"

"It's our business, but there's plenty more where that came from," Sammy said, taking over the meeting.

"How much more?"

"We're not stupid, Able. What we want is a partnership. We sell it to you and you flood the streets with it."

"At how much?"

Sammy and Khye weren't drug dealers, so they didn't know the going rate for a kilo exactly. For a moment, they both look stumped. Able laughed. "Do y'all know what the fuck y'all doing?"

"Look, we might be new to this, but we ain't stupid," said Sammy.

"So, what's not to stop us from taking the shit and giving you nothing?" Able said.

"And then what, you sell a kilo make a couple dollars, while we find some proper buyers and make them rich?" Khye chimed.

Able stopped laughing.

Khye was ready to speak up and make it happen.

"We might not be drug dealers, but we both need each other. Able, think about the future. We need to trust you and you need to trust us. No lies, no secrets. So, we have forty kilos hidden," she mentioned.

"Khye—" Sammy uttered, being perturbed that she told them how much.

"Forty? Damn, from where?"

"My ex boyfriend."

"That punk." Able laughed.

"Anyway, the past is the past and I'm only focused on the future right now, Able, and I know you are too. So, we'll do a trial run, start you off with eight keys to sell, you do well, we get in bed together and make it happen," Khye proclaimed.

Able turned and looked at The Gun. "What you think?"

"What we got to lose? Besides, she's cute," The Gun said.

Khye smiled.

"You ready to get ya hands dirty, little brother?" Able asked.

"I'm ready to make some money."

"This ain't sucking dick, nigga. This is a whole new ball game, Samuel—up the ass, raw dawg. But you already know about that, right?"

Sammy didn't respond to his brother's homophobic statement. Able was always trying to get under his skin.

"And you, Miss Pretty, you ready to roll in the mud wit' the bad boys and pigs and get your tits dirty? Get that pussy poppin' and felt up?" Able said.

"I'm more ready than ever," Khye fired back, softly but effectively.

Able chuckled.

The look in her eyes said she was serious. She had been through a lot, and aborting Floyd's baby signified that she wasn't about to cry about the past anymore. Now it was her time to shine; to no longer depend on any man to take care of her.

WAR ᴏꜰ ᴛʜᴇ WØRLDS

Two armed and dangerous men sat in the black Charger on Ralph Avenue smoking trees and listing to rap music. With New Year's Eve approaching, the two thugs were getting ready to have a good time with liquor and women at a local hole-in-the-wall spot on Gates Avenue. They wanted to get high before the party. The streets were a gold mine, but trouble had been brewing lately. Since Floyd's murder, Carlito and his men had been on high alert—knowing Floyd's killers were still out there, breathing, laughing and thinking they were victorious.

While the two thugs waited for the red light to change to green on the Brooklyn street, a black Navigator pulled alongside the Charger, and suddenly, a long arm stretched out from the passenger-side window with an Uzi at the end. The weapon exploded at the men inside the Charger. Rapidly, their car and bodies were riddled with bullets, blood spraying, bodies jerking violently in the front seat. Instantly, both of Carlito's men were dead.

A week later, three of Able's were gunned down in a vicious drive-by on 116th Street. Rash had sided with Able, and together, they were trying to take over control of Floyd's fledging drug empire, and even Slow Pullz Studio.

Before the year ended, seven men were killed between two warring drug crews, and a bloody war ensued for control over the city streets. Khye sat in charge of it all with Sammy by her side, The Gun and Able becoming killing machines while becoming drug lords and getting rich. The brutal fighting with Carlito was escalating, and bodies were dropping all over Harlem and Brooklyn. Carlito had put a fifty-thousand-dollar bounty on Khye's head, believing she had set Floyd up, stolen his money and drugs, and had the audacity to drive around in his friend's CL600 and his Range Rover while his friend was rotting in the ground. Carlito wanted the bitch dead yesterday.

In return, Khye put out a contract on Carlito's life. The two became bitter enemies, and Khye found herself thrust into a drug war, fighting for her life, as Carlito did the same. Carlito was strong, resilient, and determined to avenge Floyd's death.

Carlito barely escaped two hits on his life before the year ended. One, when two masked gunmen charged at him with their guns blazing while he walked to his car, coming from a nightclub. He dove head first into the backseat of his Yukon while one of his soldiers caught a bullet to his chest.

"Drive! Drive!" Carlito screamed out, hearing the bullets penetrate his SUV and glass shattering.

His driver pushed his foot against the accelerator and took off flying away from the threat, careening down the street. Carlito had to count his blessings on that one.

The second attempt on his life came as a bolder move, in public. The city streets were crowded with people when a lone wolf rushed in Carlito's direction brandishing a knife, and he was able to get close to his target, thrusting the sharp blade into his side, injuring him. It was a bold attack, but unfortunately for the attacker, he was severely beaten and taken away to be killed, while Carlito was rushed to the nearest hospital.

However, during the blood, chaos, and murders, a romance sparked between Khye and The Gun. The two started fucking around. Behind the killer persona, The Gun—Jason—was a sweetheart who treated Khye like she was gold. Out of the blue, the two had fallen in love, which was a shock for Khye, who never thought she would love anyone other than Floyd. Jason was a cold-blooded killer, but behind the layers, he was into poetry and easy to talk to when you got to know him. And day by day, Khye had gotten to know him.

But under a watchful eye, Able was stressed about their relationship and a little envious; he'd always had a crush on Khye and wanted to push up, but his friend had beat him to the punch.

As the New Year marched in with blood, pain, and gunplay, Khye and The Gun were becoming the new Bonnie and Clyde. Their relationship was growing stronger every day—blossoming into something special, something real. Jason would wine and dine Khye, taking her to exclusive restaurants in the city with his blood money, buying her things and loving her. He constantly wrote her poetry, and they talked like best friends. Even Sammy started to feel uneasy with Khye and Jason's unexpected relationship, feeling like he was losing his best friend once again to a murderous thug.

With more money came more problems and a life that swept them all up into itself. Khye felt back on top again: Her apartment was lavish, her cars high-end, and the money seemingly never-ending. Her life seemed to be straight out of the pages of *Untouchables* and *Feds*. As time went by, Floyd slowly became a memory, and Jason became her everything. He would kill for her, and had done so on a few occasions. Anyone who looked at his woman wrong found themselves staring down the barrel of his gun.

He loved her, and she loved him.

The Gun was her protector, and with him around, Khye felt completely safe.

However, things were about to hit close to home for everybody.

***

Sarah's belly was growing, and so was her problem. She was almost three months pregnant and had no support at all. Adewale had lost his job once again, and their situation had grown worse. There was no money, no food, and her kids were about to be taken away by ACS. They had missed too many days of school, their clothing was always dirty and torn, and a teacher had reported the family to social workers. Khye wasn't around anymore; she was too busy getting rich while her family was suffering. They were about to be evicted from their home, and they had lost everything. Sarah was stressed out with a capital S. The money and the men she went to for help were gone.

James suffered a mild heart attack three days after Christmas and was recovering at a local hospital. Gino was dead. Some unknown stranger blew his brains out right outside their building the moment he stepped out of the lobby, two days after New Year's Day. He became the fourth homicide that year. Tensions were so high in Harlem, residents were scared to leave their apartments.

Sarah left her apartment and walked toward the Robert Kennedy Bridge in the winter cold. For her, all hope was lost and she didn't care anymore. The only thing she had on were flip flops and a light jacket. She walked like a zombie, moving through the busy street with only one purpose on her mind.

She walked on the bridge, the wind pushing against her, as it was a very breezy and nippy day. Cars flew by her without a care in the world—a pregnant woman strolling aimlessly and not properly dressed for the cold. She had already made up her mind as she climbed up the bridge above the roadway and peered down at the long fall and the cold, murky water below. She would rather choose suicide than failure and embarrassment. While her daughter was living the high life, she felt like damaged goods.

Sarah didn't hesitate jumping into the water, leaping to her death, taking her own and her baby's life. She landed in the water and died on impact.

EPILØGUE

Khye woke up to a terrifying nightmare, dreaming about her own death. She was sweating profusely in the middle of the night and found it difficult to breathe. The dream felt so real, like she was drowning and struggling for air. It took a moment to compose herself. She took a deep breath and went into the kitchen to get a cold glass of water. She was alone in her Manhattan apartment. Jason wasn't home, and Sammy had his own boyfriend, who he'd started to spend the nights with.

She needed to talk to Sammy. His phone rang, and when he answered, it sounded like some confusion on his end.

"Sammy, where are you?" she asked.

"Khye, let me call you back," he said.

"Why, what's going on?"

She heard someone yelling, and whoever it was sounded very upset. Sammy hung up abruptly without giving her any explanation. But strange thing, Khye's phone rang back and it was Sammy calling. She answered, but got no response. His phone had redialed Khye's number back again and everything that was being said into the room was being heard by Khye.

"Y'all gonna do me like this!" she heard a man shout.

Khye suddenly heard Sammy shout, "If it wasn't for my information, then you wouldn't have been able to get her boyfriend at the studio. I set that up for y'all—gave y'all everything."

"And we took care of him, that white boy and that bitch," The Gun retorted. "But you getting too greedy, think you running shit."

"Greedy?" Sammy was incensed. "Able do you hear this muthafucka? Are you co-signing with him against your own flesh and blood, nigga?!"

The reply was muffled, and Khye couldn't hear what was said. There was a lot of movement, and she was sure it was Sammy flailing his arms and making over-the-top gestures.

"We sent you over to her crib to do one thing. Find the fuckin' paper and the yayo," a male voice stated.

Khye was taken aback. Was she hearing her best friend correctly? That he'd set up Floyd to get robbed and murdered? Khye listened to everything attentively, and the more she heard, the angrier she became. Her heart felt knotted and she felt betrayed.

"How was I supposed to know she was going to find his money and drugs?" Sammy said to someone.

Sammy was behind the whole thing. His big mouth gave him away, and Khye heard it all as clear as day. He was jealous of her. He always had been. But why? He had no idea that Khye would find the money and drugs before he had a chance to search the apartment, nor that he, his brother, and The Gun would make a come up, twice. The more he talked without knowing Khye was listening, the more furious Khye grew. She felt her insides turn into fire. The tears started to stream down her face, and the hurt was so deep, it cut her to the core. She listened as Sammy called her so many names, and spoke of her as if they were archenemies.

Khye realized that what Sammy had done could have cost her everything. With Floyd gone—murdered in cold blood, Sammy was hoping Khye would end right back in the ghetto. Khye thought about her baby, the abortion, and she knew if Floyd was still alive, though he was upset with her, he would have been there for his baby, and never allowed her to raise it alone. She was sure he would have left Rita. He would have been there for his child, not like his own father. And they took it all away from her, like a thief in the night.

Khye couldn't hear anymore. She ended the call. Her face flooded with tears and grief, along with anger and bitterness. She stepped out onto the terrace in the winter cold. The way she felt, the chilly weather didn't bother her one bit. She felt immune to the cold with her blood boiling on the inside. She clenched her hands around the railing tightly and seethed. Her tears continued falling, her mind spinning with resentment and bleeding for revenge.

She wasn't about to allow Floyd's murder to go unpunished. Something had to be done. They had to go. They deserved to be murdered like they did Floyd—Sammy, Able, and sad to say, even her new love, Jason, The Gun.

But how, and with what army? They were her army. They were the ones who protected her. And with Carlito constantly trying to murder her, how would she kill them all—especially Jason?

Khye cried for hours, until dawn.

She had one thing on her mind—to kill them all, even if it meant sacrificing her own life.

TO BE CONTINUED